PART ONE

The Traitor

Vengeance is mine; I will repay.
    Epistle of Peter to the Romans

One

The Act of Vengeance

'Franz, my dear fellow!' Colonel Rudolph Kessler shook hands with his fellow officer, then stepped back. 'Heil Hitler!'

Colonel Franz Hoeppner responded. 'Heil Hitler! Welcome to Bordeaux.'

Behind them the train continued to hiss noisily and doors banged as the other passengers were allowed off. But the two officers remained isolated, surrounded by their guards. 'I am sure it will be a pleasant change from the Ukraine,' Kessler agreed.

Actually, Hoeppner thought, for someone just returned from the Russian front, his replacement – a short, somewhat stout man with heavy features – looked exactly as he remembered him from their last meeting, which had been before the Eastern campaign had even commenced.

'It is very quiet here, now,' he said. 'The car is outside.' The soldiers cleared a way through the throng, everyone casting surreptitious stares at the two resplendently clad German officers. In contrast to his companion, Hoeppner was tall, strongly built, and moved athletically. With his crisp yellow hair and bold features he was a very typical representative of the 'master' race.

'Frankly, I did not expect to find you still here,' Kessler remarked.

'I felt it my duty to remain to hand over to you.'

'But after such a humiliation . . .'

'I was lured into a trap,' Hoeppner said quietly. 'And taken prisoner.'

'And then released by the guerrillas, unharmed,' Kessler commented disparagingly. The two men emerged into the bright autumnal sunlight of the station yard. Here there were even more people, openly staring at the two officers, but kept at a respectful distance by the guards, who prodded at them with their rifle butts.

'I had served my purpose,' Hoeppner agreed equably.

Kessler got into the back of the open tourer and sat down. He paid no attention to the watching crowd. 'Which was to enable Liane de Gruchy to escape from custody. Did you actually meet her?'

Hoeppner sat beside him. 'I was driven more than a hundred kilometres with her pressing a pistol into my ribs.'

'And is she as fearsome as they say?'

Hoeppner tapped the driver on the shoulder. A soldier took his place in the other front seat, this one armed with a tommy gun, which he rested across his knees. 'She is certainly as beautiful as they say. As for being fearsome . . . Well, she had me at her mercy, but she did not kill me.'

'She preferred the propaganda value of releasing you to walk back to Bordeaux.'

'Possibly. I prefer to think that she only kills when she has to.'

Kessler snorted. 'And now she is dead.'

Hoeppner sighed. 'They are all dead. Weber and his thugs wiped them out.'

'You sound almost regretful about that. Why are we not moving?'

'What is the trouble, Willi?' Hoeppner asked.

'There is a farm cart broken down immediately outside the yard, Herr Colonel.'

'Well, sort it out, there's a good fellow. We cannot sit here all day.'

Willi obligingly got out of the car, as did the guard. Kessler gave another of his snorts. 'You are too soft on these people. That is going to change, for a start.'

'They acknowledge our rule,' Hoeppner said. 'Life is simplified, on both sides, where there is no excessive demonstration of that rule.'

'That is a point of view with which I do not happen to agree. What is this?'

Despite the protective ring of soldiers, the crowd had pressed closer, and now a young woman ducked under the outstretched arms and prodding gun butts and ran towards the car. Men shouted and grabbed at her, but she evaded them with a swivel of her hips and reached the vehicle. Kessler continued to regard her with a mixture of distaste and contempt; Hoeppner stared at the flying dark-brown hair, the so-familiar face, with a mixture of both consternation and horror. 'Amalie?' he gasped.

The woman was beside the car. Kessler at last realized that they were being attacked, and unbuttoned his holster. But within seconds he was dead. The woman had drawn an automatic pistol from inside her coat and shot him twice in the head, with both composure and accuracy. Blood flew across the car and across Hoeppner. He was endeavouring to draw his own weapon, but he knew he had no chance. He stared at the woman – she was hardly more than a girl – and she stared back, her gun levelled. 'Amalie,' he muttered again.

For a moment she continued to stare at him, her knuckle white against the trigger, then she turned away, into the arms of the soldiers who had surrounded the car. They grasped at her arms and her threadbare coat and dress while she uttered no sound, but now they were themselves surrounded, by the crowd, which surged forward, ignoring the flailing rifles, seized the Germans' weapons, grasped the car itself to overturn it and send Hoeppner and Kessler sprawling in the dust. Someone fired a shot, and then another, and then there was a volley. The crowd fled in every direction, leaving half a dozen bodies behind them. Hoeppner sat up and instinctively reached for his cap, which had come off. 'Cease firing!' he shouted.

A sergeant appeared beside him. 'Those people . . .'

'Are largely innocent.'

'They have made off with the assassin.'

'Well, we will have to find her. Get this car turned right side up.'

'Yes, Herr Colonel. And the Colonel?'

Hoeppner looked at the body at his feet. 'As you say, Sergeant, the woman was an assassin.' And also a ghost, he thought.

* * *

Oskar Weber replaced the telephone slowly. Then he produced a handkerchief and wiped sweat from his brow. Then he pressed his intercom; it was better to do what had to be done before he lost his nerve altogether.

'Herr Colonel?' the woman asked.

'I wish an appointment with General Heydrich, immediately. Make it, and order my car.'

'Ah . . . Yes, Herr Colonel.'

The woman had hesitated; the bitch must have detected the agitation in his voice. That had to be controlled. A senior officer in the SD – the *Sicherheitsdienst*, the secret police within the Gestapo, and thus the most powerful force in Germany, hated and feared even by the *Schutzstaffel* – did not allow himself to be agitated, even when his career might be hanging by a thread. Weber opened his deep drawer, took out the bottle of French brandy, regarded it, and then put it away again. Were Heydrich to smell alcohol on his breath . . . Besides, his immediate panic was receding and he was having an idea on how the business could be handled.

He got up, took a turn around the office, and paused to look out of his window at the busy Berlin streets. No one had had much sleep because of the RAF raid. Another RAF raid, despite Goering's assurances that it could never happen. The raid had not caused a lot of damage, but the mere fact that it had happened was bad for morale – quite apart from the sleepless night. He sat down again.

'The car is waiting, Herr Colonel,' the woman said.

Weber got back to his feet, slowly. Of medium height, he was heavily built, with receding black hair and a strong jaw. He wore civilian clothes, and paused for a moment to straighten his tie and then dry his hands before leaving the office.

'Oskar!' Reinhard Heydrich said. 'I am delighted to see you. Come in and sit down and have a drink.' Weber hesitated in the centre of the double doors that led to the large, beautifully furnished office, dominated by the great, deep windows to either side of the huge desk. Between them there hung a full-size portrait of the Führer. Entering this office was always an experience, but more often than not it was a terrifying one.

Weber had never seen his boss, with his carefully brushed blond hair and his coldly handsome features, in what could be described as a jolly mood . . . With an open bottle of champagne on his desk, from which he was now filling two glasses.

'Come along,' he said. 'A toast! The future.'

Cautiously Weber approached the desk. He did not think the future, overall, looked all that bright. The weather in Russia was so bad that there did not now appear any possibility of Moscow falling before Christmas, as had been confidently predicted following the amazing victories of the summer. That in itself was not catastrophic, but the suffering of the troops, ill-equipped for the winter that was now closing upon them, was distressing. But he took the glass and raised it. 'The future! Which future were you thinking of, Herr General?'

Heydrich laughed, again a sufficiently rare event. Then he drained his glass and sat down. 'My future, Oskar. I am to go to Prague.'

Weber also sat down. 'Prague? A visit?'

'Idiot! I am to be Reichsführer. I am to rule a country, Oskar.'

'You mean you are leaving Berlin? For how long?'

'Well, of course I am leaving Berlin. As for how long, I cannot say. The Czechs are proving troublesome, and I have been given the task of bringing them to heel. Oh, I shall do that, you may be sure. But it could take a little while. Czechoslovakia is quite a large country.'

'But who will take over here?' Weber's brain was whirring as he considered that what he had to say might be better kept for this demonic man's successor.

'Heinrich will take overall command.' Weber swallowed. If there was anyone in Germany he feared more than Heydrich, it was Himmler. 'So, now, tell me what is so urgent?' Heydrich invited.

Weber licked his lips. 'There has been trouble in Bordeaux.'

'What sort of trouble?'

'The new commanding officer, Kessler, has been assassinated.'

'Isn't that a matter for the Wehrmacht?'

'Yes, it is. But there are disturbing elements . . .' Heydrich refilled his glass and waited. Weber licked his lips again. 'Kessler was sent to replace Hoeppner.'

Heydrich nodded. 'I know. Hoeppner was so incompetent as to allow himself to be kidnapped by the de Gruchy guerrilla gang. Then you wiped the gang out. How are you, by the way?'

'I am fully recovered from my wound.'

'Excellent. Well, this is clearly some kind of revenge killing. It must be dealt with most severely. Who is in command down there?'

'Well . . . Hoeppner. He remained to hand over to Kessler.'

'Well, you had better tell him to do something worthwhile for a change. The assassin must be hanged, with the greatest publicity.'

'The assassin got away,' Weber said miserably.

Heydrich put down his glass. 'Would you like to repeat that?'

'There was a riot, and in the chaos the woman escaped.'

'The woman. The assassin was a woman?'

'This is the problem. This woman ran up to the car, shot Kessler through the head and then stared at Hoeppner, who was sitting beside Kessler. She had every opportunity to shoot him, too, before the guards could get to her, but she did not.'

Heydrich regarded him for several seconds. Then he said, 'I do not think you can stop there, Oskar.'

Weber drew a long breath. 'Hoeppner is convinced that the woman was Amalie de Gruchy.'

Another long stare. 'Amalie de Gruchy is dead.' Heydrich continued to speak quietly. 'You killed her, Oskar. You told me this yourself.'

'That is not quite correct, Reinhard.'

'You told me the de Gruchys were destroyed when you raided their lair two months ago. Are you now telling me something different? Are you going to tell me that that shewolf, Liane de Gruchy, is actually alive?'

'No, no. Liane de Gruchy is dead.'

'You saw her body?'

'I saw her immediately before she died. I was about to shoot

8

her when I was hit myself. I do not know who fired the shot, but I was rendered unconscious, as you know. However, she was despatched by Fräulein Jonsson, who was at my side.'

'Always Fräulein Jonsson,' Heydrich remarked. 'Did you not tell me that she and Liane de Gruchy had been at school together? That they were lovers?'

'I believe that is so. But they had quarrelled, and de Gruchy had rejected her. Hell hath no fury, eh? Anyway, Jonsson shot her and her immediate companions.'

'But you did not see the bodies.'

'Well, no. I was unconscious, as I said. So Karlovy took command, and, as our time was nearly up, and he was worried for my life, and as the guerrillas were clearly defeated, he opted to pull out.'

'But he saw the bodies.'

'He saw Liane's body, yes.'

'Did he examine it?'

'I don't know. As I say, things were rather fraught, and both Karlovy and Jonsson were worried about me.'

'So no one saw the girl Amalie's body at all.'

'It was assumed that she died in the fighting deep inside the cave. There was very little light.'

'Assumed by Karlovy. And Jonsson, of course. But now it appears that they were mistaken. Where is Jonsson now?'

'On a mission to England.'

'So you still trust her absolutely?'

'I do. Yes.'

'Because she is your mistress?'

'Well . . .' Weber flushed. 'I have no reason not to.'

'Save that she is an American. I know she pretends to be a Nazi sympathizer, but that is easy to do, is it not? She is also a self-confessed lesbian.'

'Oh, come now, Reinhard. That was when she was a school-girl. And it was one relationship, which has gone sour. And is now over, in any event.'

'I hope you are right, Oskar. I think you should know that both Heinrich and the Führer have taken a great interest in the de Gruchy business, certainly in their leader. The Führer described her as a monster of destruction. When I reported to him that she was dead, he snapped his fingers with glee and said, "Good. Good. That is very good." Now, if I have to return to him and tell him that she is actually alive, someone's head is going to roll. I strongly suggest that you line up a candidate for that unfortunate position, or it is going to be yourself.'

Weber swallowed. 'She is dead. I know she is dead.'

'Very good. So we may presume that this woman Amalie is the last of the brood left.'

'Except for Frau von Helsingen.'

'You seem to have an inordinate desire to get your hands on that woman, Oskar. But you were not able to implicate her in the Hoeppner affair, and she is in the Führer's inner circle. She is also about to give birth to his godson. So if I were you, I would forget about her. If she has been aiding her sisters in any way, she has gone about it in a damned clever fashion. Concentrate on this Amalie; we don't want a reincarnation of her other sister on our hands. Have Hoeppner confirmed as remaining in his post for the time being, but send Roess down to clean things up.'

'Roess is presently commanding the Paris Gestapo.'

'I know that, Oskar. I made the appointment. But he can spare a few days. He knows Amalie de Gruchy. He once had her in his cells until Hoeppner interfered. He is the man to put her back there. He will enjoy that. Have him round up a hundred Frenchmen and then issue a statement that unless Amalie de Gruchy is handed over, or surrenders herself, in one week, he will shoot them.'

'A hundred men?'

'She killed a German officer. Do you not consider that a German officer is worth a hundred lives?'

Weber looked longingly into his empty glass, but Heydrich was clearly not going to refill it – his sunny mood was a thing of the past. 'I would like to hear of this woman's capture before I leave for Prague,' Heydrich said. 'Good morning, Oskar.'

'Well, hi there,' said Joanna Jonsson.

'Oh, good lord!' Rachel Cartwright remarked. 'Every time

I see you I don't know whether to smile, scream, or spit. Well, come in. You're blocking the draft.'

This was certainly true. Nearly six feet tall and built to match, Joanna Jonsson filled the doorway. Now she entered the room and seemed to fill the little office as well. As always, her long, thick yellow hair, carefully arranged to half obscure her right eye, lay below her shoulders like a mat, and both her dress and her mink coat had clearly come from Fortnums. Her court shoes merely added to her height, and her bold, handsome features went with her American drawl to enhance the larger-than-life image.

By contrast Rachel, only a few inches shorter, was so slender as to be considered thin. Her dress was dowdy, as required by her position, although she was even more of an aristocrat in private life than the Swedish-American. Her long black hair was confined in a tight bun on the nape of her neck, and her pertly pretty features were partly concealed behind her horn-rimmed spectacles. Yet for all their natural antagonism, the two women respected each other. They had fought together, and killed together – and survived together.

'This city can be bleak in winter,' Joanna agreed. 'And this bit is the bleakest. When does the Thames freeze?'

'It doesn't, as a rule. And the East End suits us. It's not where people expect to find us; nobody asks questions in this part of the world.'

'Because, like you, they're all up to some nefarious activity?' Joanna suggested. 'So where is he?'

'Just hold on a moment. Let's have the password.'

'Oh, for Christ's sake. Suppose I said I'd forgotten it?'

'Then I would have to place you under arrest.'

'You think you could arrest me? I could—'

'Break me in two? I imagine you possibly could. But you'd have to find your way around this.' She levelled the large Browning automatic pistol she had taken from her drawer.

'Holy shit. I never knew you people carried guns.'

'We don't carry them, as a rule. We just keep them handy, to deal with people who want to be funny.'

'All right, all right. The password is Pound. I am Pound Three. You are Pound Two. Right?'

11

'Thank you. Pound One is at a meeting. He'll be back for lunch.'

'Shit.' Joanna seated herself behind the big desk. 'You guys keep liquor on the premises?'

'You do realize it is only eleven o'clock in the morning?'

'Look, in the States we drink when the mood takes us. Not when the clock says we can.'

'Please yourself. We have some Scotch. But the only mix is water.'

'So who wants a mix?'

Rachel went into the tiny flat adjoining the office, poured, and brought the glass back. 'So what's the rush? Can't you stay to lunch?'

Joanna regarded the quarter-filled glass with disfavour. 'I guess rationing is really starting to bite. I can stay for lunch, but it'll have to be quick. I'm catching a boat out of Harwich tonight, and they want us onboard by six. And I have to check with MI5 before I leave London.'

Rachel sat down and crossed her knees. 'You're going back to Germany?'

'Well, back to Sweden first. But of course I'm going back to Germany. I'm the SD's tame messenger girl, remember?'

'Do you know what you're carrying?'

'Nope. And I don't want to. Oskar gives me the letter, I bring it to England, give it to MI5, they steam it open and note the contents. Then they give it back to me and I mail it from the Dorchester. I get a reply and take it along to MI5. They steam that open, note the contents, and return it to me, and I carry it back to Germany.'

'But MI5 must act on the information, surely? You'd know about that.'

'I don't think they do intend to act on it. If they did, they'd blow my cover. I think they just like to know what the other guys are doing . . . as long as they're not doing anything too drastic.' She held out the empty glass.

Rachel took it into the other room to refill it, then brought it back. 'But the time will come when they *have* to act. Do you have any idea what your Nazi friends would do to you if they found out you were actually working for us?'

12

'Honey, the only people in all the world who know I am working for you are you, me, James, my contact at MI5, and the brigadier.'

'And your French friends. The de Gruchys.'

Joanna grinned. 'They're all dead, remember? I said so.'

'And the Nazis believe you?'

'Oskar will believe anything I tell him. He's nuts about me.' She regarded Rachel's somewhat invisible bosom speculatively. 'It must be my tits. And I saved his life, as far as he knows. But anyway, even if we fall out, what can he do? I'm an American citizen, and a well-known one. My mom is a millionairess who plays bridge every week with Mrs Stimson.'

'There's such a thing as an accident.'

'He wouldn't dare. Now tell me, you guys got anything going?'

'After the catastrophe in September? Orders are for everyone to lie low for a few months, certainly until Monsieur Moulin gets back. Anyway, it is going to take that long for the Group to re-establish itself. I hear James.'

'You guys sleep together?'

'Do you mind? He's my boss.'

'Then you *do* sleep together.'

'Oh . . . bugger off.' She stood up as the door opened. 'We have a visitor, sir. Pound Three.'

'I was just talking about you,' Major James Barron said, handing his hat and coat to Rachel and stamping his feet; it was raining outside. He was a big man, not yet thirty – he was, in fact, several years younger than Joanna – with the powerful shoulders of an athlete, as he had been before the war, even if at the moment he moved rather sluggishly – he was still recuperating from the wound he had suffered three months before. His face was rugged rather than handsome, and wore a perpetually surprised expression. This was because, even after very nearly two years, he had still not fully come to terms with his position. A captain in a line regiment in France in 1939, he had regarded his secondment to Military Intelligence at the beginning of 1940 as a bit of a jolly. But after being wounded in the Dunkirk evacuation, he had been offered a job in the newly formed Special Operations Unit.

This had undoubtedly been because of his extensive French contacts, especially the enormously wealthy wine-growing family of de Gruchy. Pierre de Gruchy, the family son and heir, had escaped with him from Dunkirk and had already been training as an agent to return to France. It had seemed natural to the powers that be to make his friend Barron his control. James had been happy to take on the job, if only because it gave him an opportunity, hopefully, to keep in touch with the eldest daughter, Liane, with whom he had fallen in love at their first meeting. It had never occurred to him that Liane would become a leader of the Resistance, would cut such a swathe of destruction – and indeed, murder – through the German occupying forces that she was now the most wanted woman in France, or that she would wind up under his control as well. If he was not actually responsible for her life or death, he was still the man who gave her group its orders, which too often involved life or death situations.

It had also brought under his aegis this reincarnation of some Norse Valkyrie, who laughed, drank and sexed her way through life, apparently without a care in the world. James knew that wasn't true. He knew that Joanna cared as much about Liane as he did, but he also knew she was the loosest cannon in the business. He trusted her absolutely, but he never knew what she was going to do next. And now that she was playing the most dangerous game of all, that of the double agent . . .

Joanna vacated the desk and came towards him. 'Aren't you going to kiss me?'

'Ah . . . I'm on duty. And I assume you are, too.' He had never been able to shake off the feeling that if he once got into Joanna's arms he would never get back out again.

Joanna pouted. 'You are on duty twenty-four hours a day,' she pointed out. 'So is Rachel. But you kiss her, all the time, when you're not doing something better. She just admitted it.' James looked at Rachel, who took off her glasses to polish them. 'Anyway,' Joanna said. 'What's the old buzzard on at now?'

James sat behind his desk and Joanna pulled up the only other chair in the room. 'The usual. He feels we should have more control over, or at least information on, your movements.'

'And I hope you told him that is impossible. I work for the Gestapo. I do what they tell me, go where they send me, stay where they want me to stay. When I'm going some place, they tell me the day before. You want me to give that up?'

'I would, personally. When I think what they would do . . .'

'Don't you start. She's already been on at me. They're not going to do anything to me.'

'Because you're an American? Not to mention a Swede.'

'Because they trust me, or at least Oskar Weber does. It's my business to make sure he goes on doing that. Besides, if I chucked it, I'd be no more use to you, right?'

James sighed. 'Right.'

'So, I'm going back tonight. You got anything for me?'

James sat up. 'Yes. There's been trouble in Bordeaux. You remember Franz Hoeppner?'

'How could I forget?'

'Well, after Liane kidnapped him in September, he was relieved of his post.'

'That figures. He must have wished she'd shot him.'

'Probably even more so now. Anyway, he waited in Bordeaux to hand over to his successor, a fellow called Kessler.'

'Don't tell me he's been shot?'

'Hoeppner hasn't been shot. Kessler has, virtually as he stepped off the train.'

'Great stuff. I'm glad they missed Hoeppner, though. He gave me the impression of being a nice guy.'

'Well, maybe he's changed. He's just taken a hundred hostages and says that if the assassin is not handed over he'll shoot them.'

'*What?*' Both women spoke together.

'It could have been orders from Berlin. Our problem is the assassin. According to the report we have received, it was Amalie de Gruchy.'

'Oh, my God!' Joanna cried.

'They've shot Amalie?' Rachel was equally aghast.

'She got away. That's why he's taken the hostages.'

'Thank God for that,' Joanna said. 'I mean that she at least got away.'

'But wait a moment,' Rachel said. 'Did we command the assassination?'

'No, we did not.'

'And didn't you command them to spend the next couple of months regrouping and re-arming, and to do nothing until the return of Moulin?'

'Yes, I did.'

'Then what can have gone wrong?'

'That is what we have to find out. You get on the buzzer to Pound Seventeen in Limoges. I wish to speak with Liane.'

'Yes, sir.' She seated herself before the radio.

'I cannot believe Liane would have disobeyed your orders,' Joanna said. 'Or that she would have allowed Amalie to take such a risk. Isn't it likely that Hoeppner was mistaken?'

'Not a chance, for three reasons. One is that the Nazis believe that all the de Gruchys were killed in that shoot-out in the Massif Central; why would they throw out Amalie's name, thus giving the lie to their earlier claims, which, incidentally, were *your* claims?'

'Hmm,' she commented.

'The second reason is that Hoeppner knows what Amalie looks like. He rescued her from the Gestapo back in June of last year, remember?'

'Yes,' she said thoughtfully. 'Because Freddie von Helsingen asked him to. Freddie was coming over heavy on Madeleine even then, and he couldn't risk her sister being executed or sent to a concentration camp.'

'Quite. Which provides the third reason for Hoeppner's claim to be correct. Gratitude. If Amalie set out to kill the new German commandant of Bordeaux, don't you suppose that she'd have killed the man sitting beside him as a matter of course? Apparently she stared at him from a distance of six inches and didn't pull the trigger, even though she must have supposed she was about to die herself.'

'She always was a crazy, mixed-up kid.'

16

Rachel had been tapping away at her key and writing down the returns. Now she signed off. 'Pound Seventeen has had no contact with the de Gruchys for four weeks. He assumed, like us, that they were lying low.'

'Holy shit! What did you tell him?'

'To contact us the moment they surface.'

'Shit, shit, shit!'

'Amen,' Joanna agreed. 'Are you saying that the boss knows about this?'

'He knows about the business in Bordeaux, and that if it is true they have acted without orders. He is hopping mad, and told me to sort it out. If I have to go back to him and tell him I have now lost contact with them, and therefore cannot control them, he is going to go straight through the roof. And I can tell you what else he's going to do: he's going to cancel that funding for the route that Liane has applied for. He never has liked the idea of dealing with a brothel.'

'Someone is going to have to go in.'

James looked from face to face. 'I'll do it,' Rachel said.

'Now wait a moment . . .'

'You're not fit enough. And Pound will never let you, after the last time.'

'We'll talk about it. But you can help, Joanna. I want every scrap of information you can collect on just how much your friends know about the present situation. We know that the de Gruchys were top of their wanted list before the shoot-out. They'll be even higher on the list if they appear to be coming back from the dead.'

Joanna nodded. 'I'll do what I can.'

'Incidentally, how do you propose to handle this? It was your evidence that convinced Jerry they were dead.'

'Mine and Captain Karlovy's. And all I claimed was that Liane was dead. I showed him her body, while agitating all the while that we had to get Weber out of there before he bled to death, and as it was dark and Karlovy was in a hurry he didn't look very closely. As for the others, I reported that they had retreated deep into the cave and were probably dead. They were happy with that; it was Liane they were after. So I was optimistic about Amalie. They'll buy that.'

'I hope to God you're right.'

'So let's get on it. There was a rumour going about that you were going to take me out to lunch.'

Rachel threw her hat into the corner as she and James entered the office. 'You know, I cannot bring myself to like that woman. But has she got guts.'

James closed the door behind them. 'So have you. But I don't think . . .'

She stood against him, put her arms round his neck, and kissed him on the mouth. 'I'm the only one who knows the situation. Besides, I enjoyed the last time.'

'You damn near got killed.'

She kissed him again. 'That's because I had you along, and you were the one who nearly got killed.' She went into the flat. 'I think we could both do with a lie down. That was an alcoholic lunch. It always is with Joanna.'

He followed her into the bedroom, watched her undress. This was something he could do by the hour, no matter how often he had done it before. Her movements were gloriously erotic, but there was more to it than that. James came from a relatively humble background – his father was a housemaster at a public school. Thanks to that, he had been able to attend the school himself, and had thus gained entry to Sandhurst – there would have been very little point in his attempting Oxbridge. Thus his life's course had appeared to be set in a regular motion, occupying dead men's shoes while slowly working his way up the ladder of promotion. He had set his sights no higher than retirement as a half-colonel.

The outbreak of war in September 1939 had had a tremendous effect on his life, as it had done on everyone in the Army, if only because it suggested that there might be more than the usual number of dead men's shoes to fill in the near future. Besides, it was what they had all been trained for, without any real expectation that their training might ever be put to practical use. And, for more than six months, virtually nothing had happened. Thus he had welcomed the transfer to Intelligence as a relief from the boredom of drilling and digging and waiting. Until May 10th 1940.

18

By then he had stumbled, inadvertently, into the glamorous, exotic world of the de Gruchys. It had begun with a chance meeting at a dance thrown by the British Ambassador for such officers who might be on leave in Paris, just before Christmas 1939. There he had met Madeleine de Gruchy, and been swept off his feet by her looks and her chic, her clothes and her aura. That she had made some time to spend with him had seemed a miraculous turn of fortune, a glimpse of how the other half lived, on both sides of the Channel, for Madeleine's mother was an English aristocrat, and she and her sisters had been educated at Benenden, and regarded England as a second home. Her sisters! He had supposed that evening had been no more than an unrepeatable incident. But out of the blue had come an invitation for him to attend the marriage of the youngest, Amalie, to Henri Burstein. He had obtained leave, and had gone to Chartres in a mood mostly of disbelief that he should have been included in such a family affair, knowing that it must have been engineered by Madeleine, which had to mean that she was interested in him. He had looked forward to seeing her again while not daring to consider to what else he might look forward . . . And then he met Liane.

Madeleine was a lovely girl, if somewhat serious. Amalie was both pretty and vivacious. But Liane was a goddess! A goddess who lived according to her own rules – rules neither understood nor approved of by her family. Liane had preferred to live in her Paris flat rather than do the rounds of the family houses in England and France, and spend her evenings with the left-bank would-be authors and painters than at fashion-able cocktail parties. Unmarried at thirty, her private life had been a family scandal, beginning with her expulsion from her Swiss finishing school for having an affair with her best friend – Joanna Jonsson.

Not then knowing her background, that she should have looked twice at him and then offered him her body had appeared another miracle. That he should find himself respon-sible, however indirectly, for her fate, had been a macabre twist. That she had a disconcerting habit of taking that fate and its possible savage ending into her own hands was both frustrating and terrifying.

Most frustrating of all was the uncertainty of whether her feelings for him were anything like as intense as his desire for her. On the half-dozen occasions they had lain naked in each other's arms she had given herself to him with an uninhibited passion. But this was an aspect of her personality, and he had no means of knowing if she gave herself to other men, or women, with equal abandon. And when he wished to talk about afterwards – because there had to be an afterwards; the war could not go on for ever – she always gently turned him aside with the reminder that she was an outlaw and a murderess. But in a war, where did lawful killing end and murder begin? The more important question was, when it was over, how did one revert to being a normal human being, a domestic housewife? Could one? But that question applied equally to the male.

He loved Liane, but without this woman now lying naked on the bed in front of him, carefully taking off her spectacles and placing them on the bedside table, he knew he would have gone mad. The amazing thing was that Rachel Cartwright was out of a drawer every bit as top as Liane de Gruchy. Her father was a general, and his ancestors had been generals right back to the Great Rebellion. He knew that to her, also, the war had been a bit of a lark, in the beginning. But as a general's daughter she had felt obliged to do her bit, and, after joining the ATS, she had rapidly volunteered for special training, which had brought her to this office. They had regarded each other with suspicion at first. But due to Special Operations' policy of working in small, isolated sections under an overall commander – to lessen the risk of penetration by or betrayal to the enemy – they had found themselves spending most of every day alone together, and this had soon carried over into the nights. He could reflect that, while he had broken every rule in the book by taking someone who was essentially an enlisted 'man' to bed, the idea had been entirely hers. And she was an adorable companion, on either side of the sheets; utterly loyal, always anxious to please, and while she knew all about his feelings for Liane, she was also filled with the wartime spirit of living for today and worrying about tomorrow when it came – because tomorrow might never come.

But she was also a young woman who could follow her own agenda with unremitting purpose. Thus, as he lay panting into her neck, she gently uncoiled the long legs she had wrapped around him and, with some effort and a few grunts, managed to slide her body out from beneath his. 'About the drop,' she remarked.

He rolled over. 'Why are you so anxious to commit suicide?'

'I have no intention of committing suicide. I just want to do my bit.'

'You are doing your bit right here in this office. And I am not referring to sex.'

She got up and put the kettle on while he watched her movements, so utterly graceful. 'Do you have any idea what it is like to sit here like some gigantic spider, issuing directives, orders, commands, to people you have never seen?'

'You saw them, most of them, in September.'

'That makes it worse. I know you feel just the same. You get over there every chance you can.'

'I have been to France three times since the evacuation, and the last was inadvertent. I am still suffering for it. And you have been once. That should be enough for anyone.'

She poured tea, sat beside him to drink it. 'This is urgent. Someone has to go. And you know that I have all the qualifications. I am a trained parachutist. I can even fly an aircraft. I speak French like a native, and I know both the people and the situation on the ground. Come on, James.'

'Today is December the fifth. You'll get chilblains on your fanny.'

'Then you can smother it with cream.'

'You'll miss Christmas.'

'Of course I won't. I'll be back in a week. Well, a fortnight.' She gave a wicked smile. 'I'll be able to give Liane your love.'

James played his trump card. 'I'll have to have a temp.'

'Of course. I'll organize it.'

'You mean you're going to go looking for a battleaxe.'

'Not necessarily. Just someone who will understand that you're my property.'

*   *   *

21

'Right,' James said. 'Here is the drill. Your papers, ID card and some personal documentation will be ready tomorrow; your name is Brigitte Ferrand and you are a schoolteacher who has lost her job in Paris and is looking for employment in Vichy. You're not going to jump; you'll be flown in. Your pilot will be Brune, who you know. You'll be landed in the Limoges area, which means there won't be any nasties around. Pound Seventeen will be informed of zone and time and hopefully one of his people will be able to meet you. Your brief is to regain contact with the de Gruchy Group, find out why they have resumed operations without reference to us, and insist that they conform to orders in the future.'

'And after ticking Liane off, I'm to give her your love.'

'If you would.'

'And give her a hug and a kiss?' She winked at his glare. 'Just testing. Now, I have Jennifer waiting outside. Shall I bring her in?'

'Jennifer?'

'My temporary replacement. We were at school together.'

'Is that a recommendation?'

'Well, let's say we know each other very well.' She opened the door. 'The Major will see you now, Sergeant.'

James stood up instinctively as the woman entered the room and stood to attention. 'Sergeant Jennifer Mayhew, sir. Reporting for duty.'

As required, Jennifer Mayhew wore civilian clothes, but, in the strongest possible contrast to Rachel, she was short and plump, her features soft, her brown hair curly and worn short.

'Glad to have you, Sergeant,' James said. 'I gather Cartwright has put you in the picture?'

'Yes, sir.'

'And you understand the covert nature of our work here?'

'Oh, yes, sir.'

'Well, then, Sergeant Cartwright will show you around.'

'The flat is through here.' Rachel opened the door, and left it open.

James listened.

'There's only one bed,' Jennifer Mayhew remarked.

'So you sleep one at a time,' Rachel pointed out.

James grinned, and the telephone rang. Rachel hurried back in, but he had already picked it up. 'Pound One.'

'Pound,' said the brigadier. Unusually for him, he sounded breathless. 'Have you heard the news?'

'Ah . . . What news, sir?'

'It's just come through. At seven this morning, Hawaiian time, the Japanese attacked Pearl Harbor and destroyed the American Pacific fleet.'

'Ah . . . Would you repeat that, sir?'

'For God's sake, James, wake up. The Japs and the Yanks are at war. So are we, in the Pacific. Reports are coming in that Singapore has been bombed.'

'God Almighty! Where does that leave us?'

'Nationally, I'm waiting to find out. On the ground we have to look after our people. Starting with Jonsson.'

Two

Necessity

'I take it you know where she is,' the brigadier said.

'I know that she left this country three days ago.'

'To go where?'

'In the first instance, Sweden. She goes there ostensibly to visit her father. From there she crosses the Baltic to one of the German ports.'

'So she should still be there. In Sweden. Get on to your man in Stockholm, tell him to get hold of her and tell her under no circumstances to go on to Germany. She should return here immediately.'

'With respect, sir, has Germany also attacked the United States?'

'Not so far as I am aware.'

'Then the two countries are not at war. Her situation hasn't changed.'

'James, Germany and Japan are allies. We do not know the exact terms of the alliance, whether Germany is committed to aiding the Japanese in any war with a third party, but the fact that Japan is also attacking our territories makes it almost certain that Hitler will declare war on the US at some time. In any event, Jonsson is now totally exposed. You get her back.' He hung up.

James slowly replaced the phone, looked past it at Jennifer and Rachel, who had been listening on the extension. 'It's nice to know the old buzzard cares about his people,' Rachel commented. 'Even Joanna.'

'Don't you believe it,' James said. 'He's only worried that if she's arrested by the Gestapo and tortured she'll tell them all she knows about our operations, which is quite a lot.'

'Shit! What are we going to do?'

'Obey orders, for a start. That's your first job, Jennifer. Get on the line to Pound Twenty-Three and tell him to find Pound Three and instruct her to come home immediately.'

'Yes, sir. Ah . . . what number do I have?'

'In Rachel's absence, you are her. Pound Two.'

Jennifer looked at Rachel. 'Just the number,' Rachel said. 'Until I come back.' Jennifer sat before the set. 'Does this affect my mission in any way?' Rachel asked.

James shook his head. 'We have to find out what's happening over there.'

'Willco. Liane, here I come.'

'Only if she's there. You stay out of the occupied territory. That's an order.'

The woman pushed open the iron gate and walked up the path. The grounds to either side of her, though extensive, were nearly as decrepit as she. The lawns were uncut, the hedges unclipped, the trees untrimmed. The woman, straggly grey hair escaping from her bonnet, threadbare shawl clutched around her shoulders, back bowed beneath the weight of her pack, stumbled slowly up to the front door of the big, four-square house, set well back from the road to diminish the roar of the Paris traffic – not that on a December afternoon in 1941 there was a great deal of Paris traffic, apart from the vehicles of the occupying army. The woman made her way slowly up the shallow front steps and rang the bell. There was a delay, and then the door swung in.

'We do not open until six,' this woman said. Tall and raw-boned, she was clearly used to repelling unwanted callers. Then she realized that she was facing a woman. 'And we need no labour. Be off with you, granny.'

'What a way to treat a poor old lady,' the woman remarked, her voice crisp and sharp, yet with a peculiarly soft lilt. 'I thought you would be pleased to see me, Marguerite.'

Marguerite stared at her, for some seconds unable to speak. Then she gasped. 'But you are dead! The Germans say you are dead.'

'The Germans say a lot of things that are not necessarily true. Now let me in.'

25

Marguerite stepped back and the woman entered the hall, at the same time straightening and shrugging the pack from her back with the ease of a strong and healthy body, quite belying her earlier hesitation. Marguerite ran across the hall, a wide area, and knocked on the door to the left. 'Madame! Madame! Mademoiselle de Gruchy is here.'

'Sssh!' Liane de Gruchy followed her more slowly. 'You will wake the dead.' She smiled as the door opened. 'Hello, Constance.'

The woman standing there, long-legged and voluptuous, with dyed red hair, was in her mid-forties, but no less attractive for that. Now, like her maid, she stared at Liane. 'My God!' she whispered. 'But . . .'

'Everyone thinks I am dead. Shall we keep it that way for the time being?'

'But . . .' Constance peered at her. 'What have they done to you?'

'*They* have done nothing that a hot bath and a bottle of shampoo won't fix. In fact, that is the top of my list.'

'Marguerite,' Constance commanded, 'draw Mademoiselle Liane a bath. In my apartment.'

Marguerite hurried off and Constance held out her arms. Liane went to them and was embraced. 'My God!' Constance said. 'You smell like a sewer.'

'Well, that we are about to put right. But to stink is the best way to put men off getting too close, whether they be German soldiers or French lechers.' She went into the office. 'It is also some time since I had a drink.'

'Cognac!' Constance hurried to the sideboard and poured two glasses. 'But why are you here?' She leaned on the desk 'It is so dangerous.'

Liane brushed glasses. 'Damnation to the Boches! It is not dangerous at all, as long as your people are still loyal.'

'Of course they are. But if you were to be recognized . . .'

'Like this?'

'But after you have had a bath, and washed the dye from your hair and the make-up from your face, you will have to stay in your room.'

'I don't think that will be necessary. The Germans have

one photograph of me, which is three years old and is of a very chic, long-haired blonde. They also have a description of the woman who shot five German soldiers in a minute, a woman with short black hair and a generally dowdy appearance.'

'Liane, no man who has ever got close to you is going to ever forget any part of you.'

Liane blew her a kiss. 'You are so sweet. I think you should dye my hair red. Then you can say I am your sister come to visit with you.'

'I do not have a sister.'

'You do now. We will make up a joint family background.'

'The Gestapo know my family background.'

'Then we will embroider it and add a few details. As to why I am here, well, I wish to know that everything is running smoothly.'

'With the Route? There has been no problem so far. We have two Evaders in residence now. They are to be moved tomorrow. Do you wish to see them?'

'I do not think so. Certainly they must not know who I am. One of these people is going to be captured, one day.'

'And you think he would betray us?'

'Hopefully not. But it is better to be safe. Is the money being paid regularly?'

'Yes. Monsieur Brissard is not happy . . .'

Liane nodded. 'I wish to see him. Tell him to come here.'

'You expect a man like Brissard to come to a brothel?'

'Even an old stick-in-the-mud like Brissard must feel like a woman other than his wife occasionally. I assume he also thinks I am dead?'

'Everyone thinks you are dead.'

'Then to tell him I am alive may give him a heart attack. He must come here where he can see me for himself and where I can speak with him. Tell him you wish to see him, urgently.'

Constance nodded and looked up as the door opened. 'The bath is ready, Mademoiselle Liane,' Marguerite said.

Liane finished her drink and got up. 'You had better send Hercule to me.'

'Hercule is not here.'

'You let him go out? He is a wanted man.'

'I could not keep him. When he heard of your death he went berserk. He took to the bottle, then he left.'

'Shit! Was he armed?'

'He had that gun you left here.'

'Shit, shit, shit!' Liane led the way up the stairs.

'That man worships you.' Constance followed.

'And I am very fond of him. He saved my life.' Liane faced a pretty young woman wearing a dressing gown. 'Hello, Louise.'

'Mademoiselle Liane! But . . .'

'It's a long story, which Madame Constance will explain to you shortly. For the time being, pretend that you have seen a ghost.' She entered the bathroom and stripped off her filthy clothes. 'I have worn those for twelve days. I think they should be burned.'

Constance regarded the naked body in front of her. 'Why do you always look good enough to eat? Did you not love Hercule? You were his mistress.'

Liane sank into the tub with a sigh of satisfaction. 'I was not his mistress, Constance, except in his eyes. I shared his bed because I had to have a base in Paris.' Constance undressed as well, and knelt beside the tub with a bottle of shampoo. In some contrast to Liane's hard-muscled perfection, she was overweight. 'Have you never loved any man? Or woman?' she added hopefully.

Liane soaped, slowly and luxuriously, while Constance soaked her hair. 'I have loved a woman. I think I probably still do. We were at school together.' *And she, too, has saved my life*, she thought. It was such a feeling of reassurance to know that she and Joanna were now working together, for the same end.

'But no men,' Constance suggested, more hopefully yet.

Liane considered. 'There is one,' she said, and giggled. 'My boss.'

'You have a boss?'

'Did you think I could create all this, the network, the Route, have access to my gun and ammunition, all on my own? I work for the British.'

'I do not like the British. They deserted us last year. Lean back so I can rinse.' Liane obeyed, and then there was a tap on the door. 'What is it?' Constance called.

Marguerite opened the door. 'Captain Hoffmann is here.'

'He is always early. What time is it?'

'Just past six, madame.'

'Are the girls down?'

'Three of them.'

'Well, tell them to entertain him. I will be down in a little while. If he is impatient, they can give him a trick. He can pay later.' Marguerite closed the door.

'As popular as ever,' Liane remarked.

Constance poured water and massaged Liane's scalp. 'Of course. I run the best house in Paris. Now get out and I will use the dye. You are sure you wish to be red? It will not go with your colouring.'

'Who is going to look at my colouring?' Liane got out of the bath and towelled herself dry. 'I feel almost human again.' She leaned over the basin. 'You must not hate the British, Constance. They took their army away to fight another day. What would have been the point in their surrendering three hundred thousand men to the Germans? In any event, you are working for them now, too.'

Constance was busy with the shampoo. 'You told me I was working for France.'

'We are all working for the defeat of Nazi Germany. We in particular are under the command of the British Secret Service.'

'And you have fallen in love with one of them?'

'I did not say I had fallen in love with him. But I think if I was going to love any man it would be him.'

'Have you ever met him?'

'Oh, I have met him,' Liane said dreamily.

'There,' Constance said. 'That is fine. Actually it suits you.'

Liane straightened to look at herself in the mirror. 'I look forty years younger.'

'When the war is over you should join the Folies Bergère. Or will you merely go back to being a millionairess?'

'I don't know there will be anything left to go back to, after the war.'

'Well, you know . . .' Liane was still looking at herself in the mirror. Constance slid her hands over her buttocks and then round in front to caress her pubes. 'There will always be a place for you here.'

Liane blew her a kiss. 'After the war, maybe. But as I am here now, let's go and see what the latest breed of Nazi officer is like.'

Henri Brissard closed the gate behind him, and looked nervously left and right. He was sixty-two years old, and for forty of those years had been the epitome of respectability. He had worked his way up from junior clerk to be the manager of De Gruchy and Son's Paris office, which, apart from the headquarters in the village of Paulliac, outside Bordeaux, was the most important of the firm's agencies. The bulk of the orders for Gruchy wines came through Paris. Of course, since the invasion, the only orders came from Germans, but even Germans could appreciate good wine, and de Gruchy was the best. So, although the family itself, by identifying with and then leading the Resistance, had outlawed themselves, the Germans were content to let the vineyards continue to produce their superb grapes, and the business to continue without interruption. They counted the staff as of no importance, clerks who were only happy to have retained their well-paid jobs. They had no idea what went on beneath the surface, and particularly here in Paris. But that was known only to himself and a bunch of whores.

That he had become involved with such people – financing them in their surreptitious activities of smuggling downed British airmen out of France – had been because Mademoiselle Liane had commanded him to do so, illegally using company funds for the purpose. But no man he had ever known had been able to resist Mademoiselle Liane's beauty and charm, particularly when these were backed up by the deadliness of the dedicated assassin. But following the news of her death, Henri had not been able to suppress a sigh of relief. If he had often dreamed of having her as a mistress, he had also known that it had never been the least possible. Nor could he still dream of her memory without the disturbing apprehension of her next appearance in his life, requiring him to carry out some new task that would endanger both himself and his family.

He would even be able to tell Madame Constance that he could no longer support her activities. How he had got away with it for so long without the books being audited and his repeated embezzlement uncovered, he had no idea. He had told her last messenger that it would have to stop . . . But now he'd received this peremptory summons, and to such a place! At least there was no one about in the middle of the afternoon, but the thought that he might be spotted – entering a brothel!

He rang the bell and was faced with Marguerite. 'I am to see Madame Constance,' he announced.

'Monsieur Brissard, is it?'

'My name is not important.'

'I am sure it is, to someone, monsieur. Come in. Give me your hat and coat.'

'That will not be necessary. My visit will be brief.'

Marguerite shrugged. 'This way, monsieur.' She led him across the hall while he looked around himself and up the stairs, wondering . . . Presumably at three o'clock in the afternoon they were all asleep. Marguerite knocked. 'Monsieur Brissard is here, mademoiselle.' Brissard's head jerked.

'Ask him to come in, Marguerite,' said the woman beyond the door. Brissard gasped, but Marguerite had opened the door. 'Henri!' Liane had risen and come round the desk. 'It is good of you to come so promptly.'

'But . . . They said . . .'

'Thank you, Marguerite. Please don't say it, Henri. Everyone says it, and it is becoming tiresome. Unless you believe in ghosts, I cannot possibly be dead.' She embraced him, kissed him on both cheeks. 'Do I feel like a ghost?'

'Oh, mademoiselle . . .' With difficulty he kept his arms at his sides. 'There is so much—'

'I know. Sit down.' She indicated the chair before the desk. 'Madame Constance tells me you are concerned about the money.'

'It is a serious matter, mademoiselle. The books should have

31

been audited in October. I do not know why they were not. But it must happen soon. And then . . . I shall go to prison.'

Liane leaned against the desk, almost touching him. Now she squeezed his hand. 'Of course you are not going to prison, Henri. I have arranged it. There will be no audit until next April. When it happens, any irregularities will be overlooked. I have also arranged for funds to be supplied from England, so you will no longer be involved. You will be able to go into honourable retirement, knowing that you have played your part in our eventual victory.'

Brissard did not look entirely convinced. 'But . . . Monsieur Bouterre . . .'

'Monsieur Bouterre is on our side.'

'You have spoken with him?'

'In my father's absence, he is managing director, and as such he takes his orders from me. So you see, you have nothing to worry about. All you need to do is continue to supply the funds here in Paris until the English source takes over. Then you can forget all about us.'

'I could never forget about you, mademoiselle. Will you be staying in Paris?'

'For a while, certainly. Now, as you are here, would you like someone to accommodate you? It will be on the house.'

'Oh, mademoiselle . . .'

'Come on, Henri, be a devil.' She had remained half-sitting on the desk, her hip almost against his arm. Now he gave a heavy sigh as he gazed, not at her face, but at her groin, and the penny dropped. 'Why, Henri,' she said. 'You *are* a devil, after all.' She held his hand again and drew him to his feet. 'Come upstairs with me.'

'Have you heard the news from Bordeaux, Herr Colonel?' Captain Marach asked.

Johann Roess raised his head. He was a small man with a toothbrush moustache and sharp features, precise in his manner and his dress. Only recently appointed head of the Gestapo in Paris – although he had served in France for over a year – he always wore uniform, his tie knot tight against his collar. 'I have heard the news.'

'Do you believe it, sir? You were there when the de Gruchy gang was wiped out.'

'I was in Bordeaux,' Roess said carefully. 'I did not take part in the raid on the de Gruchy hideout, and so had to accept the report made by Colonel Weber and that American harpy he trails around.'

'Then you think this assassin could have been the de Gruchy woman?'

'*That* de Gruchy woman, very probably. But she will go the way of her sister. Do you know, I once had that woman, Amalie, in my cells in Dieppe, and was forced to let her go. By this same idiot, Hoeppner. That is why she did not shoot him as well as Kessler, you know. She owes him her life.' He flicked the paper on his desk. 'Now they want me back, to find her all over again. Would you believe it?'

'You are going to Bordeaux, sir?'

'That is what I have just said. I am going to find and arrest the last of this devilish brood. And this time I am not going to let her go. You will have to hold the fort here for a few days.'

'Yes, sir.' Marach, an eager young man, delighted to be working with such a famous officer, bristled with enthusiastic curiosity. 'Did you ever meet her sister, sir? The famous one.'

'If I had ever met Liane de Gruchy, Hermann, her fame would have ended there and then.'

'I wonder if she was as beautiful as people say.'

'Very probably yes, judging by her photo. But she was a cold-blooded murderess. Remember that.'

'Yes, sir. Speaking of the American woman, sir, what will happen to her now that we have declared war on the United States?'

'That will be very interesting. If she has any sense she will not return to Germany.'

'But if she does . . .'

'She will either have to declare her allegiance to the Führer, and become a traitor in the eyes of the Americans, or she will be executed.'

'May I ask, sir . . . What is *she* like?'

'Oh. Very Aryan. Her father is a Swede, you know. What

with her American millionairess mother, that is why she carries so much clout.'

Marach studied his expression. 'I do not think you like this woman, sir.'

'I do not like Fräulein Jonsson, Hermann. I think she is leading Weber up the garden path. In which direction I do not know. But I will tell you this: I would give a month's pay to have her down in our cells, right this minute.' He looked at his watch and stood up. 'I will go home now. I have some packing to do. I am to leave on tomorrow night's train.'

Marach held his topcoat for him. 'Do you think this American development is bad for us, sir?'

'I don't think you need lose any sleep over it. It had to come. That it has come sooner than perhaps we intended is neither here nor there.'

'But this talk of American power . . .'

'It may be a powerful country, Hermann, in terms of industrial production. But the production is all consumer oriented. The Americans live in luxury, and believe in it. They are not going to give up one iota of that luxury to fight a war. And, incidentally, how are they proposing to fight this war? The two oceans, which have protected them from foreign invasion, must also inhibit their ability to invade other countries. They are more than three thousand miles of water away from us, and more than six from Japan. Let them fight a naval war for a year or so, supposing they can find the ships. By then this Russian business will have been completed, and we will be able to deal with them ourselves. Have a good evening.'

'Thank you, sir. Ah . . . Would you not care to have a good evening?' Roess raised his eyebrows. 'I was thinking of going to Madame Constance. Have you been?'

'A couple of times, last year.' *Before I became commandant*, he thought. Dignity above everything. Besides, he remembered how critical Constance had been when he had told her his requirements.

'It is really very good,' Marach said. 'And you know you will meet no one but German officers there. No one else is accepted.'

'I know that, Marach. But the same six girls, night after night . . . Don't you get tired of them?'

'Well, actually, sir, there is a new girl. Constance's sister. She is an absolute knock-out. I'm sure you would enjoy her.'

Roess considered this. But when Constance had refused him permission to indulge his sadistic tastes, he had been a mere captain, and of no great importance. Now he was Commandant of the Paris Gestapo. She would not dare refuse him anything. But a sister?

'Constance does not have a sister.'

'Well, that is what she says she is. They have the same colour of hair.'

What does one do, Roess wondered, with an army composed of innocents? On the other hand . . . 'Do you know, Hermann,' he said, 'I think this may be worth investigating.'

At nine p.m. Madame Constance's was full. She had a large reception room opening to the right of the central hall, which had an inner staircase leading up to the bedrooms in use. There was a bar where the clientele could help themselves to whatever they wished, and if there were only eight women, including Constance herself, there were a dozen men, all in uniform. Three of the women were already upstairs with their clients. A further nine men were downstairs with the remaining five prostitutes, drinking and choosing their partners. The talk was vivacious, the 'champagne' flowing. It was, in fact, exactly as Roess remembered it.

Constance advanced to greet the two new arrivals, smiling as always, but her smile faded when she recognized the colonel. Then it returned more brightly than before.

'Herr Colonel! Captain Marach! We are honoured. It is not every day the Gestapo pays us a visit, except officially. You are not on an official visit, I hope?'

'I am told you have a new girl,' Roess said. 'Your sister. Introduce her to me.'

'She is presently upstairs.'

'Then I will wait, eh?' He had already handed his cap, coat, gloves and stick to Marguerite. Now he strolled into the room, acknowledging the respectful and somewhat apprehensive greetings of the other officers.

35

Constance hurried behind him, anxiously; she had no idea how Liane would react to the idea of being whipped, but she didn't want to have to risk it. 'You don't want to wait, Herr Colonel. I have just the girl for you. Louise, Louise, come over here. Do you remember Colonel Roess? He commands the Gestapo.'

'It is my pleasure, Herr Colonel.' Louise was a dark-haired, voluptuous young woman whose décolletage was slashed to her navel, and who, perhaps more importantly, had a large backside.

'I am charmed,' Roess said. 'But I will wait for . . . your sister's name?'

'Jeanne,' Constance said.

'Jeanne. I will wait for Jeanne.'

'I will come with you, Louise,' Marach said, as eager as ever.

'Ah, Captain, you also will have to wait. There is someone in front of you.'

'But . . .' Marach looked from woman to woman.

'Colonel Roess is a colonel, Herr Captain,' Constance explained in her most dulcet tones. 'And Louise is entertaining a major, who is waiting for you now, Louise. But your turn will be next.'

'The privileges of rank, my dear Hermann,' Roess said to the frustrated young man. 'My word!'

Constance turned to watch Liane descending the stars. 'Shit,' she muttered under her breath. There would be no holding Roess back now. As with all the women, Liane had showered and renewed her make-up following her trick. The décolletage on her blue dress was every bit as deep as Louise's, and her deep-red hair floated above her shoulders as she moved. Although all the men in the room, save Roess, had seen her before, every head turned.

'She is quite beautiful,' Roess said, and went forward. 'Jeanne, is it?'

Liane glanced at Constance; she had instantly recognized both the uniform and the insignia.

'Jeanne,' Constance said, 'may I present Colonel Johann Roess, Commandant of the Paris Gestapo.'

36

Liane's expression of eager anticipation never changed, but then, as Constance had suggested, she was a consummate actress. 'I am charmed, Herr Colonel,' she said softly.

'As am I, mademoiselle. It is mademoiselle?'

'At the moment, yes, sir.'

'And will you accommodate me, mademoiselle?'

Liane gave Constance another glance as she said, 'I will be pleased, sir.'

'It will be one hundred francs,' Constance said.

Roess raised his eyebrows. 'She is that good?'

'Yes. And it is to cover your special requirements. There will be a further hundred if you mark her.'

'Very good. Captain Marach will pay you.'

Constance looked at Liane and waggled her eyebrows. Liane held the colonel's hand and led him to the stairs. 'You have special requirements, Herr Colonel?'

'I have . . . tastes.'

'Well, let me see if I can gratify them.' She climbed the stairs in front of him, his gaze an almost physical presence on her buttocks. She felt a mixture of anticipation and apprehension. She genuinely enjoyed sex, but if sex with James was sublime, it was a rare event in their circumstances, and her Bohemian years before the war had accustomed her to more rough and ready methods – as typified by Hercule more recently. But always, even with Hercule, while he knew she needed his support, she had been in control, because of her money and the prestige of her family, as well as her own dominant personality. She had never encountered a man who, when Liane de Gruchy held up her hand and said enough, did not immediately obey.

But that was outside of this brothel. She had only worked here on a few occasions, when Constance had first hidden her from the Gestapo before she had hurried back south to resume control of the Group last August. It had been a strangely satisfying experience, to be forced to surrender herself absolutely to a man's lust, yet knowing that it would be over in half an hour. This time she knew it was going to be different. She had never seen, much less met, Colonel Roess before, but she had heard of him; his reputation was known throughout France.

Thus it was extremely unlikely that he would be interested in straightforward sex – and Constance had seemed agitated.

On the other hand, for her to have sex with a man who would give his all to be able to hang Liane de Gruchy was a hoot. The last time she had been here she had entertained the even more fearsome Oskar Weber, and counted that her biggest triumph. But his desires had been oddly straightforward.

She led Roess along the corridor to the room she had been allotted, which was situated immediately beneath the attic in which two RAF officers were concealed. She wondered if they could hear what was happening beneath them? Obviously they would know they were being hidden in a brothel; they could hardly fail to be interested in what was going on. Roess shut the door behind them. 'Constance speaks highly of you,' he remarked.

'I am her sister.' Liane released her gown and let it slide from her shoulders to gather round her ankles. She wore nothing underneath. She stepped out of it and felt him behind her. His hands closed on her arms, slid down them to her wrists, then moved inside them and grasped her hips. She waited, controlling her breathing, while he came up her sides to her armpits, then slid round to hold her breasts. So far he had been utterly gentle.

'You are very desirable,' he said into her ear.

'Thank you, sir.'

'I wish your lips.'

She turned into his arms. His kiss was also gentle.'And again.'

'Of course. Do you prefer to lie, sit, or stand.'

'I will sit.' He chose the one chair, which had arms, and sat down with his legs apart. Liane knelt between them, released his breeches, and did as he wanted. It was very quick. He sighed, predictably. 'You are very good.'

Liane swallowed. 'I am a professional. Will there be anything else?' As if any man would pay a hundred francs for a simple blow job.

'Yes. Now I would like to attend to you.'

It could only be with his hands or his mouth, at least for the immediate future. 'How would you like me?'

'On the bed.' She lay down. 'On your face.' She rolled over. 'Spread you arms and legs wide. Grasp the bedposts with your hands. You understand that I do not wish to bind you, but you must not move. You may scream, if you wish. I would like to hear you scream. And then you must beg. I will beat you until you beg.'

Oh, shit, she thought. But she obeyed, wrapping her fingers round the bedposts, extending her toes as far as she could, clenching her buttocks and praying that he only meant to hit her there. She listened to the sound of him undressing, turned her head, and saw that he was already becoming erect again, in anticipation. Now he drew his belt, made of heavy leather, out from his breeches. His holster he laid on the chair. Then he stood by the bed. Time to beg, she decided.

'Please, sir . . .'

'That is too soon. I wish to see your ass turn red.' He swung the belt.

The pain was so immediate and intense it took Liane's breath away as it seemed to cut through her body into her groin, and before she could recover there was another blow. She got her breath back for the third, and uttered a piercing shriek.

'Ha ha!' he shouted. 'I like that.'

Liane knew that she was not going to be able to stand much more of this, and was terribly aware of the proximity of the holstered pistol. But to resist, and perhaps kill this appalling man, would not merely be to commit suicide – the house was full of German officers, and their cars and drivers were parked outside – it would also mean the deaths of Constance and all her girls, not to mention the destruction of the Route she had worked so hard to establish. She could not let that happen. So she clenched her teeth – she could no longer clench her muscles – received the next blow, and became aware of a very loud noise from downstairs, shouts, screams, and then several shots.

'What the shit . . .' Roess turned to the door, hearing heavy feet in the corridor.

Liane rolled across the bed, sat up, giving a gasp of pain, and watched the door swing in. She stared at the big, unshaven, roughly dressed man standing there. Hercule!

39

He was armed with a Luger automatic pistol. 'Bitch!' he shouted, and then looked at Roess. Liane's brain raced. Hercule was levelling his gun, and there could be no doubt he meant to shoot the Gestapo officer. She could hear feet on the stairs; there could equally be no doubt that they were about to be joined by every other officer in the building. If Hercule were taken, they were all as dead as if she had shot Roess herself. She had been this man's lover for several months now. But that had been expedience; she was fighting a war to save France, and the rest of the people in this house were fighting beside her, utterly loyal to her. But Hercule, as she had agreed with Constance, had become a menace.

The decision was instantaneous. She tumbled out of bed on to her knees, reached the colonel's holster and drew the gun. Roess had backed against the wall, still holding the belt, but clearly close to being paralysed as he stared death in the face. Hercule was distracted by Liane's violent movement and turned towards her. As he did so, she aimed and fired. The bullet struck him in the face and he fell backwards without a sound as his head disintegrated into a mass of flying brains and blood.

'My God!' Roess gasped. The room filled with men and women, but the men were to the fore. Hands grasped Liane and tore the pistol from her hand. 'Don't harm her!' Roess shouted. 'She saved my life.'

Constance pushed her way through the throng. 'Li— Jeanne?'

'That man . . .' Liane panted, and now she was not acting.

Roess was pulling on his pants. 'He broke in here, waving a pistol. How did he do this?'

'He suddenly appeared, Herr Colonel,' Marach said. 'Meitner tried to stop him, and he shot him. I think he is seriously hurt. Then he ran up here . . .' He looked at Liane.

'And this gallant little girl did what none of you *gentlemen* were able to do,' Roess snapped. 'Take your hands off her. Jeanne, my dear, are you hurt?'

Released by the officers, Liane sank on to the bed, and immediately stood up again. 'Only in my ass.'

'Yes. Well, you have been paid for that. But now you are

a heroine.' He glared around the officers, daring anyone to argue. Then he looked at Constance. 'Who is this man?'

'I have never seen him before in my life,' Constance declared, without hesitation.

Roess looked at Liane. 'He seemed to know you.'

'I don't know how. I only arrived a few days ago.'

'Perhaps he was on the train with you. Yes, that must be it.' He surveyed the waiting men. 'This must be kept quiet.'

'But, Herr Colonel,' Marach protested, 'the man tried to kill you.'

'Undoubtedly I was his target. He must have been stalking me. But a killing in a brothel is bad publicity. Major Steuben, have this carrion removed and dumped somewhere. Ladies, you will speak of this to no one. Off you go.'

They filed out, reluctantly, except for Constance.

'I will put a guard on the house,' Roess announced.

'A guard? Whatever for?' That would cripple the Route.

'This man may have friends, who may come looking for him.'

'We can take care of ourselves, Herr Colonel.'

'Ha ha.' He smiled at Liane. 'I know that she can. But she has no weapon.'

'May I not have a weapon, Herr Colonel?' Liane's tone was demure.

'It is not legal, but . . . take that fellow's gun, before the ambulance arrives. I will tell Steuben I have given you permission.'

'He fired most of his bullets.'

'Take those from my pistol; they are both Lugers of the same calibre. I wonder where he obtained his.' He watched her remove the magazine. 'Where did you learn about guns?'

'On our father's farm, before the war. We both did.'

Roess turned to Constance. 'I understood that you were born and bred in Paris.'

'Ah . . . Well, I was. But then my father went to live in the country, before Jeanne was born. She is younger than I.'

'By several years, I would say,' Roess remarked ungallantly. 'But I am very glad she is here now. You take care, little lady.' He stroked Liane's head. 'I will see you again soon.'

41

The door closed behind him. 'You have made a conquest,' Constance remarked. 'If he ever finds out the truth . . .'

Liane sat on the bed again, gasped, and rolled on to her front.

Constance bent over her. 'The bastard! What surprises me is that you didn't shoot him when you had the chance.'

'And have us all hanged?'

'Jesus! You must let me put something on those stripes.'

'In your room. I don't want to look at Hercule any more.'

'But you shot him.'

Liane got off the bed, ignored her dress, and went along the corridor to Constance's apartment. There was a good deal of confused sound from downstairs, but she did not suppose any business was being done. Constance followed her. 'Lie on the bed.'

Liane obeyed. 'You had better go upstairs first and put the Britishers in the picture. They must be going mad.'

'I'd forgotten about them. I'll be back in a moment.'

The door closed and Liane, lying on her stomach, gazed at the wall. The paper, like the bed covers, was pink. *I have shot Hercule*, she thought. Oh, Hercule! Hercule had owned the bar in Montmartre for several years before the war. She had first met him when she and some of her actor friends had stumbled in there for a drink after a performance. She had known from the moment of that first meeting that he had fallen hopelessly in love with her, but she had not at that time been in the mood to take up with lower-class barmen. When she had had to return to Paris the previous year, heavily disguised, a wanted woman for killing a Gestapo officer, he had been the obvious choice for a refuge. She had known what would be his price, and in the upside-down world of a country at war she had been happy to pay it. Her business had been to set up the Route, and she would have done anything to accomplish that goal. Besides, he had been good in bed.

And he had never let her down. If she had been given the credit, it had been Hercule who had shot them to safety when the Germans had finally caught up with them, and brought them both to a refuge at the house. When London had ordered her to return to the south and the Group, he had been upset at being unable to accompany her, but she had promised to return in a couple of months. As she had done. She had not suspected that he would go crazy at the news of her death. And now . . .

Constance closed the door behind her. 'You were right. They were agitated. But I have soothed them.' Again she surveyed Liane's backside, then fetched a jar of cream from her dressing table and started work. 'One would have supposed that even a man like Roess would have preferred to fondle these than beat them. Why did you have to shoot Hercule?'

'Because in a moment he would have said my name. Once he did that we were finished. And even if he had shot Roess, we would all have been arrested and it would have come out. The Route would have been destroyed and we would have been hanged. I could not permit that.'

'Your cold-bloodedness frightens me.'

'I am not the least cold blooded. What I did horrifies me, too. But it was a decision that had to be made, and I made it. What is that noise?'

'Those are the people coming to remove Hercule.'

'I did not hear the siren.'

'That is because there was no siren. Roess does not want the world to know that he visits my house, remember? That may be useful for us. I had better go. Will you come?'

'No. I do not wish to look at him again.'

'I had better see how the girls are getting on as well. Stay awake. I have something important to tell you.'

'What?'

'I will be back in a little while.'

She closed the door. Liane got off the bed and twisted round to look at herself. Even through the cream she could see the weals; the skin was broken in several places. Well, presumably they would disappear eventually. What she had to do was stop moping, both about herself and about Hercule's death, and determine how her elevated status could be used to the advantage of the Resistance. She had no doubt it could, even if getting too close to the Gestapo was highly dangerous. But there were only four living and important Germans who actually knew her by sight, as opposed to a battered photograph.

43

Her personal war had begun within a week of the invasion in May 1940, when she and Joanna had been captured by six deserters and gang raped. But all six had been hanged. They had been interviewed by the local commander, a man named Rommel, who had been both apologetic and solicitous for their well-being, but as far as she knew he was fighting the British in North Africa. They had been interviewed then by two Gestapo officers, Colonel Kluck and Captain Biedermann, mainly in an attempt to persuade them not to publicize their ordeal for fear of embarrassing the Wehrmacht. She had regained Paris, and Biedermann had visited her there – Joanna having left, ostensibly to flee back to the security of the United States, but as she now knew, to get *her* revenge by working for British Intelligence. Liane had killed him, thus beginning her tally, and becoming very rapidly the most wanted woman in France.

Kluck was still alive, as far as she knew, but had been returned to Germany in disgrace for his failure to catch her. Then there was that unfortunate fellow Franz Hoeppner, whom she had had to use to extricate her parents from their home in Paulliac. She did not suppose he would ever forget her. But he was now in Bordeaux.

And lastly there was Oskar Weber, a man who from all accounts would make Roess seem like a babe in arms, but who was being led, like that babe, by the nose because of his lust for Joanna. Weber was based in Berlin, but he did visit Paris from time to time, and it had been on one of those visits that he had come to the brothel and she had met and serviced him. Back then she'd had black hair. But he had seen her again after that shoot-out in the Massif Central, briefly, before he had been shot himself, by Joanna. She knew that Joanna had claimed it had been a dying partisan who fired the shot, just as she had claimed that moments later Liane herself had been shot and killed. In the confused darkness of the cavern, and with their commander badly wounded and perhaps dying, none of the German soldiers had disputed her version of events. Thus Weber, and everyone else, thought her dead. In that lay her ultimate security.

She found the bottle of cognac she knew Constance kept

in the room and poured herself a glass, drinking it walking up and down. She turned to face the door as it opened.

'What a shambles,' Constance said. 'Everyone is having hysterics.'

'They won't do, or say, anything stupid?'

'No, no, they are absolutely trustworthy. They hate the Boches, and they know their necks are in it as much as ours. Anyway, all the clients have gone home; they seem to be quite off sex. This has been a calamitous evening. We have hardly taken a franc. Do you know, that louse Marach was supposed to pay me a hundred for what Roess did to you, and he went off without a word.'

'You'll get your money. You say you had something to tell me.'

'Oh, yes.' Constance poured herself a glass of cognac, and thoughtfully topped up Liane's glass.

'You think I am going to need this?' Liane asked.

'Yes. There are two things I learned tonight. I don't suppose one is very important, but did you know the Japanese have attacked the US?'

'Good Lord. Why did they do that?'

'I am not Japanese. But apparently they have been bickering for a long time. The point is that Hitler has now declared war on America as well.'

'What?' Liane lowered her glass.

'Well, it's the sort of thing he would do. I don't see how it can affect us. America is a very long way away.'

'But . . .' Liane bit her lip. Constance knew nothing about Joanna, nor should she. But if America and Germany were at war, Joanna had lost her immunity. On the other hand, while she had no idea where her oldest and dearest friend was at that moment, she would surely have the sense either to get out or stay out of Germany. She had to believe that. 'You're probably right. You said there was something else.'

'Brace yourself. The commander of the Bordeaux garrison has been killed. Shot down in broad daylight.'

'Not that poor chap Hoeppner?'

'No, that wasn't the name. It was someone else.'

'Then Hoeppner must have been replaced. Ah well . . .'

'It is the name of the assassin that matters. Marach said it has thrown the Security Services into a frenzy.'

'Tell me!' Liane almost shouted.

'Amalie Burstein. She is your sister, is she not?'

'Yes,' Liane said, her voice now low. 'She is my little sister.'

'Of course, you have another sister. The one who turned traitor and married a Nazi.'

Liane opened her mouth to argue, but then closed it again. That Madeleine had also betrayed her husband and his people by helping their parents to escape in September had to be her secret alone. And Joanna's. 'Yes,' she instead said.

'Marach says they had supposed that Amalie was killed in the same battle in which you supposedly died.'

'Well, obviously she wasn't,' Liane snapped, trying to think.

'So they are wondering how many of your people managed to escape.'

'They think I escaped?'

'No, no. They are sure you are dead. One of them identified your body.'

'Yes,' Liane said. But if Joanna was now persona non grata . . . But what on earth had induced Amalie to do such a thing when they had been commanded to lie low until orders came from London? How could Pierre have permitted it? How could Henri, Amalie's husband, have allowed his wife to take such a risk? *She* had just killed an old friend and lover to protect the secrets of the Resistance. Amalie had just endangered the Group by killing – and for what purpose?

What would Jean say? Jean Moulin, who had been Prefect of Chartres when the Germans had invaded, had been arrested and savagely tortured by the Gestapo, but had escaped and made his way down to the Massif Central in Vichy. There he had created the band of guerrillas that had become known as the de Gruchy Group. Jean would never have permitted something like this to happen without discussing it with James. But Jean was in England, summoned there by General de Gaulle, the man who was claiming to command all Frenchmen and women who were still resisting the Nazi invaders. Jean was supposed to be returning, but he had not yet done so. Thus, with her absent as well, the breakdown in discipline was perhaps inevitable. But by her own sister? Most important of all, what would James say? Worse, what would James *do*? For all his urbane exterior, Liane knew James to be utterly ruthless when it came to his job, which was controlling his various agents in France. Despite his love for her, which she was sure was genuine, she knew that if he felt her Group had been compromised to the extent that it might endanger other groups, or even agents, for whom he was responsible, he would close it down without hesitation, cut off all supplies of arms, ammunition and information, all contact with London and, most importantly, the promised funding for Constance.

If only she could get in touch with him. But the only radio in the brothel, carefully hidden in an attic bedroom, was a receiver. It had not been considered necessary or desirable for them to make calls out, only to receive advice regarding the arrival of the next lot of evaders, as the downed RAF personnel using the Route were called.

'What will you do?' Constance asked. 'She has probably been caught by now, anyway.'

'If she had been caught, would the Germans not be shouting it from the rooftops? I must get down there.'

'No! It would be too dangerous. Anyway, you cannot leave Paris. Roess has said he wishes to see you again, and I would say it is going to be quite soon.'

'Ah,' Liane said. 'But he owes me a favour. His life.'

'Jeanne?' Johann Roess rose from behind his desk, an honour he never accorded any of his usual visitors. 'My dear girl! But you should not be here.'

Liane glanced right and left. The walls of the office were bare, save for the portrait of Hitler. But then, all the walls in this building were bare, and cold. 'It does give me the shivers,' she said, and she was not lying.

'It should only do that to enemies of the Reich,' he said. 'Not to those who protect the Reich.' His secretary hovering just beyond the door – she had in any event been astonished when this rather cheaply dressed if good-looking young woman had been granted instant admission to the Commandant's office

– raised her eyebrows and returned to her desk in the antechamber.

'But you are not pleased to see me,' Liane suggested.

He held her hands to escort her to a chair. 'My dear girl, I am always pleased to see you. But after what happened last night . . .' He frowned. 'There has been no trouble for you?'

'No, no.'

He nodded, squeezed her shoulder, and went back behind his desk. 'I gave orders that you were not to be implicated. So tell me what is bothering you.'

'We have heard from Limoges. Our father is gravely ill.'

'Limoges? You come from Limoges?'

'Why yes. Have you ever been there?'

'I have passed through it. It is just that I did not know you were from the south. I am sorry about your father.'

'I must go to him. He may be dying.'

'Go to him? You mean leave Paris? No, no. Let Constance go.'

'She and Papa are estranged. I told you, when Papa left Paris to return to his home, he abandoned Constance here.'

'You mean she would not go.'

'Well . . .' Liane shrugged. 'Either way, they quarrelled. She hates him. She does not care whether he lives or dies. I must go, Johann. I would hate myself for ever if he were to die and I not be there.'

Roess considered. 'I do not want you to hate yourself, Jeanne. If you feel so strongly . . . How long will you be gone?'

'Well, if you will give me a train pass, so that I can travel quickly, and a passport to cross the border, I should be gone not more than a fortnight.'

'A *fortnight*?'

'I do not know how long he will take to die. And then there will be the funeral arrangements . . .'

'A fortnight. I cannot do without you for a fortnight. I want you again. I want you now.'

'I will come to your apartment tonight. Free of charge.'

'I am leaving Paris tonight. For Bordeaux.'

'Bordeaux? Whatever for?' As if she could not guess.

'It is a case they seem unable to handle. Listen, Jeanne, I intend to take you out of that brothel and set you up in a place of your own, as my mistress. Would you like that?'

'Oh, I should adore it, Johann. The moment I come back from Limoges.'

He gazed at her for several moments, then grinned. 'I know what we will do. We will go to Limoges together.'

'What? You will cross the border?'

'I do not think Vichy will object. I told you, I am required to go to Bordeaux on business. So we will go down together. I will drop you off in Limoges, continue to Bordeaux, and pick you up on the way back. Would you not like that?'

Liane drew a deep breath, but yet again her decision had to be instantaneous. 'I would like that very much.'

'Then hurry home and pack. We are leaving on tonight's train.'

Three

Betrayal

The dripping hawsers were dragged on board and secured, then winched tighter, and the Baltic ferry was slowly brought alongside the Lübeck dock. Apart from the stevedores there were not many people there to welcome her. Most of Germany was still holding its breath, waiting to see what, if anything, was going to happen next. A great number of Germans had relatives living in the United States, and it was not believable that a stroke of a pen could turn these into deadly enemies.

It was also very cold. Joanna hugged her mink tighter about herself as she waited, with the handful of other passengers, for the gangplank to be run out. Then the officer stood back, saluted, and the passengers disembarked. Joanna was in the centre, and on reaching the dock she and the others went to the customs and immigration building. This was a routine she had followed many times before, and as usual she was carrying only an overnight bag; she kept a complete wardrobe in the suite she maintained at the Albert Hotel in Berlin. But today her heart was pounding as she presented her passport. Pound Twenty-Three, a rather nervous young man, certainly when in her company, had been aghast at her decision to disobey a direct order from London and proceed with her journey. She felt he had been close to placing her under arrest. But his nerve had failed him. Not only was she bigger than he – and undoubtedly stronger and better trained in martial arts – but in Sweden she was the daughter of a well-known government minister, and not to be trifled with, at least in public, as they were when he caught up with her on the Malmo dockside.

'You understand that I must report this to London. It is my duty,' he had said.

'And you must do your duty,' she had agreed. 'Just remind them that I am doing mine.'

'But why take the risk? You wouldn't be letting anyone down by quitting; London has ordered you back. It's their decision.'

'And it's mine to go on with the job.'

He had finally given up, and she had boarded the ferry. She wondered herself why she was doing it. Perhaps because she was, if not an Anglophile, certainly a Francophile. She felt as devastated at what had happened to France over the past eighteen months as if it had happened to Connecticut, where she had been born and spent her childhood. The fact that her oldest and dearest friends were so closely involved was an additional factor in her determination to fight beside them until the job was done.

Then there was the desire for vengeance. This was not just on account of the rape she and Liane had suffered at the start of the invasion. It was also because of Aubrey. Aubrey had been her kid half-brother, ten years younger than she, the product of her mother's second marriage. Like Joanna, he had come to France to attend Amalie's wedding. And, like her, he had been caught up in the excitement of that unforgettable day in May. They had both volunteered to accompany Liane on that mad drive to return Pierre de Gruchy and James Barron to their respective units on the Belgian frontier. That had been successful enough. It had been on the return journey, when they had got enmeshed in the endless stream of refugees, that catastrophe had struck, first in the form of a strafing attack by German planes, which had left Aubrey's body torn to pieces by machine-gun bullets. Then, when she and Liane, both shaken and grief-stricken, had sought refuge in an abandoned village, they had been raped by the deserters.

But she knew she would be lying to herself if she did not admit that she enjoyed the life she had lived for the past year. Like Liane, gifted with too much money, too much animal magnetism, and too little parental control, she had spent the half-dozen years before 1940 living an utterly hedonistic life.

Unlike Liane, she had obtained a job, but the job – as a roving reporter for a leading American newspaper – had been secured for her by her mother, who was a personal friend of the editor, and had actually encouraged her lifestyle by requiring her to roam from Berlin to Vienna to St Moritz, to Cannes, to Rome and to Paris, reporting on what European women were wearing, eating, saying and thinking. And, incidentally, drinking. She had known she was drifting. Perhaps Liane had known it too, about herself. Neither of them could possibly have expected what was actually going to happen to them, yet both had reacted as if it was something they had anticipated all of their lives. A certain amount of luck had been involved, of course. Gaining London after her flight from France, bruised, battered and outraged, both mentally and physically, knowing that she had to do *something*, yet having not a clue what she *could* do, she had bumped into, quite by accident, the same James Barron she had last seen about to go into a disastrous battle. From the lunch they had shared that day had come this.

James, while immediately recognizing her potential value as a neutral who possessed both Swedish and American passports, and was well known and accepted in all the important capitals of Europe, had mistrusted the motivation behind her volunteering to work for him, and she had a strong suspicion that neither he nor the brigadier – not to mention Rachel – had ever been able truly to trust her. Her decision to allow herself to be 'turned' by Oskar Weber had added to their doubts. But as her value to them had doubled, they continued to employ her.

She was under no illusions. She thought that James was a great guy, and she wouldn't have minded getting between the sheets with Rachel – if only to be amused at how shocked that prissy English aristocrat would be – but she had no doubt that their apparent concern for her safety was caused by fear of what she might divulge were she to be 'interrogated' by the Gestapo. And the fact was, they had absolutely no employment for her apart from the information she brought to them from Germany, and more recently, the information she provided them about what German agents in England were up to. If she once went crawling back, they would pat her on the head and send her home to the States.

So what was the risk? Presumably some people at home would call her a traitor, but when the war was over, she would have the testimony of James to prove that she was actually pretty much a heroine. As for the Germans, as long as Oskar was panting to get his hands on her body, she was inviolable. She had reminded herself of this throughout the brief voyage. Yet now that the man behind the desk was actually examining her passport, she was aware of a certain shortage of breath. Because she had encountered this man before, on her last trip.

He raised his head. 'I did not expect to see you again, Fräulein Jonsson.'

'Didn't you? I regard Berlin as my home now.'

'That is very nice. What have you done with your American passport?'

'I left it in Stockholm. With my father. I didn't think you would let me in as an American.'

'That is a good point. Would you go with this gentleman, please?'

A door at the back of the room had opened and a man stood there. He wore plain clothes but was very obviously a policeman. 'Am I under arrest?' Joanna enquired pleasantly.

'Not at this moment, Fräulein.'

'Then I am entitled to refuse to be interrogated by the Gestapo.'

'In that case you *would* be placed under arrest.'

Joanna considered. But there was no point in making a fuss out here; there were several people in the line behind her, waiting patiently, and making it quite plain by their studied indifference that they had absolutely nothing to do with her. So she smiled at the officer. 'Then I had better see what the little man wants.' He gestured her round the desk, and she went to the waiting policeman, who stepped aside to allow her past him, then closed the door behind them. Inside the small, windowless room there waited another man, as well as a table with two straight chairs, one on either side. Joanna's travelling bag, already open and disturbed, waited on the table.

53

'There had better be nothing broken or missing,' she remarked, and sat down.

'I did not give you permission to sit,' the first man said.

'I reckon I've been standing long enough,' Joanna said. 'In that line out there.'

'Well, now you must get up again.'

'Why?'

'Because I wish you to undress.'

'Why?'

'It is standard procedure, when an arrest has been made. You have to be searched.'

Joanna had been searched by the Gestapo before. 'You can forget that.'

'Do you think you can defy the Gestapo?'

'That's what I'm doing. In the first place, you haven't arrested me yet. In the second, you have to allow me to make a phone call.'

'I do not have to allow you to do anything. You have no rights.'

'Have it your way. Then you make the call.'

'We do not play games here, Fräulein.'

'I am sure you don't. But I bet you like to survive. If you do not call the number I shall give you, and ask to speak with Colonel Weber, you and your friend here are going to lose your jobs, your pensions and your futures. I won't talk about your lives, or those of your families.'

The man glared at her, but she met his gaze with her smile. 'I will make that call,' he said. 'And when I come back, I am going to take you apart.'

'Sounds like fun. By the way, if you're going out, bring me back a glass of cognac, will you?'

'You understand, Fräulein,' the Gestapo officer said as he escorted Joanna to the waiting black Mercedes saloon, 'I was but doing my job. Your name was on a list given to me.'

'I understand entirely,' Joanna said. 'And I will tell Colonel Weber that you have been most helpful, even if I'm afraid I cannot recommend your taste in brandy.'

54

She sank into the leather upholstery and he saluted. 'Perhaps we shall meet again, Fräulein.'

'What an exciting thought.' She rolled up the window, and the car moved away. Now at last she could allow herself to relax. She opened her handbag to find her handkerchief, took off her gloves, and dried her fingers. She had not allowed herself to consider her situation had Oskar refused to acknowledge her. But as he had, she could only wait to discover what plans he had for her. If James felt that her cover was blown in Germany, Oskar had to feel that her cover was equally blown in England. She would have to persuade him otherwise.

The drive took a couple of hours, and she actually dozed off before they arrived at the Albert. 'How good to see you back, Fräulein,' said the reception clerk. Joanna waited for the 'we did not expect to see you again' routine, but he merely said, 'Colonel Weber is waiting for you.'

'Thank you, Walter.' She rode up in the lift, again feeling a slightly anxious anticipation – she did not doubt that the coming hour was going to be boisterous. She turned the key, opened the door, and stepped inside. The lights were on, as the day outside the windows remained gloomy, and for a moment she did not see him. Then she was swept from her feet in a bear hug, carried across the sitting room and through the open bedroom door, and flung on to the bed.

'Oskar!' she protested.

He was on top of her, pinning her to the bed with his weight. With her training in unarmed combat she could easily have disposed of him, but he was her future in Germany. He squirmed on her as he sought her lips, his hands running up and down her coat and at last getting inside to reach her dress and fondle her breasts. Then he was scooping her skirts up to her waist, dragging off her knickers, and unfastening his pants to be inside her in a matter of seconds. Totally unprepared for such a greeting she gasped and bit her lip, but got her arms round him to hug him against her, and remained lying there when he was finished. He rolled off her, pulled up his pants, and went into the sitting room to pour her favourite cognac. Joanna sat up, slowly, then stood up, kicking off her shoes as she did so, and taking off the mink. Weber returned to hand her a glass.

'I did not expect ever to see you again.'

'You knew I would never leave you, Oskar. Here is Burton's message.'

He took the envelope, slowly. 'But your people . . .'

'The English aren't my people, Oskar. And they know nothing of Burton.'

'They can stop you going back.'

'I do not think they will. I am not the least important, and I am travelling on a Swedish passport.'

'But they are allied to the Americans. *They* will call you a traitor.'

'But they can never reach me, Oskar. I have renounced my American citizenship. I am Swedish now.'

'I would prefer it if you renounced that as well, and became a German.'

'Then I would be useless to you. The British would never accept me back under those circumstances.'

'You mean you would be prepared to go back?'

'Of course. The moment you have something for me to take.'

He gazed at her for some moments. 'I have never known a woman like you.'

'I should hope not. Now, Oskar, I simply have to have a bath.'

'Those stupid bastards did not harm you?'

'No, no. Although I imagine they would have liked to.' She undressed while he sat on the bed and watched her. 'So what is the news here? Has Madeleine delivered yet?'

'Yes. A girl. A week ago.'

'And is Helsingen coming home?'

'Not even Helsingen can obtain compassionate leave right now. The Führer is determined to have Moscow by Christmas, and that is only a fortnight off.'

'Will he make it?'

'Between you and me, no. The weather out there is simply unbelievable. Do you know, our panzers are having to light fires under their tanks each morning before the oil in the engines will liquify sufficiently for them to start up? And more men than ever are coming down each day with frostbite.'

'Sounds horrendous.' Joanna went into the bathroom and turned on the taps, but left the door open. 'Do you have any objection if I visit Madeleine? It must be a miserable business being a new mother and not knowing if bits of your husband are dropping off.'

'If you must.'

'You still don't trust her.' She gathered her hair and inserted it into a cap. 'Because she is – was – a de Gruchy?'

'That is a reason, certainly. I am still not satisfied with her part in what happened in September.'

'I thought she was entirely innocent.' Joanna sank into the water with a sigh of contentment.

Weber stood in the doorway to watch her. 'She was *there*.'

'Tied up in her bed.'

'By her own mother and sister.'

'Well, in view of the way she betrayed them, I think she's lucky they didn't shoot her.'

'It was all too pat,' he grumbled. 'And now . . . you know about Bordeaux.'

Joanna soaped, slowly and luxuriously. That way she could adequately disguise the beating of her heart; she had known this moment had to come. 'What about Bordeaux?'

'The commanding officer has been murdered.'

'Oh, good Lord! Hoeppner? He really is an unlucky fellow.'

'Not Hoeppner. His replacement. But he was there. And he claims the assassin was Amalie de Gruchy.'

Joanna soaked, slipping right down into the bath so that only her head was exposed. 'That's not possible. He has to be mistaken.'

'He should be able to recognize her. You said she was dead.'

'I said she was almost certainly dead. I didn't see her body. I'm sorry. I was so worried about you . . .'

'I understand that, and I will always be grateful. But still, there is a problem. If Amalie somehow survived, who else did so?'

'If you are thinking of Liane, I saw *her* body, and put a bullet in it myself.'

57

'I know. But the brother, Pierre – he was never accounted for.'

'That's true.' Joanna got out of the bath and began to towel herself; the crisis seemed to have passed. 'But Liane was the leader, the inspiration for everything they did. Without her . . .'

'They have still managed to kill a German officer. This has to be attended to.'

'But . . . was Amalie not arrested?'

'Not yet. There was a riot after the shooting and she got away.'

Joanna pulled off the cap, let her hair tumble past her shoulders. 'But surely she will be caught.'

'One would have supposed so. But it hasn't happened yet. Frankly, I do not think Hoeppner's heart is in it.'

'Oh, but . . .' Joanna checked herself in time before she mentioned the hundred hostages; she was not supposed to know anything that had happened. 'Surely some of the locals would know where to find her?'

'Again, one would have supposed so. We have sent Roess to sort it out.'

'Roess?'

'I know he is not your favourite man, but even you must admit that he is good at his job. However, at the end of the day, it is our baby.'

Joanna realized that he was giving her the opportunity to do even more than James had wanted. 'Of course it is. I will go down there and find out exactly what is going on.'

'Do you think you can handle it?'

'Of course.' She went into the bedroom, lay on the bed. She didn't bother to put any clothes on; she needed him to find concentration difficult. 'Listen. Nobody down there knows I work for you, save for Hoeppner himself.'

He sat beside her and stroked her legs. 'And Roess.'

'Roess will surely be happy to work with me, if he knows I am coming from you. As far as the rest of the world knows, I am a journalist. I have been to Bordeaux before. Better yet, I was once arrested by the Wehrmacht there, for irregular activities. These things will be well known to the locals. And I am also an old friend of the de Gruchys. It is entirely natural for me to hurry down there to see if there is a story. Equally, it is highly likely that once I am known to be there, Amalie, or someone who knows where she is, will wish to get in touch with me. All I need is for you to inform Roess of what I am about, and tell him to give me every co-operation. You should also brief Hoeppner.'

'And should Amalie get in touch with you?'

'I hand over to Hoeppner and return here.'

'You are prepared to betray your oldest friend?'

'My dear Oskar, I shot my oldest friend, remember. I do not have any friends left, except you.'

He squeezed her thigh. 'Suppose Amalie knows that?'

'How is she to know that? We only entered that cave after the assault had been successfully carried out. Every one of the guerrillas who was in the cave mouth was killed, either outright or immediately afterwards. Those who did not die, and in this category we must now include Amalie, had obviously long retired to the deep interior, and equally obviously stayed there until we had withdrawn, or they would have died too.'

Weber leaned over the bed and kissed her. 'You are a treasure. I must get back to the office. I will see you again before you go. But you must leave tomorrow. This matter is urgent.'

'Fräulein Jonsson is here, Frau Helsingen,' announced Hilda the maid, disapprovingly. She certainly did not approve of Joanna. But then, considering her tight features and stiff shoulders, it was difficult to suppose she approved of anything.

Joanna ignored her as she entered the room. 'Madeleine!'

Madeleine von Helsingen stood in the centre of the drawing room. The tallest of the sisters, now that she had regained her figure she had also regained her natural elegance, which was her principal asset. Being a de Gruchy, she was also a handsome woman, even if her features were too softly rounded to equal the beauty of her elder sister. As always when meeting Joanna, her expression was apprehensive.

'How well you look,' Joanna declared, advancing into the room. 'Motherhood becomes you.'

'It becomes most people,' Madeleine pointed out. 'You

59

should try it some time. But what are you doing here? *How* are you here? How did you get in?'

'I am a Swedish citizen.'

'Oh, really, Joanna.'

'Your government is quite happy with that, so why should you not be? Don't you have a kiss for me?' Madeleine reluctantly allowed herself to be embraced, and Joanna whispered in her ear. 'And get rid of that harpy. I need to talk to you.'

'And I have no desire to talk to you. About—'

'Things of mutual interest, darling. Do it.' Joanna gave her a hug and released her. 'I've come to see baby.'

Madeleine sighed. 'Hilda!' she called. 'Will you make some tea, please?'

'Tea?' Joanna demanded.

'Believe me, it is better than any coffee I can offer you. It is quite impossible to buy real coffee in Germany any more, for love or money. Anyway, it is virtually teatime.' She led the way to an inner doorway. 'Now, you must be quiet. Helen is asleep.'

She opened the door and tiptoed in. Joanna followed her example, stood above the cot. 'What a lovely child. She looks like you.'

'No she does not. She looks like Freddie.'

'Well . . . Does the boss approve?'

'The Führer sent me a bouquet of red roses.'

'And he is still going to be its godfather?'

'*Her* godfather.' Madeleine led her back out of the nursery and closed the door. 'Of course. I think he would have preferred her to be a boy, but he always keeps his word.'

'I'm sure.' Joanna sat down, crossed her knees, and watched Hilda bring in the silver tray and place it on the table. 'How is Freddie, by the way?'

'Thank you, Hilda, that will be all.' Madeleine waited for the maid to leave the room. 'He is very well. But the letters he writes are terrible.'

'I know,' Joanna agreed. 'Frozen engines and frost-bitten men. Now tell me about Amalie.'

Madeleine glanced at the open door, and then sat beside Joanna on the settee. 'I know nothing about Amalie except that she appears to have committed suicide, and in doing so has compromised everyone.' She got up again, poured two cups of tea, and brought them back to the settee.

Joanna regarded hers with disfavour. 'What is that?'

'A slice of lemon.'

'With sugar?'

'There is no sugar.'

'You mean you have run out of sugar as well.'

'There is a shortage, yes. But you are not supposed to put sugar in this tea.'

Joanna sipped and made a face. 'OK, I'll suffer. Amalie has not compromised anyone except herself. Her folks – your folks – are safely tucked away in England . . . Aren't you interested in how they're getting on?'

'Of course I am. But I can do nothing about them now. You do not suppose that Liane has been compromised by this stupid murder?'

'The Germans are satisfied that Liane is dead.'

'Do you not suppose she commanded this assassination?'

'I cannot believe that.'

'You do not think she would sanction such a thing? You think you know Liane very well, but the Liane you knew before the war no longer exists. What about that man, Biedermann? She cut his throat while he was sleeping.'

'He had just raped her.'

'She still did it.'

'Which at least proves that she does not delegate,' Joanna said stubbornly. 'If anyone in her group was going to shoot a German officer it would have been her. But she would never disobey orders, certainly those given by James Barron. And her orders were to do nothing until instructed by him.'

'Well, all I can say is that it's a mess, and I want nothing to do with it.'

'We're talking about your family.'

'And I helped my family, in September. I am happy Mama and Papa got away, but I will always regret having Franz so humiliated.'

Joanna finished her tea. 'I'll give him your love,' she said.

*   *   *

'Well?' The brigadier was a stockily built man, bald except for a fringe of dark hair, with a pronounced jaw. He invariably barked, at least to his inferiors, and the fact that he was paying the office a visit, rather than requiring James to visit him, indicated that he was upset.

James, standing by his desk, which the brigadier had just appropriated, drew a deep breath. 'I'm afraid she's gone in, sir.'

'I gave precise instructions that she was to abort and return here.'

'And those instructions were delivered, sir. Pound Twenty-Three assures us of that. But apparently she decided to ignore them.'

'That woman is a fucking menace.' He glanced at Jennifer, whose ears were pink. 'Who are you?'

Jennifer looked at James. 'Cartwright's replacement, sir. Temporary.'

'And what about Cartwright? Or have you managed to lose her also?'

'We know she was put down safely. Flying Officer Brune told us that when he got home, and this was confirmed by Pound Seventeen. This was a week ago. Since then there has been nothing. But I am certain Pound Seventeen would have called if anything had gone wrong. So I am assuming she is making discreet enquiries. Perhaps she has made contact with the Group, and is sorting things out.'

'Perhaps and perhaps not. Pound Seventeen must be able to get in touch with her. Have him do so and report. It may be necessary to pull her out.'

'Ah . . . We did allow her a fortnight, sir.'

'That is if all is going well. I want to know that. But Jonsson is a more serious problem. You are quite sure she has returned to Germany?'

'That is what Pound Twenty-Three reported, sir.'

'Then she's almost certainly been arrested by now. And blown our entire operation sky-high.'

'I don't think that will have happened, sir.'

'James, I know you regard Jonsson as the best we have, but there is no one, and certainly no woman, who is going to be able to hold out once the Gestapo get their claws into her.'

James reflected that it was a very good thing Joanna was not here to listen to that piece of male chauvinism. 'I meant, sir, that as she is travelling on a Swedish passport, she remains outside the reach of the Gestapo, quite apart from the fact that she is protected by being an SD agent.'

'James, has it ever occurred to you that she *is* an SD agent? That it is *we* who are being hoodwinked?'

'I can't believe that, sir. She hates the Germans. Or at least, the Nazis.'

'Because she claims to have been raped by some German soldiers. Do you have any proof whatsoever that that actually happened?'

'It was corroborated by Liane de Gruchy, who was there. And suffered the same fate.'

'Liane de Gruchy. Another young woman who follows her own agenda and makes up the rules as she goes along. I'm sorry, James, but this is a risk we cannot carry any longer.' He looked from James to Jennifer and back again. 'Who have we got in Berlin capable of carrying out executive action?'

James swallowed. 'With respect, sir, you ordered executive action to be taken against Jonsson last year, and were very happy that it was never carried out, in view of the inform- ation she brought to us.'

'That does not mean that she has not actually been turned. I believe that is what has happened. I want something done about it now.'

'I'm afraid I have no professional assassins on my books, at least in Berlin.'

'Well, then, one will have to be brought in. Get on to the Basle station, and tell them what we want. Be sure to use code. And tell them the matter is urgent.' The brigadier stood up. 'Keep me informed. And about Cartwright.' The door closed, and Jennifer and James looked at each other.

'You heard the man,' James said. 'Code a message for the Basle office and send it. Request a confirmation.'

'But . . . You mean . . . Well, he can't be serious.'

'I assure you that he is very serious.'

'About murdering one of our own people?'

'We happen to be fighting a war, Jennifer. If, just for example, Jonsson were to be interrogated by the Gestapo, or if she has truly been turned, the lives of all our Pound agents in the field will be at risk. That includes Rachel. Incidentally, the word to use is execute, not murder.'

'But . . . Do you believe Jonsson is a traitor? You know her well, don't you?'

'I know her very well. No, I do not believe that she is a traitor. But I accept that she has put herself into an impossible position. Now send that message. And then bring in that bottle of Scotch.'

Footsteps. On the stairs. Rachel sat up, then swung her legs off the bed. She did not bother to put on her shoes, but took the revolver from her bag. It was not a heavy army issue Webley, but an altogether smaller and lighter Smith & Wesson thirty-two.

Her heart was pounding. But then her heart had been pounding almost non-stop from the moment she had said goodbye to Brune. Up till that moment she had been utterly confident. She had flown with Brune before and knew his capabilities – and besides, he was always so confident himself, so calm in every crisis. Not that there had been any crises. The meadow had been lit with flares, and there had been several people waiting for her, even including two women. That had been reassuring. But then Brune had said goodbye, got back into the Lysander, and soared into the night. Then she had been alone with a bunch of complete strangers, terribly aware of the capsule she had placed in her mouth on leaving the aircraft. It was wedged between her gum and her cheek, to obviate any risk of her biting it inadvertently, but it was there to be used if she had been betrayed. She had been assured that she would be dead in ten seconds. But what would happen in those ten seconds? What terrible pains would rip through her body, what horrifying thoughts would inflame her mind? Besides, she did not wish to die. Not in ten years, much less ten seconds.

The people had taken her to the house of Pound Seventeen,

a man with whom she had communicated on many previous occasions, without the slightest idea of what he might look like or be like. He had turned out to be a baker named Anatole, in a village only a few miles south of Limoges. A stout, good-humoured man who clearly enjoyed his own bread, and equally shaved only when necessary, for instance when going to mass. His wife, Clotilde, no less plump and pleasant, was equally welcoming, but they had both made it clear that they considered her presence a danger to them. This close to the border the *gendarmerie* were inclined to be less accommodating than their fellows in the Massif Central.

Thus, while they had given her a job in the bakery, keeping the accounts, they had also found her this room in a boarding house, so that no one could suppose she was too closely connected to them. The people in the boarding house seemed to accept her as what she claimed to be – a schoolteacher who had been forced to leave Paris because of some trouble with the Germans. This was necessary as her French, although flawless, was of the *langue d'oïl* variety rather than the *langue d'oc* of the south. But while they might sympathize with her, they also did not wish to get too close, nor did she wish to get too close to them. Then it had been simply a matter of waiting and worrying. The worrying was because Anatole had entirely lost contact with the Group. James had placed his faith in Liane's leadership, but according to Anatole, Liane had been the first to leave, claiming that she had business in Paris.

Aware of the orders from London that the de Gruchys were to lie low for a while following the battle in the Massif Central, Anatole had assumed that they were doing just that – that whatever business had taken Liane back to Paris had been of a private nature – and had not worried until the news of what had happened in Bordeaux had reached him. Now Rachel got the impression that he did not care if he never heard from them again, in which case his repeated assurances that he was trying to find out where they were and have them contact her had to be a load of codswallop. She was wasting her time. But to call for Brune to return and pick her up after only a few days would be too humiliating. She could not imagine

Joanna accepting defeat so easily. And now there was someone outside her door, at . . . She peered at the luminous dial of her watch. It was two o'clock. How had he, or she, got into the house?

For this trip into the unknown she had forsworn the habits of her adult life and had brought pyjamas, which she was now wearing. But there had been no room in her limited knapsack for a dressing gown, so she pulled the topcoat from its hook behind the door, retrieved her spectacles from the table beside the bed, held the revolver against her shoulder, and waited. Fingers scraped across the wood. Rachel stood against the wall beside the door, wishing she had some saliva. 'Identify yourself.'

'Pound,' came the low, masculine voice.

Should he have had a number? Rachel knew that Pierre de Gruchy was Pound Thirteen, and Liane was Pound Twelve, but the only other member of the Group who had been given a number was Moulin himself, Pound Eleven, and he was in England. On the other hand, that this man knew the code word at all had to indicate that he was a member of the Group, or that he had been sent by Anatole, although why Anatole should send someone to her in the middle of the night when he would see her in the bakery in a few hours was mystifying.

But she was here to do, not to speculate. She drew the bolt. 'It's open.' The door swung in and the man stepped through. Rachel moved behind him, closing the door and pressing the muzzle of the revolver into his neck. 'Identify yourself.'

'If you squeeze that trigger, mademoiselle, you will arouse the entire house and be arrested for murder. You would be guillotined. That is not a suitable fate for a pretty woman like you. Besides, we are old friends, are we not?'

'Monterre!' Rachel lowered the revolver.

'It is good to see you again, mademoiselle. Is there no light?'

'There are matches on the table.' She continued to point the gun. Monterre was one of the de Gruchys' senior people, and indeed she had fought beside him in the battle. But he was also a Communist, and she knew that Liane had not altogether trusted him.

A light flared and the gas was lit. 'You are as beautiful as ever, mademoiselle.'

Rachel snorted while she surveyed him in turn. He was a solidly built man, with coarse features and stubble on his chin. She remembered that even without Liane's opinion she had not liked him on the occasion of their earlier meeting. But he was the nearest she had come to locating the de Gruchys. 'How did you find me?'

'Anatole told me where you are living.'

'And you have come at this hour?'

'It is safer for me. I am a wanted man.'

'But you can take me to Monsieur Pierre.'

'I know where he is, yes.'

'How far is it?'

'It is a good distance. But I have transport.'

'You have permission to drive at night?'

'Of course. It is the vegetables, you see. I must deliver them by dawn.'

'I see. And when will you bring me back?'

'Tomorrow night.'

'Very good. Wait outside.'

He grinned at her. 'I would rather wait in here.'

'Outside.'

He hesitated, shrugged, and left the room. Rachel took off her pyjamas and put on her underclothes, added trousers and a thick shirt, a jerkin, heavy shoes, and resumed the topcoat. She decided against taking a change if she would be back tomorrow night. Then she checked her revolver and put it in her coat pocket, dropped six spare bullets into her shoulder bag, together with her capsule – she hated carrying it in her mouth and she had to presume that Monterre was loyal. Finally, she turned down the gas.

Monterre had been leaning against the wall with his arms folded. 'You were very quick.'

'I thought you might be in a hurry.'

'Never hurry,' he said enigmatically. 'Mind how you go.' Rachel had been up and down the stairs sufficient times to know her way, even in the dark, and a moment later she was on the pavement, holding her coat tight against the cold wind. 'It will be warm in the van,' Monterre assured her, indicating the vehicle that waited at the corner, giving off a high smell of overripe fruit. The unlit street itself was deserted save for a stray cat that darted in front of them and then disappeared. Monterre opened the door for her and then sat behind the wheel, started the engine and drove slowly down the street.

'Do you know why I am here?' Rachel asked.

'I am hoping you will tell me. But I imagine it is about that business in Bordeaux.'

'That is correct. Do you know why it happened? Who gave the order for it to happen?'

Monterre turned a corner. 'Nobody ordered it to happen, mademoiselle. It just happened.'

'You are saying that Madame Burstein happened to be in Bordeaux, inside the occupied territory, where she had no business to be, armed with a pistol, on the day a new commandant arrived for the garrison, and shot him on the spur of the moment?'

'No, no. She went there to kill him.'

'But why?'

'Because of her husband.'

'You'll have to explain that.'

The last of the houses fell behind, and they were proceeding along a country road behind dipped headlights. 'It happened when Burstein went into Bordeaux.'

'Why did he do that?'

'I do not know. But he did, and he was identified as a Jew.'

'Well, of course he would be. It was a crazy thing to do. So you are saying that he was arrested.'

'No. He resisted arrest and, as he was armed, he managed to kill one of the soldiers before he was overpowered.'

'My God! What happened to him?'

'They did not bother with a trial. They hanged him there and then, in one of the town squares.'

'And you think Amalie went to avenge his death?'

'I know she did this.'

'And no one tried to stop her? Pierre? Liane?'

'Liane was not there. She went away. I think she went to

68

Paris. And Pierre . . . he is a weakling. He could not stand up to Amalie.'

Rachel frowned. Pierre had not struck her as a weakling on their previous meetings 'Are you telling me the truth?'

'Of course I am telling the truth, mademoiselle. Why should I lie to you?'

Rachel considered, and then looked out of the window at the blackness surrounding them. They had now been driving for about half an hour, and the village was far behind them. They had also been driving in virtually a straight line; there had been no bends and only a couple of crossroads. 'We're driving west,' she said. 'Why are we driving west?'

'I am taking you to see Pierre. Is that not what you wish?'

'But in a few minutes we will be at the border. Are you saying that Pierre is hiding out in the occupied territory? That doesn't make sense. Surely he and Amalie would have returned into Vichy to avoid arrest.'

Monterre braked the van to a halt. 'Do you wish to go to Pierre or not?'

'Of course I do.'

'Then it is necessary to cross the border. You must get out.'

'Here? You mean we are going to walk the rest of the way?'

'No, no. But I must conceal you, beneath the vegetables. I am sorry, but this is necessary.'

Rachel deduced that he was very nervous, but that was understandable. She got out, drew her coat more tightly about herself, and walked round to the rear of the van, where Monterre was already opening the double doors. 'There is a space already cleared, with a blanket. Lie down and I will cover you up.'

Rachel peered into the distinctly noisome darkness, sighed and put her hands on the floor of the van to mount. This was apparently what Monterre had been waiting for, as he had not been sure where her fingers were in relation to the revolver he knew she was carrying. He had also, while waiting for her to come round the vehicle, taken a sack from inside, and now he dropped this over her head and shoulders, pulling it down to her hips with an effort that knocked her off balance. As the sack was even smellier than the interior of the van, for a moment she couldn't breathe, and found herself lying on the ground while Monterre scrabbled for her wrists. She tried desperately to get them free to push up the sack at least far enough to reach her gun, but he was far too strong for her, and again he had obviously prepared for this moment, for now he fitted a loop of thin rope over her left wrist and another over her right, and drew them together, securing them in the small of her back. Then he pulled the sack from her head.

This was a relief, and for a moment she couldn't speak as she gasped for air, aware that her glasses had disappeared into the night. Then she realized he was fumbling at her coat, trying to locate the revolver.

'You bastard!' she snapped. 'What the fuck do you think you're doing?'

'Many things.' He pocketed the revolver, and pushed her on to her back. Her head hit the ground with a thump. He knelt beside her and unbuttoned her coat.

'What are you *doing*?' she demanded again, determined to keep the fear out of her tone.

'Many things,' he repeated. 'But if you are good to me, I will not hurt you.'

'You . . .' She kicked, but could not get her legs up far enough to reach him.

He spread the open coat to either side, still kneeling beside her. 'You are from the English,' he said. 'The Secret Service.'

'Yes,' she said, starting to pant. 'And they have long arms.'

'But they have to know where to look.' He unbuttoned her jerkin. 'You have come to make contact with the de Gruchys.'

'You know that.'

'Then you know where they can be found, eh?' Carefully he opened the jerkin. The cold air got through her shirt and she began to shiver.

'You know I do not. You are taking me to them.'

'I do not know where they are. But I wish to know. So do my friends. So you will tell me.'

'I do not know where they are. I wish to find out. Did Anatole not tell you that is why I am here?'

'Anatole? I have nothing to do with Anatole.'

'But didn't he send you to me?'

70

'I have said, I have nothing to do with Anatole. But I know who he is. *What* he is. When one of my friends told me that there was a strange woman in the village, working for Anatole, I knew at once it had to be an agent, so I discovered where you were living. It was very easy.' He unbuckled her belt.

Rachel made herself keep calm. 'If you harm me, be sure that *my* friends will seek you out.'

'I am not going to harm you, mademoiselle. I am doing you a favour. Because if I take you to my friends, and give you to them, you will probably never be able to have sex again. Would that not be a waste? You are an attractive woman.' He released her buttons, his knuckles roaming up and down her groin.

I am going to be raped, she thought. *My God, I am going to be raped!* She opened her mouth to scream, and then closed it again. There could not possibly be anyone within earshot. And besides, she was not some empty-headed young girl. She was a highly trained operative who, if she could get her hands free, could probably dispose of this lout in a matter of seconds. She must not panic. She must wait, and seize the first opportunity that arose. Yet the panic was there, lurking in her subconscious. She had only ever had sex with two men in her life. One was a forgotten nightclubber in that esoteric world she had known before 1939. The other was James. Oh, James!

Monterre pulled down her trousers and knickers, and then took them right off. Rachel drew up her knees. He grasped them and pushed them flat again, then stood up to drop his own trousers. Rachel rolled on her side and swung her right leg as hard as she could, catching him on the ankle when he was off balance. He gave a shout of pain and alarm as he fell down. Rachel rolled and reached her knees, but before she could get to her feet he was back at her, seizing her shoulders to throw her flat again with a thump that left her winded. While she gasped for breath, he kicked off his trousers and came at her again. Now she could take a deep breath, and as he straddled her she brought up her knees as hard as she could.

Monterre uttered a scream and fell away from her, clutching his genitals. Once more Rachel rolled the other way and again reached her knees. This time she actually got to her feet and took a few steps, away from the van, before he recovered. Then he came at her again, but no longer with rape in mind.

'Bitch!' he snarled, punching her in the back so hard she once more lost her breath. 'Bitch!' Two more punches brought her back to her knees, and he began kicking her. Now she did scream, in agony, and fell down, trying to roll away from him, but he kicked her again several times, and she subsided into moans, tears dribbling down her cheeks.

She seriously thought he was going to beat her to death, but he suddenly stopped, and grasped her shoulders to drag her up and across to the van, bundling her in through the open rear doors. She fell on to a relatively soft cushion of fruit and vegetables and braced herself for another assault, but he merely slammed the doors, then returned to the front, got in, and started the engine. For a few minutes Rachel couldn't think. Her head was swinging, and her body was aching. She wasn't sure she hadn't broken a bone, although the pain was dull rather than sharp. But her brain was in an even greater turmoil. Monterre had fought beside her in the Massif Central. Yet clearly there had been a split in the ranks of the guerrillas, and she had fallen into the middle. She should have insisted upon the pair of them visiting the bakery for confirmation of his position. But his apparent desire to operate in the dark had been entirely plausible. And now, he was taking her to his 'friends' who, from the way he had treated her, were hardly likely to be *her* friends.

What to do? Think, and be patient, she reminded herself. Until she could . . . She almost despaired, because now her ability to think was being hampered by the cold, which, as she was naked from her hips to her boots, was making her shiver and was seeping upwards into the rest of her body. She tried rolling to and fro, and managed to turn over and sit up, but now she was embedded in the soft mass around her. She simply had to get her hands free, but work them as she might, she didn't seem to be making any progress.

The van stopped, so suddenly that she fell over again, and now there were lights outside. She made herself lie still to listen, and she heard a voice saying, in French, but with a foreign accent, 'Papers'. *Oh, my God*, she thought, *we're at the border.* But could that help her? Did she dare declare her identity, as a French schoolteacher, kidnapped for the purpose of rape? But it was her only hope. Her bag, with her false identity, was still in the front of the van, as far as she knew.

She listened to Monterre. 'You know me, Sergeant. I am Monterre.'

'I know you,' the sergeant replied. Rachel drew a deep breath, but the sergeant was still speaking. 'And what have you got in there today?'

'Something very special.' His door opened and closed. 'Come and have a look.'

Rachel's brain seemed to freeze with the rest of her. But before she could decide what to do, the doors were opened and a bright flashlight was shone into the interior. 'What the shit . . .?' the sergeant demanded.

'She is a present for Colonel Hoeppner,' Monterre said proudly. 'A British agent, come to contact the de Gruchys. She knows where they are.'

PART TWO

Friends and Enemies

May we never want a friend in need.
                              Charles Dickens.

Four

Desperation

Eva, a plumply handsome young woman who wore her yellow hair in a ponytail, stood in the doorway of the office. 'Sergeant Globus wishes to see you, sir. He has the man Monterre with him.'

Franz sighed. He disliked Communists, and agreed with the Führer that they should be locked up. He also disliked traitors, no matter which side they betrayed. Most of all, he disliked Jacques Monterre. But the man was his only real hope of finding Amalie de Gruchy – and thus salvaging his own career – and he had proved his worth as an informer more than once already. 'Bring them in,' he said.

Eva stood to attention. 'The colonel will see you now.'

Globus entered and stood to attention. 'Heil Hitler!'

Franz nodded and looked at Monterre, who was attempting to follow the sergeant's example, but sloppily. 'Heil Hitler!'

'You have something for me?'

'Some*one*, Herr Colonel,' Globus said enthusiastically.

Franz frowned while his heart began to pound with a mixture of anticipation and distaste. He did not actually want Amalie de Gruchy to be captured alive, with all the horror that would necessarily follow, and which he would be required to supervise. Having saved her once from the Gestapo, he felt an almost proprietary interest in her. If she had to die – and sadly, after shooting Kessler, she did have to die – he wanted it to be in a shoot-out, shouting defiance to the last, rather than standing on a scaffold before a salacious crowd, her body already ruined by long hours in a Gestapo torture chamber. 'You have captured Amalie de Gruchy?' he asked.

'No, Herr Colonel. But we have captured someone who will lead us to her. *I* captured her,' Monterre said proudly.

'Who?'

'An English spy.'

'You have captured an English spy? Here in Bordeaux? How do you know he is a spy?'

'It is a she, a woman who was with the guerrillas in the Massif Central when they were raided. I saw her there. I spoke with her. She escaped and returned to England, but now she is back, seeking to reopen contact with the de Gruchys.'

Franz studied him. Monterre had only been in his pay, one might say, for just over a month. He had appeared out of the blue, claiming to have been a member of the de Gruchy Group. Franz's first reaction had been to hang him out of hand, but what he had had to say correlated with other information he had been given, and he had been able to pinpoint the where-abouts of one of the gang – the Jew, Burstein.

The capture and execution of Burstein, known to be a prominent member of the de Gruchy gang, had been a feather in his cap, even if he knew it must have led directly to the assassination of Kessler by Burstein's wife. In betraying Burstein, Monterre had clamed to have quarrelled with the de Gruchys, and broken with them, and thus had no knowledge of Kessler's murder. That had also made a certain amount of sense. But some of his other claims had been absurd, such as that Liane de Gruchy had also escaped the famous shoot-out. That was not credible, in view of the eyewitness accounts of her death. But suppose it were true? Because the evidence was largely provided by the American woman, someone about whom Franz had mixed feelings.

He had not reported Monterre's claim to Berlin. Because Liane was someone else he did not wish to see captured and tortured? Even more than Amalie, who he had only ever actu-ally met once, Liane was imprinted on his consciousness. He had, as he had confessed to Kessler, spent five hours sitting beside her in the back of his car, with her pistol pressed into his ribs. She had leaned against him, made him put his arm round her shoulders, so that when they had stopped at the border checkpoint they had appeared to be enjoying each other's company. He could remember the feel of her, the scent of her, the aura that she exuded. The evidence that she could kill with dispassionate efficiency was overwhelming, but again as he had told Kessler, once they were across the border it would have been the simplest thing in the world, and certainly the most sensible, to shoot him and his driver before making off with his car. Instead she had turned them loose to walk back to Bordeaux.

Everyone supposed that she had been interested only in the propaganda coup of humiliating a German officer. But if that had been her intention, and if she had survived the Massif Central massacre, she had not yet attempted to capitalize on her achievement, and she remained the most compelling woman he had ever met.

But perhaps this British agent might be able to unlock the mystery of what had actually happened in that corpse-strewn cavern. 'I will see this woman,' he said.

'Yes, Herr Colonel.' Globus hurried from the room.

Franz looked at Monterre. 'Was there something else?'

'Well, Herr Colonel . . . She is my prisoner.'

'Who you have now turned over to the Wehrmacht. I congratulate you. If she gives us the information we need, and we take Amalie de Gruchy, I may even reward you. Now you may get back to your vegetables.'

Monterre stood on one leg and then the other. 'She resisted arrest.'

'You mean she is hurt.'

'No, no. I do not think so. But . . . I had to wrestle with her. She will claim that I attempted to rape her.'

Franz considered him for several seconds, then asked, 'Did you rape her?'

'No, no, Herr Colonel. I am not that sort of man. But as I say, I was trying to restrain her, to disarm her.'

'She had a weapon?'

'Oh, yes, Herr Colonel. She had a revolver, and threatened to shoot me. So I had to tackle her.'

'Which was very brave of you,' Franz agreed drily. 'Thank you, Monterre. I will bear what you have said in mind.'

Monterre hesitated a last time, turned to the door, and

encountered Rachel, who was being marched in by two of Globus's soldiers. She stared at him, blinking short-sightedly. She had been allowed to put on her pants and button her shirt, but was dishevelled and there were bruises on her face. She walked uncertainly; her arms were still confined behind her back, but now with handcuffs rather than rope. She also smelled highly of rotten fruit. She turned to face Franz. 'That man attempted to rape me,' she said in French.

'What did I tell you, Herr Colonel?' Monterre asked.

'Yes, Monterre,' Franz said wearily. 'She looks done in, Globus. Take off those cuffs.'

'Be careful, Herr Colonel,' Monterre said. 'She is trained in unarmed combat. She is a dangerous woman.'

'I have said that you may go, Monterre. Kindly do so.' Monterre hesitated a final moment, then left the room. Globus unlocked and removed the handcuffs. Rachel brought her arms round in front and rubbed her wrists with a sigh of relief. 'I am sure you would like to sit down,' Franz suggested. 'Sergeant.' Globus placed a straight chair before the desk and Rachel sank into it. 'Thank you, Sergeant. Has she any possessions?'

'This bag, Herr Colonel.' Globus held up the shoulder bag.

Franz beckoned with one finger and the bag was placed on his desk. 'Has anything been taken out?'

'No, sir. You will see . . .'

'Monterre mentioned a weapon.'

'This revolver, sir.' Globus placed the gun beside the bag. 'And we found these bullets in the bag.'

'Very good. Thank you, Sergeant.'

Like Monterre, Globus hesitated. 'If she *is* an English agent, sir . . .'

'You think she will attack me? Will you attack me, mademoiselle? It is mademoiselle, is it not?'

'Yes,' Rachel said, her voice hardly more than a whisper.

'And are you going to attack me?'

Rachel licked her lips as she stared at him. 'No.'

'You see, Sergeant. You may go. Leave the door open. Eva,' he called. 'A glass of cognac.' The three soldiers tramped out and Eva hurried in with the glass of brandy. 'I

80

think you will feel better if you drink that,' Franz recommended.

Rachel held the glass in both hands to disguise her shivering, and sipped. 'I would feel better for a bath. Can't you smell me?'

'Then you shall have a bath. After we have talked a little.' Franz emptied the contents of the bag on to the desk, flicked the bullets, picked out the identity card. 'This says that your name is Brigitte Ferrand.'

'Yes,' Rachel said. She was actually feeling better for the brandy, even if she knew she was lost. But this man appeared to be a gentleman.

'A schoolteacher. Monterre says these papers are false, that you are actually a British agent.'

'Well, he would say something like that, after trying to rape me.'

'A schoolteacher, armed with a gun?'

'It is Monterre's gun.'

'And these cartridges?' Rachel bit her lip. 'And . . .' Franz sifted through the other items in the bag. 'A capsule. I suppose it contains cyanide. It should have been in your mouth, mademoiselle. Although that would have been a shame: you are a very attractive woman. Now tell me the truth. I wish your name, the name of the agency you work for, and, most important, the whereabouts of the people you have come to see. The de Gruchys.'

Rachel drew a deep breath. 'My name is Brigitte Ferrand. I am a schoolteacher who had to leave Paris for personal reasons. I am working in a bakery in Vichy until I can obtain a new position. I was kidnapped from my bedroom by that beast, for reasons of sex. When I resisted him, he beat me up and drove me across the border. That is the truth.'

Franz regarded her for some moments. Then he said, 'I have just explained that I should have hated to be looking at your dead body. You may believe that I would like it even less, having to see you being tortured by the Gestapo. I think you should know that my superiors take the de Gruchys very seriously. This means that they take anyone who is connected to the de Gruchys, or who might be able to give us information

81

as to their whereabouts, very seriously, too. I should tell you that the top Gestapo commander in France is on his way here now. He does not know you exist, as yet. But he is coming to take over the entire investigation into the death of Colonel Kessler. That means he will take you over as well, unless by the time he arrives – which I imagine will be this evening – you have told us everything we require, and certainly the whereabouts of Amalie de Gruchy. If you do that, I can save you from being interrogated. I may even be able to save your life and have you sent to a prison camp for the duration of the war. If you do have to die, I promise you that it will be quick and clean and painless. But your co-operation must begin now. Monterre tells me that your real name is Rachel Cartwright. Will you confirm that?'

Rachel stared at him. *This man is actually trying to help me*, she thought. *But all he can offer me is a quick death.* And the interrogation would not end with a mere admittance of her name, rank and number, so to speak. She did not know what game Monterre was playing, but it did not appear as if he had told the Germans about Anatole. Once she started giving information, there was no telling what they might be able to drag out of her. Another deep breath.

'My name is Brigitte Ferrand. I am a schoolteacher from Paris. I have never heard of anyone named de Gruchy. That man kidnapped me for sex, and when I refused him and fought him, he brought me here with this absurd story, to prevent me from having him arrested.'

Franz had been staring at her as well. He continued to do so for several more seconds, then sighed. 'Eva!' he called.

'Yes, Herr Colonel.' She stood in the doorway.

'Is Globus still there?'

'He is waiting outside, Herr Colonel.'

'Send him in.' He looked at Rachel. 'This is your very last chance, mademoiselle.'

'My name is Brigitte Ferrand, and I am a schoolteacher from Paris.'

'Very good, mademoiselle. I am truly sorry. Globus, you will place Mademoiselle Cartwright in a cell until the arrival of Colonel Roess. She is not to be ill treated, she will be fed three good meals a day, and given a half-bottle of wine with her lunch and dinner. Do you understand this?'

'Yes, Herr Colonel.'

'You promised me a bath,' Rachel said.

'So I did. Fräulein Cartwright is to be allowed to use the showers.'

'Yes, sir.' Globus's eyes gleamed.

'Under female supervision. And she is not to be touched.'

Globus gulped. 'Yes, Herr Colonel.'

'Very good. You will go with this man, mademoiselle.'

Rachel stood up. 'I would like to thank you, sir.'

'What for?'

'For being a gentleman, sir.'

'I have Pound Seventeen, sir.' Jennifer was excited, even as she continued writing down the message conveyed by the clicking key.

James waited, frowning as he watched her expression beginning to lose its animation. Then she signed off and raised her head. Never had he seen so stricken an expression. 'Tell me.'

'Pound Seventeen reports that Pound Two has disappeared.'

'You must have more.'

'He says that she did not come in to work at the bakery this morning, and so he went to her lodging house, and she was not there. He looked into her room, and says there was no sign of a struggle, and her weapon and some personal effects were also missing.'

'If there was no struggle and she has taken her gun with her, it seems pretty obvious she left of her own free will,' James pointed out. 'She must have got a lead on the Group.'

'Yes, sir.' Jennifer did not look reassured. 'Are we going to report to the brigadier?'

'I don't think that is necessary at this moment. Pound Seventeen is obviously a bit agitated. We'll wait for Rachel to report in.'

'Yes, sir. Suppose she doesn't, sir?'

'Jennifer, one of the most important things you have to learn about this job is never to overreact. That almost inevitably leads to disaster. Rachel is following a lead. She'll get back to us just as soon as she can. Have we heard from Basle yet?'

'Yes, sir. They have found someone who will do the job.' She stared at him with enormous eyes. 'Oh, sir . . .'

'Pour yourself a drink,' he recommended. 'And pour me one as well.'

'Limoges is the next stop,' Roess said. 'Do you know, I have never actually stayed there.'

'You mean to stay there now?' Liane asked in consternation.

'I thought I might, with you, for a day or two. I would like to see your home, meet your father, even if he is about to die.'

'But you are booked through to Bordeaux.'

'That is not a problem. I shall simply get off here and telephone Hoeppner to say that I shall be a day or two late.'

'Ah . . .' Liane had been comfortably relaxed throughout the journey, confident that all her options were open. As Roess's mistress, however basically *un*comfortable that was, she was superbly placed both from the position of obtaining information and perhaps even harming the Reich, and she was sure she would be able to locate Amalie and find out what was going on and be back in Limoges in time for him to pick her up on the way home. She did not suppose *his* investigations were going to get him very far very quickly. While if she did not make it in time, well then, she would just have to disappear and leave him confused and fuming. But that plan had been based on his leaving her here and continuing on his way. Now she was suddenly skating on thin ice. Even if she had known anyone in Limoges who could play the part of her family – she dared not involve Anatole – there was no time to make any arrangements, for she did not suppose he was going to let her out of his sights. Desperately she tried to think. 'I really do not think you would enjoy that, Johann,' she said. 'We live in a ghastly slum. I am very ashamed of it.'

'But that is terrible. We shall have to do something about that.' The whistle whined as the train began to slow, and he got up and turned to lift their suitcases down from the rack.

Liane stared at his back. For the second time in a week she was faced with an irrevocable and terrifying decision. Roess might be infatuated with her, but he was not a fool, and she knew him to be every bit as ruthless as herself. If they got off this train together, she was done for. As for the alternatives . . . Constance had accepted her as her sister. On the other hand, they had both agreed that they had lived apart for several years, and Constance could hardly be expected to know what her baby sister might have turned into in that time. She would just have to face it out, and join Roess in his condemnation of her.

As always, her mind was made up in an instant, even as the pros and cons flitted through it. The safest thing would be to kill him, but that would also be fatal for her. She had no knife, and though she intended to take his gun, there were several other German officers on the train who would be instantly on alert at the sound of a shot. So she stood up behind him, drew a big breath, and, as he lifted the first suitcase down, she unfastened the holster on his belt, took out his Luger pistol, whipped off his cap – all in virtually the same movement – and hit him as hard as she could on the back of the head. His knees sagged and struck the edge of the seat, and she pushed him forward so that he fell on to it. He uttered a groan, so she hit him again. Blood dribbled down his neck. The suitcase had fallen under him. She dragged it out and lifted his legs on to the seat, stretching him out, then hastily lowered the window blind as the train came into the station. The corridor blind was already down, as he had been kissing and fondling her during the journey.

She put the pistol in her shoulder bag, retrieved her own suitcase, much smaller and lighter than his, and stood above him as the brakes squealed. She could not be sure if he was breathing, so she put two fingers on his neck and found a pulse. She supposed she should hit him again, but he was so fond of her . . . Had been so fond of her. And what difference would it make? If she were ever caught, her fate would be the same whether he was there to administer it or not.

The train stopped. Liane opened the door and stepped into the corridor, carrying her case. A guard appeared. 'Oh, guard,' she said. 'The colonel is resting and does not wish to be disturbed until you are approaching Bordeaux.'

'Of course, mademoiselle.'

'Thank you.' She made her way along the corridor, passed two compartments filled with German officers, who eyed her appreciatively, but offered no comment; they knew she had been travelling with Colonel Roess. There were only six people getting off, and four getting on. By the time Liane had crossed the platform and presented her travel pass, the train was already moving. She reckoned she had a few hours in hand.

'Fräulein Jonsson is here, Herr Colonel,' Eva said.

Franz looked up. 'What did you say?'

'Fräulein Jonsson, Herr Colonel. You remember . . .'

'I know who Fräulein Jonsson is, Eva. And you say she is here? *Here*?'

'Yes, Herr Colonel.' She was clearly mystified at his reaction.

'In this office?'

'Yes, Herr Colonel.'

'Show her in.' He stood up. He had no idea what to expect.

But Joanna was as *soignée*, as flawlessly and expensively dressed as ever, and, wearing her mink with a matching hat, looked in perfect health.

'Hi, there! I'm not a ghost.' She closed the door on an outraged Eva.

'What are you doing here?'

Joanna drew up a chair and sat down. 'I've come to see you, Colonel. To help you.'

Franz also sat down, slowly. 'You have come here to see me? To *help* me? You are an American.'

'Wrong. I am a Swede.' Joanna delved into her handbag and took out her passport. 'There we are.' She laid it on his desk.

He glanced at it, but did not open it. 'Do you really think you can get away with that trick?'

'It is not a trick, Franz. You don't mind if I call you Franz, do you? And you must call me Joanna, as we are going to be working together. The situation is simply this: I have renounced my American citizenship, and am thus entirely a Swede. And as you know, I work for Oskar Weber. He has sent me down here to assist you in locating Amalie de Gruchy, and anyone else who may have survived the battle in the Massif Central. He feels I may be of importance in this business, because I know both Amalie and her family, and their habits.'

'You expect me to believe that?'

Joanna opened her handbag again, took out Weber's letter and laid it on the desk. This Franz picked up and scanned. Then he laid it down again.

'So,' Joanna said. 'Are you happy?'

'No. But I suppose I must accept Colonel Weber's recommendation.'

'Good boy. So, tell me what you have been able to discover. Up to the time I left Berlin two days ago it does not seem to have been very much.'

'Whatever I have "discovered" is confidential.'

'Would you like to read that letter again?' Joanna's voice remained quietly pleasant. 'Oskar requests you to co-operate with me in every possible way.'

Franz regarded her for several seconds, then shrugged. 'We haven't done too badly. We have, at this moment, an English agent in our cells.'

Joanna frowned. 'What has that got to do with finding Amalie de Gruchy?'

'This woman was sent here to contact the de Gruchys.'

'Did you say woman?'

'A very attractive woman, at the moment. Unfortunately, she refuses to co-operate with us in any way, and so I am forced to hand her over to the Gestapo. And sadly, as you may know, Roess himself is also on his way here to assist me. I had expected him by now. He will certainly wish to get his claws into her. It is going to be very unpleasant.'

Joanna's brain was whirring. If the captured agent was a woman, it could only be Rachel. But what on earth had happened? 'Surely London would be in touch with the de Gruchys by radio?'

'That link appears to have broken down, probably because

they are on the run. In fact, their entire organization seems to have broken down and is in the process of breaking up. This woman, her name is Rachel Cartwright . . .'

'She told you her name?'

'No, no. She persists in trying to pretend that she is a French schoolteacher. But she was identified by a man who until recently was a member of the de Gruchy gang. He is a vile fellow, but he has some value. He has already identified another member of the gang, who has been executed. And he actually brought this Cartwright woman to us.'

'Just like that? Does this traitorous virtuoso have a name?'

'He calls himself Monterre.'

Joanna kept her face impassive with an effort. *Holy shit*, she thought. Monterre had been with them in the cave. He hadn't been at the entrance when she had shot Weber, but he could well have learned her part in that. And he certainly had to know that Liane had survived. Yet this rather pleasant man did not appear to know of that, or surely he would have mentioned it. 'So where is this Monterre now?'

'We have set him up with employment on a vegetable farm, and we have given him permission to cross the border as and when he likes.'

'You mean you trust such a man?'

'Not at all. But he is a magnet for those of the guerrillas who appear to have escaped the destruction of their camp. They contact him and he informs us. As long as he goes on doing that, we can use him.'

'And what if, one day, he goes across the border, with your permission, and just doesn't bother to come back?'

'That is not a problem. We have his name and description, and the Vichy administration in Limoges is very anxious to keep on good terms with us. We can extradite him with a snap of our fingers.'

Monterre would clearly have to be sorted out as soon as possible, but she would have to go slowly to discover exactly what the situation was, how much this man knew and was not telling her. 'But he has not been able to deliver Amalie de Gruchy.'

'He does not know where she is. As I have told you, he

broke with her and her brother, before Colonel Kessler's assassination.'

'That is what he says.'

Franz shrugged. 'I do not think he is lying about that, although I will agree that he is a consummate liar. But he certainly seems to have it in for the de Gruchys. Do you know, he actually claims that the famous one, Liane, survived the battle!'

Joanna drew a quick breath. 'That is impossible. I shot her myself.'

'I know this. And he has been able to provide not a shred of evidence to support his claim. One would have supposed that, *if* she were alive, she would be with her brother and sister. In fact, one would have supposed that she would have carried out the assassination herself, if her reputation is anything to go by. But still, it is a worrying business. You say you shot her yourself. Are you sure she was dead?'

'Of course I am sure,' Joanna snapped.

'Of course. Well, there it is. But I have high hopes of this Englishwoman, even if I regret what may have to be done to her to make her tell us where the de Gruchys can be found.'

'What makes you think she knows that?'

'Why else would she be here, enquiring after them?'

'Franz, if she is enquiring after them, she can hardly know where they are.'

'Well, she must have a reason for being here, which she will have to tell us. And I think she will produce results. So I would say you have had a journey for nothing, Fräulein.'

'And you intend to turn Fräulein Cartwright over to Roess when he gets here?'

'Well, he is coming to take over the investigation. By the orders of Weber himself.'

Joanna nodded while her brain continued to race. 'I know this. Well, I must report to the colonel and receive his further orders. I wish the use of a telephone.' Franz indicated the phone on his desk. 'I'm sorry,' Joanna said. 'My calls to the SD are required to be confidential.'

'I see. Where are you staying?'

'Nowhere, yet. I came here directly from the station.'

89

'Eva!' He waited for her to appear. 'Telephone the Splendide and arrange a room for Fräulein Jonsson. Then arrange a car to take her there. Also inform the hotel that she is to be allowed to make whatever calls to Germany that she requires.'

'And that the calls are not to be monitored,' Joanna said.

'You heard the Fräulein.'

'Yes, Herr Colonel.' Eva bustled off.

'I hope that is satisfactory?' Franz asked.

'Entirely. Thank you.'

'Then perhaps, when you have settled in, and before you begin your journey back to Berlin, you will dine with me. Shall we say, half past seven?'

What to do? Joanna paced up and down her surprisingly luxurious bedroom. She had often wondered just how tough Rachel was, but she knew that they had both been warned at training school that there was no one in the world who could stand up to torture as applied by experts. In any event, the very idea was unthinkable. Rachel was a highly educated, blue-blooded intellectual. Her life was built around clean sheets and even cleaner underwear. Her sexual habits, if perhaps amoral, still demanded mutual respect and tenderness. The idea of all that refinement at the mercy of a beast like Roess was horrifying.

Could she be saved? Joanna felt sure that she could get her out of Bordeaux. But Berlin would not be a step forward. Although she had never seen him at work, she had no doubt that Oskar could be every bit as brutal and unpleasant as Roess. Therefore, while Rachel had to be extracted from Hoeppner's cell, she also had to escape before reaching Germany. It would have to be very convincing to fool Oskar. And having escaped, what then? Rachel would be stuck in central France. Her only chance would be to make it to Vichy territory, and thence across the Swiss border . . .

And where would that leave Joanna? Even if she could hoodwink Oskar into accepting her story, she would be able to do nothing about Amalie and Pierre – and Monterre. If only she knew where Liane was, and what she was doing. And if she could be contacted. But Rachel was the most immediate problem, and one that had to be solved before Roess arrived. She picked up the phone, gave the number in Berlin, and waited.

Franz Hoeppner looked at Johann Roess in astonishment. The Gestapo colonel was unable to wear his cap because of the bandage round his head, and he moved uncertainly, as if unsure of his balance. Coming into the office, he almost slumped into the chair Eva had hastily placed for him.

'My God!' Franz said. 'What happened to you?'

'I was attacked by a bitch from the pit of hell,' Roess muttered.

Franz looked above him at Eva, who was waggling her eyebrows. 'Would you care to explain?' he asked.

'I was travelling with this treacherous female, and without warning she attacked me.'

Franz put up his hand as if he would have scratched his head, but decided against it, and stuck to essentials. 'Have you seen a doctor?'

'Of course I have seen a doctor. He bandaged me up and gave me some pills. My head hurts abominably. I have double vision.'

'You should be in bed.'

'I will go to bed when I have watched that woman hanged.'

'May I ask where this incident took place?'

'In Limoges railway station.'

'That is in Vichy.'

'Don't you think I know that?'

'Then how are you hoping to find her in Bordeaux?'

'Because I naturally began the search for her as soon as I recovered consciousness and had my wound attended to, and I was informed that a woman answering her description had been seen crossing the border and travelling south. That means she is passing through the territory under your command.'

'I would have supposed she would stay in Vichy.'

'Well, she has not. With good reason. The Vichy police are quite as outraged as I am, and are conducting house-to-house searches. I wish that done here.'

Franz sighed. 'What time did this attack take place?'

91

'Just after dawn this morning. We had travelled overnight from Paris.'

'And it is now five in the afternoon. She has a considerable head start. On the other hand, I assume that she is on foot.'

'I do not know. The fact is . . . well . . .' Roess flushed. 'She is in possession of a travel document.'

'You mean a railway pass. But surely she left the train after attacking you.'

'The pass gives her the right to travel freely by any means of transport she wishes, for an indefinite period, throughout occupied France.'

'Would you repeat that? No, don't bother. But I think you should explain it. Just who is this woman?'

Roess glanced at the open door. 'This needs to be confidential.' Franz got up and closed the door. 'She is . . . an acquaintance of mine,' Roess explained. 'With whom . . . Well, of whom I am – was – rather fond.'

'You mean she was your mistress.'

'Well . . . we were in the middle of a liaison, yes.'

'I assume that she is French?'

'Oh, yes. She comes from Limoges.'

'So you were taking her home. And having got to her home, she attacked you. There must be a reason for this. What had you done to her?'

'I did nothing to her that she did not appreciate. She just went berserk. Her first blow laid me out. I think she must have a history of insanity in her family.'

'You know her family?'

'I know her sister. She has always appeared a very sensible woman.'

'And the rest of the family?'

'I do not know. I never met them. I have some of my people looking for them now. They are not in the telephone book.'

'Their name?'

'Clement. The woman we are looking for is Jeanne Clement.'

Franz wrote it down. 'Description?'

'Well, she is quite beautiful.' Franz raised his head. 'I mean it. I have never seen anyone to match her. Her features could have been carved by Michelangelo.'

'I do not think Michelangelo sculpted women.'

'Well, by somebody like that. Her figure is superb. Her hair is like silk. But it is not just the looks. It is the aura. The way she moves, sheer grace. The way she smells, heavenly. The way she makes love . . . And as for her voice. It is the voice of a goddess.'

'Are you sure you want this woman hanged?' But Franz was frowning. The eulogy was how he would have described Liane de Gruchy. It could not be possible. 'You say her hair was like silk. What colour was it?'

'Deep red.'

'That cannot be a natural colour.'

'Oh, well, of course not. You know what these women are like.'

'What women?'

'Well . . . she is a prostitute. No, no, a courtesan. A re-incarnation of Nana, or the Lady of the Camelias. Actually, she looks a little like Greta Garbo.'

My God! Franz thought. Monterre was telling the truth. But he had to be sure. 'Assuming her hair *is* dyed, what is its natural colour?'

'I have no idea.'

And this man is a policeman, Franz thought. 'My dear Roess, you have described this woman as your mistress, with whom I assume you have had sex on a regular basis. Does she come to bed with her clothes on?'

'Well, of course she does not.'

'So what colour is her pubic hair?'

'Well, it is very fair. Almost blonde.'

Franz stared at him. The thought of this unutterable little rat having sex whenever he chose with Liane de Gruchy, who was certainly the most beautiful and the most desirable woman *he* had ever known, made him feel physically sick. But at the same time, the knowledge that the legend, supposed by everyone to be dead, was actually alive and kicking in every possible sense gave him a most powerful weapon, to be used as and when he thought fit. 'Eva!' he called.

93

The door opened. 'Yes, Herr Colonel.'

Franz handed her the paper on which he had written the description. 'Have that typed up. I want twenty duplicates to be circulated to all border posts and control centres. You will also arrange somewhere for Colonel Roess to stay.'

'The Splendide?' she asked brightly.

'Ah, no. I don't think he would enjoy the Splendide in his condition. It is very noisy. Somewhere quiet.'

Eva bustled off. 'Someone said something about a British agent you have captured,' Roess said.

'Time enough for that tomorrow, when you have had a good night's sleep. You look completely done in. And by tomorrow, who knows, we may have captured your beautiful madwoman.'

'Did you manage to get through to Weber?' Franz asked Joanna at dinner. She was, as always, beautifully dressed and groomed, voluptuous, and utterly feminine. He wondered if she would be as good in bed. He wondered if he dared do anything about that – she was clearly Weber's woman, in every way. But he might hold her very life in the palm of his hand.

'We had a long chat,' she said. 'I put him in the picture.'

'I hope he is pleased with our progress.'

'He is very pleased.' Delicately Joanna scattered grated cheese over the bouillabaisse. 'He wishes to see this English agent for himself.'

Lifting a glass of Pouilly Fuissé, Franz asked, 'He is coming here?'

'No, no. He wishes the woman taken to Berlin.'

Franz considered. 'I will need written confirmation of that.'

'There is a letter in the post. But he says you are to telephone him if you have any reservations. However, I am to take tomorrow's train.'

'Why is she so important?'

'I have no idea. He obviously has some information we do not.'

'And Roess?'

'You told me that Roess is coming here to take over the search for Amalie de Gruchy. He will not be interested in a British agent.'

94

'He will be, if this British agent has information regarding the de Gruchys.'

'Well, if she has, we will find it out and inform you. In any event, as we will be gone long before Roess gets here, you don't even have to tell him about her.'

'Roess is already here. He arrived at five o'clock this afternoon.' Joanna spilled some soup, fortunately from her spoon back into the plate rather than on her dress. 'He was delayed,' Franz explained. 'Because of a most remarkable occurrence.'

He told her the story. Having recovered from her dismay, she listened without obvious emotion. 'I can't say I'm going to weep,' she commented when he was finished. 'It's a pity the lady didn't hit him a little harder. Do you think you will find her?'

'I do not see any reason why not. He has given us a very detailed description. Would you like to hear it? You never know, it might be someone you have met.'

'A French prostitute? Not my scene, Franz.'

'This sounds like something special. He describes her as the most beautiful woman he has ever seen, a sort of re-incarnation of Greta Garbo, only better.'

Joanna finished her soup. 'Greta Garbo isn't dead.'

'Is that important?'

'Certainly. If she isn't dead, she can't be reincarnated. Right?'

Franz subjected her to one of his long stares. 'Very droll. Very American. But I would like you to envisage Greta Garbo, superb figure, beautiful movement. Her hair is apparently a deep crimson at present, but it seems fairly certain that its natural colour is blonde. She wears it straight and shoulder length. He says she is unparalleled in bed.'

'And she is a whore? She *should* be on the stage.'

'Yes,' Franz said. They gazed at each other. 'But do you know what he says is the most memorable thing about her? Her voice. He describes it as being like velvet. Are you sure you won't have another course?'

'Thank you, no. That soup is very filling.'

'Well, then, coffee and cognac.' He signalled the waiter.

95

'You know, of course, that I once spent some time in the company of Liane de Gruchy.'

'I have heard of it. As I understand it, throughout that time you didn't know whether, or when, she was going to shoot you. I can understand that this would have had a powerful effect on your senses. Especially as within twenty-four hours she was dead.'

Franz stirred his coffee. 'You were at school together.'

'Yes.'

'I have heard it said that you were lovers.'

'We were at school together.'

'And now you claim to have shot her.'

'Liane de Gruchy is dead.'

'An old school friend, an old lover, an old family friend – are you a monster?'

'Anyone can become a monster, in certain circumstances. I loved Liane, yes. But she took another lover, and told me she did not wish to see me again. When we broke into that cave, I was at Oskar's side. She was there. I did not intend to harm her. But when she shot Oskar, in front of my eyes, I suppose something snapped.'

Franz studied her as he drank his coffee. 'If we liken Liane to Greta Garbo, to what actress would you liken yourself?'

'I have never considered it.'

'I think you should. I would say Veronica Lake.'

'You joke.'

'Oh, I know she is only five feet tall, and you are nearly six. But the face, the hair, and the way you wear it, drooping over your eye, and of course, the figure, somewhat enlarged but the more compelling for that . . .'

'Are you trying to seduce me, Colonel Hoeppner?'

'Would you object to that?'

She considered him. 'I might not, personally. But I can think of some others who might.'

'You mean Weber? How is he to know, unless you tell him?' He leaned across the table to hold her hand. 'And you will never tell him, Fräulein Joanna, because we share a secret, you and I. Do we not?'

96

Five

The Gestapo

Roess opened his eyes, stared into blackness. For several moments he had no idea where he was. He only knew that his head hurt, that wherever he was seemed to be revolving about him. He put out his hand, scrabbled at the bedside table, and located the light switch. Then he remembered. That unutterable bitch! The most desirable woman he had ever known! She had to have been mad. Not just because only a mad woman would attack a Gestapo officer, much less the most senior Gestapo officer in France, but because to attack a man whose life she had saved only two days previously – and to whom, throughout those two days, she had been the most loving of companions – surely signalled some form of insanity.

But what had aroused her mania? Try as he might, he could think of nothing he had said or done on the train to trigger such an explosion. He intended to find out. Oh, indeed he did. When she was apprehended, and brought before him, he would wring it out of her, as he intended to wring every last scream from her body before she died. As for ever trusting a woman – any woman – again, well, he would have more sense. And more anger. He wished he could have the entire female sex lined up before him, so that he could walk up and down their ranks, sword in hand, lopping off a breast here, an arm there, a head there, listening to the bitches scream in agony and terror.

He looked at his watch. One o'clock. Only one o'clock. He knew he was not going to sleep again; his head hurt too much. The quack in Limoges had foreseen this situation and given him pills to be taken as necessary, but as they put him in a daze he decided not to try them again.

One o'clock! At least seven hours before anything could start happening. He frowned. Why should that be so? He was Johann Roess. Except possibly for the governor-general, he was the most powerful man in France. He could operate, do what he liked, at any hour of the day or night. As for Hoeppner, he was a mere colonel in the Wehrmacht.

He swung his legs out of bed and got dressed, with some difficulty as he kept losing his balance, then peered at himself in the mirror. The bandage was pink in some areas; he would have to see a doctor again in the morning. As he felt naked without his cap, he tucked it under his arm and went downstairs. The clerk at the reception desk regarded him with some apprehension; he knew who he was.

'Is my car outside?' Roess demanded.

'Ah . . . you do not have a car, Herr Colonel.'

Roess glared at him. 'Then how did I get here, cretin?'

'You came in a car from Wehrmacht headquarters, sir.'

Roess continued to glare at him, but he could not remember. 'Then get me a car. Now.'

'Yes, sir.' The clerk telephoned the taxi rank, and a few minutes later Roess was at headquarters. Sentries stared at him and hastily presented arms. There were only a handful of sleepy clerks in the downstairs offices, and these regarded him as if he were a ghost.

'You!' He pointed at the duty sergeant. 'What is your name?'

'Fehrmark, Herr Colonel.'

'Very good, Sergeant Fehrmark. You have a prisoner in your cells. A British agent. Take me to him.'

'Ah . . . it is a woman, Herr Colonel.'

Roess could not believe his good fortune. 'Well then, take me to her.'

'She is Colonel Hoeppner's prisoner, sir. His orders are that she is not to be interrogated except in his presence.'

'Do you know who I am?'

'Yes, Herr Colonel. You are Colonel Roess of the Gestapo.'

'Then you will know that Colonel Hoeppner takes his orders from me. I wish to see this prisoner, now.'

The sergeant gulped. 'Yes, Herr Colonel.' He walked round

his desk, giving the woman clerk seated beside him a violent kick on the ankle as he did so.

She gasped, but managed not to say anything, watched Roess follow the sergeant along the corridor to the stairs leading down to the cells. 'What the fuck brought that on?' she muttered. 'He could have broken my leg. I think he did.' She raised her skirt to rub her stocking vigorously.

'I think he was trying to tell you something,' said the soldier standing behind her, admiring the view. 'I think he wants you to get hold of the colonel, and tell him what is happening.'

'Me? Wake up Colonel Hoeppner? It is nearly two o'clock in the morning.'

'Well, that's what I think he wants.'

The woman bit her lip. Either way she was on a hiding to nothing. But she was actually more afraid of the sergeant than of the colonel, with whom she had never come into contact, except at a safe distance. Then she had an idea. 'I'll call Eva. She'll know what to do.'

'Would you like a cigarette?' Franz asked.

'I'd prefer a drink,' Joanna said, stretching.

'Was I that bad?' He got out of bed and switched on the lamp.

'You were excellent.'

'And you were superb. But a drink – it will mean waking up the hotel.'

'Try the bathroom.'

He opened the door, switched on the bathroom light. 'Were you expecting the worst?'

'I always expect the best. But I also always travel with my own liquor.'

He half-filled the two tooth mugs and brought them to the bed, sitting beside her. 'I do not wish to, but I feel I have to go.'

'Why? Aren't I coming with you tomorrow to pick up this British agent?'

'I think it would be bad form for us to arrive at the office together. Or for the chambermaid to find us in bed together.'

'And form bothers you. You ever thought that you have a lot in common with the Brits?'

'Should we not? We are of the same stock.'

The telephone jangled. They looked at each other. 'I'll take it,' Joanna said, swinging her legs out of bed. 'It can only be Oskar, checking up on me.'

'But he does not know where you are staying.'

'I called him, remember.' She picked up the receiver. 'Yes?'

'Oh, Fräulein Jonsson.' Eva was breathless. 'I must speak with the colonel. It is most urgent.'

Joanna looked at Franz. 'It's your secretary. She sounds agitated.'

'Eva? How did she know where to find me?'

'I'd like you to explain that, yes.' Joanna gave him the receiver.

'Eva? How did you know where I am?'

'Well, Herr Colonel, I tried your rooms, and you were not there, and I knew you were taking Fräulein Jonsson out to dinner . . .' She paused, archly.

'You should be a detective. Why are you calling me at half past two in the morning?'

'It is about Colonel Roess, sir.'

'He's not dead?'

'No, sir. He has gone to headquarters.'

'In the middle of the night? The man must have lost his senses. What is he doing there?'

'I understand that he has left again, sir. But he has taken the prisoner.'

Franz stared at the telephone for a moment. 'Taken her where?'

'They think to Gestapo Headquarters.'

'Shit,' Franz muttered. 'Very good, Eva. Thank you for letting me know.' He hung up.

'Problem?' Joanna asked, having returned to bed.

'Only that that cretin Roess does not appear to be as badly hurt as I supposed. Or he has actually suffered brain damage. He has gone charging down to headquarters, over-ruled my orders, and carried Cartwright off to Gestapo Headquarters.'

'Oh my God!' Joanna leapt out of bed and ran into the bathroom.

Franz followed her. 'I know. It is most unfortunate for the woman; she looked a thoroughly nice girl. But there it is. It was bound to happen.'

Joanna ran back out of the bathroom and began dressing. 'Hurry up.'

'Joanna, there is nothing we can do. Once the Gestapo have someone . . .'

'You have retrieved someone from the Gestapo before. Amalie de Gruchy,'

'That was different. I was a major and Roess was only a captain. And it was in an area still considered to be a combat zone, on the Channel coast, so the Wehrmacht had ultimate authority. Now that things have settled down, and certainly as he has been sent down here to take control of the investigation . . .'

Joanna buttoned her blouse, tucked it into her skirt, and reached for her mink. 'Franz, I am going to Gestapo Headquarters now. Are you coming or not?'

He began to dress himself. 'But what can you do? You have no authority over the Gestapo. Roess will probably lock you up. And this woman is nothing to you.'

'This woman is a prisoner I have been instructed to deliver to SD headquarters in Berlin. This I intend to do, and I do not wish her to be a shattered wreck when I get her there. As for authority, I have the authority of Oskar Weber. If anyone is going to be locked up, it will be Johann Roess.'

Franz stared at her for several seconds, then he finished dressing and followed her down the stairs.

Rachel was surprised to realize that she had actually slept. She was not used to sleeping in her clothes, which, despite her shower, still stank of rotten fruit, and the single bunk bed in the cell was harder than anything she had previously known. There was also the fact that her brain was in turmoil. On the other hand, as the German colonel had commanded, she had been served a very good dinner, had drunk every drop of the surprisingly good wine, and no one had yet laid a hand on her, even to sexually assault her, much less torture her. With the aid of the wine she had almost convinced herself that she might be going to get away with it. But now she was awake, staring into the darkness, listening to distant sounds on the level above her, and she knew she was not going to sleep again. Because someone was going to lay hands on her very soon, and then . . .

Oddly, she was more curious than afraid. She did not yet regret that she had not bitten the cyanide capsule. She had no idea what they were going to do to her, what it would feel like. She intended to let herself go and scream as loudly as she could. As long as she was doing that, she couldn't tell them anything. It was a matter of living in the present, from minute to minute, of feeling. Her body was alive, all of its private and intimate parts tingling. Because she knew that those parts were soon to cease being private and would belong to the men who would be interrogating her.

Footsteps in the corridor. Rachel sat up, all of her courage draining from her mind. It could not possibly be morning yet. But perhaps they were just coming to make sure she was all right. She lay down again, closed her eyes. A light came on and a key scraped. She opened her eyes again, blinking short-sightedly as two men entered her cell. She did not remember ever having seen them before, but she knew that one was an officer and the other a sergeant. It was the officer that mattered. He was not very tall, in fact was altogether a small man, his face separated by his moustache; neither half was the least attractive. And his head was bandaged. She found that incredibly odd. The sergeant issued an order, but she did not understand him. So she stared at him and he began to shout. The officer spoke, quietly, and the shouting stopped, although the sergeant continued to glare at her.

'He does not realize that you do not speak German,' Roess said in French. 'I understand that you are an English agent.'

He seemed perfectly civilized. Perhaps she was just being lucky with her German officers. Oh, how she hoped her luck would hold. 'Everyone tells me that,' she said, as insouciantly as she could. 'I don't know the reason. My name is

Brigitte Ferrand, and I am a schoolteacher from Paris.'

'I am Colonel Johann Roess, and I am commander of the Gestapo in France.' Rachel caught her breath, which she felt was not unreasonable for a schoolteacher. 'So, get up. You are coming with me.'

Rachel licked her lips. 'Colonel Hoeppner said . . .'

'What Colonel Hoeppner said is of no importance now.' Without warning he stepped forward and slapped her across the face, very hard. Her head spun and she tasted blood as she fell across the bunk. 'I told you to get up.' Rachel slipped off the bed and found herself on her knees, gasping for breath. Immediately the toe of his boot thudded into her thigh. Such primeval violence, happening with such unexpected suddenness, seemed to have paralysed her brain. 'Up!'

The paralysis was soon replaced by anger. With her training she could surely take this rat apart. She reached her feet and swung her hand, only to be struck from behind, a shattering blow in her kidneys that sent her back on to her knees, vomiting. She had forgotten the sergeant, standing behind her.

'Don't hit her again,' Roess said. 'She has spirit. I do not want her damaged yet. What took you so long?'

Rachel realized that he was speaking to some more men, who had come hurrying down the corridor. 'We came as quickly as we could, Herr Colonel.'

'You mean you were asleep. I wish this woman taken to our headquarters. Be careful with her.'

Rachel felt hands grasping her arms and shoulders to drag her to her feet. Her head was still spinning and she had no breath, while the pain in her back was agonizing, robbing her of all her strength. Her knees gave way and she was dragged through the cell door and along the corridor.

'Pick her up!' Ross commanded.

Other hands grasped her thighs and ankles, and she was carried between the four men. Their fingers ate into her flesh and she thanked God that she was wearing trousers, but she did not suppose they were going to provide more than a passing safeguard. She was carried up the stairs, too exhausted to attempt to move, aware only of pain accentuated by the fingers. Dimly she realized that she was being carried through the outer office, past several men and a woman, who were on their feet as the officer passed. The woman held a telephone in her hand and looked terrified. Then she was in the open, inhaling the near freezing air and realizing for the first time that both her coat and her jerkin had been left in the cell. She was thrust into the back of a limousine, landing on her knees as the hands released her.

'Handcuff her,' Roess commanded. 'She is a hellion.' Her arms were pulled behind her back and she felt the steel of the handcuffs as they were clipped into place. 'Now seat her,' Roess said.

She was dragged upright and made to sit in the centre of the rear seat. Roess got in beside her, and one of his men sat on the other side. Three more got into the front, and the limousine drove out of the yard. Rachel swallowed some more blood and at last got her breathing under control.

'You have no right to do this,' she ventured, hating herself because her teeth were chattering from the cold.

'I have the right to do anything I wish.' As if to prove it, he squeezed her breasts through the shirt. Rachel gasped in discomfort and revulsion; her nipples were hard because of the cold. She opened her mouth and then closed it again. Protesting was clearly not going to accomplish anything. She had simply to accept what was happening to her, and wait for it to end.

Roess's hands roamed over her shirt and then over her stomach and down to her groin. She clamped her knees together, but he forced his hand between her thighs, again to squeeze. This time she drew a sharp breath.

'Why do you not scream?' he asked. 'I like to hear women scream.' Rachel spat at him and his head jerked back, while his hand was withdrawn to wipe the saliva from his face. 'You will scream,' he said. 'You will scream so loud they will hear you in London.' The car was slowing and then turning into another courtyard before coming to a halt. 'Take her out,' Roess commanded.

The man seated on Rachel's other side got out, and then grasped her arms to pull her behind him. She stumbled but this time kept her feet; she did not wish to be dragged again like a sack of coal. Another man stood at her other side, also holding an arm, and she was pushed through an open doorway into another office, which at least provided some warmth.

Roess followed her into the room. 'Downstairs,' he ordered.

Rachel was largely unaware of the other men in the room as she concentrated on keeping on her feet. Even so she repeatedly stumbled as she was forced across the floor and down a flight of stairs. This level was brilliantly lit and consisted of a corridor along the front of several closed doors. Behind these doors there was restless movement and a mixture of shouts and groans, wails and whimpers. The men ignored these and forced Rachel the length of the corridor to another door, which was opened. Already short of breath, Rachel all but choked as she gazed at the instruments hanging on the walls, the rings let into the floor. *My God*, she thought. *This can't be happening to me!* Now she felt like screaming. But she would not give these brutes that satisfaction.

Roess came in and closed the door. 'Let's see what the bitch has to offer,' he said. The handcuffs were taken off, but there was no relief. Surrounded and manhandled by the four men, Rachel could do nothing but gasp as she was pushed and pulled to and fro while her clothes were taken away, buttons being ripped off and the material torn. The most humiliating moment was when, naked, she was thrown over one of the men's shoulders while her boots were removed. Then she was set on her feet to face Roess. Instinctively she closed one hand over her pubes and held the other arm across her breasts. Then she let them fall to her side. Modesty had no place here.

'Thin,' Roess remarked. 'But not unattractive.' He held her hands to examine her fingers. 'These have never seen a day's manual work. You are upper crust, eh?' He peered closer, looking for marks. 'And they have never known a ring, either. Can you be a virgin?'

'We can soon put that right, Herr Colonel,' said one of the men.

'Oh, indeed, we shall do that. But first we must make her feel a little. And tell us the truth about herself.' He snapped his fingers, and his men, who obviously knew what he wanted without being told, immediately raised Rachel's arms above her head and secured them to steel rings hanging from the ceiling. Meanwhile Roess went to the wall and selected a riding crop, with a thong about four feet long. 'This will make you cry,' he said, returning to stand at her shoulder. 'But first, light a cigarette.'

One of the men obeyed, inhaling to make sure it was well lit, and then handed it to his superior. Rachel drew a deep breath, and then realized that had been a mistake, as he fingered her left nipple to bring it back erect. 'Let us discover what you are made of, Mademoiselle Cartwright,' he said, and stroked the nipple with the unlit end, then suddenly reversed it and pressed the glowing tip into the pink flesh.

Rachel could not suppress a little whimper of pain, and he smiled. 'Tell me your name.'

She panted. 'My name is Brigitte Ferrand, and I am a schoolteacher from Paris.'

'Well,' he said. 'Fortunately you have two tits.' He massaged the other one.

The pain was already considerable. Rachel knew she was going to scream after all. She drew another deep breath, closed her eyes, and heard the door open.

'What is the meaning of this?' Roess demanded.

'You took the words right out of my mouth,' Joanna said.

Rachel opened her eyes in amazement. Roess had also just realized who the intruders were, or at least one of them. The other was Colonel Hoeppner, looking at once embarrassed and apprehensive, in strong contrast to Joanna, who was her usual soignée, immaculate and ebullient self.

'You!' Roess snapped.

'In the flesh. Now tell me what you are doing with my prisoner.' She stepped closer to Rachel, nostrils dilating at the odour of scorched flesh. 'My God! You bastard!' She stared at Rachel, and Rachel stared back, their eyes exchanging a wealth of signals.

'Your prisoner?' Roess demanded. 'This woman is a British agent'

'You could be right,' Joanna agreed. 'She looks British. But to burn her . . .'

'That is standard procedure. And as a spy, she belongs to the Gestapo.'

'Now there you are wrong. She is a prisoner of the SD. I have been sent here by Colonel Weber to take possession of her and escort her to Berlin for interrogation.'

Roess looked at Franz with his mouth open. 'I'm afraid that is correct, Johann,' Franz said.

'So you,' Joanna said, pointing at the policemen, 'take the prisoner down.' She walked to where Rachel's discarded clothing had been thrown. 'These are torn. Fetch a greatcoat.'

Roess at last found his voice. 'You cannot give orders to my men.'

'Then you do so. A greatcoat. And release her.'

'I think it would be best for you to do as Fräulein Jonsson requires,' Franz suggested.

'I will make an official report of this incident to General Heydrich.'

'I think that would be a very good idea,' Joanna agreed. 'In fact, it may be essential to your future, seeing that Colonel Weber is acting on General Heydrich's instructions.' Once again Roess was speechless. 'Down,' Joanna repeated. 'And a coat.'

Rachel's arms were released and she fell into Joanna's embrace. Now she could not stop herself weeping.

'She regards you as her saviour,' Franz remarked.

'So it would seem,' Joanna agreed. The coat was brought, and Rachel was wrapped in it, giving another whimper as the material brushed her burned nipple. 'We need to do something about that,' Joanna said.

'You have not heard the last of this,' Roess snarled.

'Tread carefully,' Joanna recommended.

'You have made an enemy for life,' Franz said as they drove back to Wehrmacht headquarters, Rachel between them. Wrapped in the greatcoat, she still shivered, partly from cold, Joanna estimated, but also partly from delayed shock – she had spent the better part of an hour staring into the abyss. But she had kept her nerve, and said not a word to betray either of them.

'I don't think we were ever likely to be friends,' Joanna pointed out.

'So what do we do now?' Franz asked. 'It won't be daylight for another four hours, and the train doesn't leave until eight thirty.'

'We take her to your office. We have to find clothes for her. And we have to do something about that burn and those bruises.'

'You are very solicitous. She *is* a British spy. Anyway, how do we do that at three o'clock in the morning?'

'I will fetch some cold cream from my hotel, and you will obtain some clothes from your staff.'

'They're all asleep.'

'Eva isn't, remember? I also want all of this woman's remaining gear. Everything that was in her haversack. Oskar will wish to see it all for himself.'

'Her gun as well?'

'Certainly.'

He sighed. 'I had really hoped we could go back to bed.'

'No you didn't. You were planning to leave my bed when Eva called.' She leaned across Rachel to squeeze his hand. 'You really have been a sweetie, Franz. I am going to give Oskar the highest possible praise for your behaviour.'

'Eh?'

'I meant, professionally, stupid. As for the other, well . . . We'll keep our little secret, shall we?'

'Please,' Rachel said in a small voice, 'what is to become of me?'

'You are going on a journey, my dear. Just sit back and enjoy it.'

Franz accompanied them to the station on a cold, damp morning. 'I really think you should let me send a couple of my men with you,' he said.

'Oh, come now, Franz. Do you not suppose I can handle this waif? I could break her in two with a twist of my wrists.'

He had to agree she was right. Rachel certainly looked

better than she had done in the Gestapo cell. She had been given a hot bath and breakfast, her coffee being laced with cognac, and Eva had done surprisingly well as regards clothes, which almost fitted her. What Joanna had done about her injuries he did not know, as he had not been allowed in the cell while she was treating her, but she had undoubtedly soothed the pain. Yet she was still a bruised and battered figure, more mentally than physically, he felt, although apart from her breasts there were still ugly marks on her back and thighs where she had been kicked and punched. Now she wore a topcoat and a felt hat, from which there drooped a veil, at Joanna's insistence. He wasn't quite sure why, because she was also handcuffed, in front, and was clearly a prisoner. He accompanied them on board the train and into their first-class compartment, anxiously followed by the conductor.

'These ladies are not to be disturbed,' Franz said.

'Of course, Herr Colonel.'

'Except that we will need our meals brought to us,' Joanna said. 'We will not be using the dining car.'

'As you wish, madame.'

'Mademoiselle,' Joanna pointed out. She squeezed Franz's gloved fingers. 'Again, all my thanks for your help.'

'When will I see you again? I am due for leave after Christmas. I shall come to Berlin.'

'We would have to be very discreet. But who knows, once I have delivered this bitch, Oskar may well send me back to assist in the search for Amalie de Gruchy.' She gave a throaty chuckle. 'Just imagine how pleased Roess will be.'

'I salute you. Heil Hitler!' Franz left the compartment.

Joanna drew the blind. 'I think you should sit down.'

Rachel sank on to the bunk. 'Will you tell me what is going on?' Although they had been alone in the cell for over an hour, while Joanna had tended her, she had shaken her head whenever Rachel would have spoken; she knew the cell was bugged.

Joanna sat opposite her. 'Surely you understand what is going on? I have extricated you from the clutches of the Gestapo.'

Rachel held up her manacled wrists. 'But I am still under arrest. And you are taking me to Berlin.'

'Well, you don't suppose Hoeppner would have let you go under any other circumstances, do you? As to Berlin . . . tell me what happened.' The train shuddered and started to move. Rachel outlined her experiences. 'Monterre,' Joanna mused. 'I never did like that bastard. But it was incredibly stupid of you to trust him.'

'I know that now. But I was getting desperate. The de Gruchys seem to have vanished off the face of the earth.'

'If you ever intend to be a successful agent,' Joanna said, 'or indeed if you intend to survive, you must never be impatient, never become desperate. And never trust anybody, unless you know them very, very well.'

'I am trusting you.'

'Well, in this instance, you don't have any choice. As for the de Gruchys, I can tell you that they haven't disappeared all that far. Where do you suppose Roess got that bump on the head?'

'You're not serious.'

'Liane.'

'Does he know that?'

'Good God, no. He thinks she's some floozy he picked up in Paris and was bringing down here for a prolonged bit of nooky. Liane is very good at playing that role. She enjoys it.'

'Oh. Does James know this?'

'Of course he does.'

'Yet he is in love with her.'

'So? When you're in love with somebody – I mean really – it doesn't matter who or where she fucks. Especially when you know she is doing it for the Resistance.'

This was not a point of view Rachel had ever considered before. Of course she knew that James slept with Liane whenever he had the chance, which wasn't very often, and she had never held it against him. She supposed she was just old-fashioned, had grown up with the assumption that men had a permanent *droit de seigneur*. These women were out of her class.

'And where is she now?'

'Having laid him out, she disappeared. That's why Roess

is in such a bad mood. Apart from his headache, he would dearly like to have her where he had you.'

Rachel shuddered. 'If she was going to split his head open, why didn't she go the whole hog and kill him?'

'Now that I cannot tell you. But I am sure she had a reason. Liane always has a reason.'

'You admire her, don't you?'

'I love her, too,' Joanna said simply.

'Oh. I thought . . . well, I know about the schoolgirl thing . . .'

'Our love has nothing to do with sex any more. Which is not to say . . . Oh, forget it.'

'I'm sorry. I didn't mean to upset you.' Rachel held up her arms again. 'Do you think we could take these off? My wrists are becoming quite chafed.' Joanna took the key from her handbag and unlocked the cuffs. Rachel rubbed the reddened flesh. 'So what is going to happen now?'

'If you were to get off this train at an appropriate moment, do you suppose you could find your way to Switzerland? We have all your original documents, and I have sufficient funds.'

'I think I could do that. But when will be an appropriate moment?'

'We have to work that out. In a couple of hours we are going to cross the border into Vichy. I am sorry, when that happens I will have to cuff you again, for the benefit of the border guards, who will inspect the train. Right?'

'Ye–es. But once we are across the border . . .'

'I know, it is tempting. The train stops at Limoges.'

'Brilliant! I can go back to Anatole, warn him about Monterre, and call London to get me out.'

'I said it was tempting. But it's not practical.'

'Why not?'

'There are three reasons. The first is that it was in Limoges station that Liane bopped Roess.'

'Oh, my God!'

'Good point. According to Franz, the whole area is in a state of high alert. They are looking for Liane, but they will be stopping every strange woman and interrogating her, and possibly locking her up while they investigate her further. The last thing you want with the bruises you are carrying is a strip search. The second reason is that I think you need to stay away from Anatole. There appears to be some pretty dicey stuff going on, with him in the middle, and even if he's clean, you can bet your bottom dollar that the Vichy police have a pretty good idea what he does with his spare time, and have him staked out. Right?'

'I hadn't thought of that.'

'And the third and most important reason is that *I* have to stay clean. You have to escape me, not be released by me. OK, so you were veiled when you came on board, but your figure and movements are not too forgettable. We reach Limoges just after lunch. If the conductor sees you leaving the train in broad daylight he may just be curious enough to alert the *gendarmerie*. He would certainly want to check with me to make sure it was all right, and that would ruin everything. No, what we have to do is sit it out. We should leave Vichy again mid-afternoon, and get to Dijon just about dusk.'

'And you reckon I can get off then?'

'Nope.'

'For God's sake!'

'I told you, to succeed in this business you just have to be patient. If we don't order dinner, again the conductor is going to be suspicious. So we have dinner, and we go to bed. We'll be at Metz about midnight. That's where you'll leave the train.'

'Metz?' Rachel cried. 'That far north?'

'So you'll have a long journey. I'm going to let you have a travel document which will see you most of the way. And you have a north French accent, so you'll melt into the background. You are on your way to Switzerland to visit your aged mother.'

Rachel considered this for several minutes. Then she said, 'So I get off the train in Metz. How do I do that without leaving you up the creek?'

'I think we could possibly take a leaf from Liane's book. Of course, we don't want to be too literal about it. But it has to look good.'

*   *   *

112

Roess sat in front of Franz Hoeppner's desk. His head had been re-bandaged, but he was obviously still in considerable pain, and a consuming fury.

'That bitch,' he said. 'One day . . . How did she come to be with you at two o'clock in the morning?'

'I'm afraid one of my staff took exception to your decision to remove the prisoner,' Franz said. 'She telephoned me to tell me what had happened. Well, I knew that Jonsson was acting on orders from Heydrich, via Weber, so I felt she should be informed. I'm sure you'll agree that it would be unwise to get on the wrong side of either of those gentlemen.'

'One day,' Roess said again. 'If you knew how I felt, to be humiliated by one woman after the other, and be unable to do anything about it . . .'

'I know,' Franz said. 'It is a terrible situation to be in.'

Roess regarded him for several seconds, rightly suspecting sarcasm. 'And now the doctor tells me that I cannot go on with the investigation, that I must have complete rest for several weeks.'

'I am sure he is right.'

'So, Amalie de Gruchy will also slip through my fingers.'

'I will continue the investigation as best I can, until you are fit to resume.'

'As best you are able,' Roess said contemptuously. 'The thought of those creatures out there, laughing at us . . .' Then he snapped his fingers. 'Well, at least we can wipe the smiles off their faces. You are still holding the hundred hostages you took last month?'

'They are in the town gaol. I am half-inclined to let them go. They are not serving any worthwhile purpose.'

'I agree. We will shoot them.'

'Eh? Don't be ridiculous.'

Roess pointed. 'You took those hostages on the orders of General Heydrich. Am I not correct?'

'Yes,' Franz said, a lump of lead gathering in his stomach.

'And his orders were that they were to be shot if Amalie de Gruchy was not surrendered.'

'He issued that order. But it was never meant to be carried

113

out. It was intended to frighten the population into giving the woman up.'

'And it has not worked. And you have not executed a single hostage. There is another reason for them to be laughing at you. Well, as I say, we are going to wipe that particular smile from their faces.' He stared at Franz. 'Or are you going to countermand General Heydrich's express command?' Franz gulped. Roess smiled. 'Cheer up. It may even bring the bitch out of hiding, and you will have completed the investigation before I return from hospital.'

The conductor hummed as he walked along the corridor, carrying the breakfast tray. The other passengers had got the message that there were two very important people in compartment three, and this gave him an increased sense of his own importance. He had no idea who the two women were, but the fact that they had been escorted on to the train by the Bordeaux commandant was sufficient for him. The additional fact that one of them had boarded in handcuffs – a fact known only to him – gave them added interest. He wished he knew what she looked like. But she had worn a veil, and on the two occasions he had been allowed into the compartment, with meals, her face had again been hidden. He had even hung around in the corridor, waiting for her to go to the toilet, but they had gone together, and again she had been veiled. On the other hand, first thing in the morning, when they would both be in bed, he wondered what else he might uncover . . .

He drew a deep breath, and knocked. There was no sound from inside the compartment, or at least none that he could hear above the sound of the train rushing through the dawn. He tried again, but still there was no response. Did he dare open the door? The temptation was enormous, but he resisted it for the moment. Let them sleep, or do whatever it was they were doing, a while longer. They would have to wake up at the border. Two women, one at least of whom was quite beautiful and was also obviously high in the Nazi hierarchy . . . His imagination boggled.

He took the tray away and returned half an hour later; they were approaching Saarbrucken. Again there was no response

114

to his knock, but now he was entitled to awaken them. Another deep breath and he released the door, cautiously sliding it along its groove just a few inches, so that he could see inside. Predictably, the compartment was in darkness, but it was also filled with the women's scent.

'Fräulein?' he asked.

There was movement from one of the berths. Then there was a moan. He placed the tray on the floor of the corridor, switched on the light, and gazed in consternation at the woman lying on the bunk, on her side, facing him. She was naked, and from the position of her arms, behind her, he guessed that her wrists were bound, as were her ankles, while an additional band, like the others made from torn sheets, had been passed round her waist and secured to the bunk itself to prevent her from rolling out. She was also gagged, but her eyes were open, peering at him through the strands of heavy yellow hair that drifted across her face.

He looked left and right, ascertaining that the other woman was missing. Then he tentatively approached the woman on the bunk. He had never seen a more evocative sight. His hands scrabbled at her head, fingers sifting through her hair to find the knot for the gag. It took him several minutes to release it.

'Fräulein?' he said again.

'Shut that fucking door,' she commanded. 'Oh, and bring the tray in.'

He obeyed her.

'Now get me free. Where is she?'

Trembling, the conductor bent over the naked body to release the strip of sheet holding her to the bed. 'She, Fräulein?'

'The prisoner. The woman who was with me.'

'I do not know, Fräulein.' The sheet came free and he released her wrists.

'Well, she must be found. She has to be somewhere on the train.'

'Well, there was the stop. Actually, there were two stops during the night.' He freed her ankles, and was kicked in the thigh as she swung her legs out of bed and sat up.

'What did you say? What stops?'

115

'The last one was at Metz. Did you not know of it?'

'And you say that bitch got off there? Why did you not stop her?'

'Well . . . I don't *know* she got off, Fräulein. Several people left the train; I did not look closely at any of them. And I had no reason to stop her. I did not know what she looked like.'

'What are you staring at? Have you never seen a naked woman before? Give me my robe. And that orange juice.'

The conductor obeyed. Joanna wrapped herself in her dressing gown and drank greedily. 'The train must be searched and at the same time put into reverse. How far back is the last station?'

'It will be thirty miles behind us, at least.'

'Well, then, don't just stand here. Stop the train. Pull the communication cord.'

'I cannot do that, Fräulein.'

'Listen, that woman is a wanted criminal. A British spy. She must be re-captured.'

'If she is still on the train, we will find her. But to stop the train and go back . . . it is impossible. And dangerous.'

'How can it be dangerous?'

'There are other trains using the track. One is behind us now. There could be an accident. And if the woman got off the train at Metz, she could be anywhere by now. If she had papers.'

'She has papers.'

'Well, then, I am sorry, Fräulein. But . . . how did it happen?'

'It happened,' Joanna spat at him, 'because I am a stupid, soft-hearted halfwit. She seemed so docile, so when she begged me to free her wrists, I did so. And then, last night, after dinner, she got hold of my gun.'

'She has a gun?'

'Yes, she has a gun. You say it is impossible to go back. When do we stop again?'

'At the border. That is in a few minutes' time.'

'That is something. Look, go and bring me some cognac. There is going to be hell to pay.'

*   *   *

Jennifer placed the transcript in front of James and stood to attention. James scanned it while lead balloons gathered in his stomach. He raised his head.

'Did Pound Seventeen say how this happened?'

'He doesn't seem to know, sir. When Rachel did not come in as usual, he began checking about, as we know. But she had just disappeared, with a man called Monterre. You say you knew Monterre.'

'I do.'

'Well, all Pound Seventeen knows is that they must have crossed the border. Now the Germans have announced that they have captured a British agent. They haven't named her, or even said that it is a woman, but it can't be anyone but Rachel.'

'Yes,' James said.

Jennifer licked her lips. 'What will they do to her, sir?'

'Didn't they teach you anything at training school?'

'Oh, my God! But Rachel . . . Oh, my God!'

'However, she had her capsule. We must assume she's dead.'

'How can you sit there and say something like that? I thought you were friends.'

'Would you prefer it if I broke down and wept? Yes, we were friends. Very close friends. But she knew what she was risking.' He knew he dare not let himself think or he *would* break down and weep. The thought of Rachel in the hands of the Gestapo, subjected to flogging or to having electrodes thrust into her body to tear her apart with agony, the thought of all that delicate refinement at the mercy of brutal, jeering men . . . He had to believe she was dead. But then, the thought of that joyous, eager body turned into a lump of decaying flesh was no less horrendous.

'Was Pound Seventeen able to tell us anything about the de Gruchys?' he asked.

'No, sir.' Jennifer's tone was cold. 'He has had no contact with the Group. But he assumes that Monterre was taking Rachel to them when they were arrested. He is afraid that if they were interrogated by the Gestapo, the whereabouts of the de Gruchys will now be known, and that therefore we must assume that they have been terminated.'

117

'And he's probably right.' James got up and put on his coat and hat.

'May I ask where you are going, sir?'

'To see the brigadier. I think we have just gone out of business.'

Six

The Hideaway

'There is a gentleman to see you, Frau von Helsingen,' Hilda said, standing in the doorway of the lounge.

Madeleine was playing with her baby, as she spent most days doing. Now she stood up, the child in her arms. Unexpected men calling on her always made her nervous, since the day Oskar Weber had suddenly appeared to talk with her about Joanna. She felt she had handled that rather well, as Joanna and Oskar now seemed to be as thick as thieves. An apt description, she considered. But if this was Weber, Hilda would know it.

'Has the gentleman a name?' Madeleine asked.

Hilda looked at the card in her hand. 'A Herr Fesster. He is Swiss.'

'I do not know anyone in Switzerland.'

'He says you have a mutual acquaintance.'

'Oh, very well. Show him in.' Madeleine placed Helen in the cot, and the baby gurgled happily.

'Frau von Helsingen, it is good of you to receive me.' Herr Fesster was a short, somewhat stout man, who wore a gold watch chain across the waistcoat of his three-piece suit; the chain accentuated his air of genteel prosperity. His face was round and clean shaven, his head bald save for a fringe. Madeleine placed him in his late forties.

'My maid suggested we had an acquaintance in common.'

'I believe we do. A Fräulein Joanna Jonsson.'

'Hilda, will you serve coffee?' Madeleine sat down and gestured Fesster to a chair. 'You know Joanna?'

'We are business acquaintances.'

Madeleine studied him. That could mean anything. But he

119

was not her idea of a British agent. 'I did not know Joanna had business interests in Switzerland.'

'Fräulein Jonsson has interests everywhere.'

'I know she travels a lot. But what has that to do with me?'

'It is simply that I seem to have missed her. I checked at the Hotel Albert, where I was informed she maintains a suite, but she was not there, and they had no idea when she would be returning. Apparently she often does this. But they suggested that I try you for some information. They say you are her best friend in Berlin.'

'They are mistaken. We had an . . . acquaintance, before the war. She comes to see me occasionally. But she never tells me what she is doing next.'

'But you do expect to see her again.'

'Perhaps. Is it that important?'

'It is to me.' He took a wallet from his inside breast pocket. 'If I may, I will leave you my card.' He opened the wallet, extracted the card, and a banknote drifted from his fingers to the carpet. 'Oh!' He retrieved it. 'An English pound note. I had forgotten I had it.' He stared at Madeleine as he restored the pound to its sleeve.

Madeleine had no doubt he was trying to tell her something, but she had no idea what it was. She took the card. 'When – if – I see Fräulein Jonsson again, I will tell her you called, Herr Fesster.'

He was clearly disappointed at her reaction. He finished his coffee, stood up, and bowed. 'I should be most grateful, Frau von Helsingen. Good day to you.'

'Fräulein Jonsson,' the under manager said, taking her bag. 'Good to have you back.'

'I have only been away a week, Rudolf.'

'It seems longer. Now, Fräulein, Herr Weber is waiting for you.'

'Ah. Yes.' She began to brace herself mentally.

'And . . .' He took a note from her pigeon hole. 'A gentleman called, two days ago.' He handed her the note. 'Herr Fesster, from Switzerland.'

She scanned the paper. 'I know no Herr Fesster.'

120

'He seemed to think that you do, Fräulein. He left you this as a memento, of past times, he said.' He gave her an English pound note. Joanna stared at it. 'And you see he has left a telephone number for you to get in touch with him.'

'Thank you.' Joanna folded both notes into her handbag, walked slowly towards the lifts, followed by a boy with her suitcase. What a time for London to start chasing her! But first things first. She rode up in the lift, smiling at the bellboy, then checked him at her door. 'I'll take it in.' She took the suitcase, tipped him and opened the door. 'Oskar!'

'My dear!' He took her in his arms.

'I am so ashamed.'

He kissed her, then released her to pour two glasses of cognac. 'Tell me what happened.'

Joanna told him exactly what she had told the conductor. 'When we stopped at the border, I called the local commandant, but he wasn't very co-operative. I asked him to put out an alarm along the borders with Vichy, and Switzerland as well, but I don't know if he did. I don't think he considered I had the least authority, and, as he pointed out, Metz is a long way from Vichy.'

'You did not give him my name?'

'I didn't think you would wish me to do that.'

He nodded. 'You are a good girl. But also a very foolish one. In our business, one should never be overconfident. Would not Hoeppner give you an escort?'

'He offered to, yes. But I did not think it necessary. As I said, she seemed such a depressed little waif.'

'Overconfidence,' he said again. 'It can be fatal. I will see to the borders; she cannot possibly have got anywhere near them yet. But it is a serious matter.'

'I know. As I say, I am very ashamed. But I do not think she was that important. I told you on the phone from Bordeaux that I felt she would have information about the de Gruchys. Well, it seemed logical that London would seek to make contact after Kessler's death.'

'Do you not suppose London and the guerrillas are in touch by radio?'

'There seems to have been a breakdown. I was right that

121

she was to do with the de Gruchys. But she had no idea where they were. That is why she was sent, to re-open contact, and she had not yet succeeded in doing this when she was captured.'

'She told you this? Without being interrogated?'

'Well, she was in the hands of Roess for an hour before I extricated her. She was terrified, and talked on the train.'

'You should have left her with Roess for another hour.'

'He would have reduced her to a gibbering wreck. I thought you would want more than that.'

'Instead I got nothing, and you might have been killed . . . Oh, I am not angry with you. No one knows you were bringing a spy home. Except of course Roess and Hoeppner. Now, tell me, what is the truth in the rumours I have been receiving about Roess?'

'Hasn't he reported?'

'He has reported that he was attacked by a madwoman in Limoges. That is all. But he was apparently so badly injured that he has had to go to hospital.'

'Well, I suppose that is the truth. Save that this "madwoman" shared his compartment all the way from Paris, overnight.'

'What is your interpretation of that?'

'That she found his sexual preferences unable to stomach. He really is a horrible little man.'

'He does his job,' Weber said mildly. 'We shall wait and see, and hope he comes up with something. When he gets out of hospital.'

'Am I to go back down?'

'Not at this time.'

'You *are* angry with me.'

'I am not in the least angry with you. I am thinking of you. Don't you realize that your position has been compromised?'

Joanna frowned. 'In what way?'

'This British agent who has got away knows who you are. If she were to regain England . . .'

'Oh, come now. There are something like forty million people in England. We are hardly likely to bump into each other.'

'She will be able to describe you. You will admit that you are not the sort of woman one easily forgets.'

'I usually travel in dark glasses and with my hair up. And this woman does not know I have ever been to England. The risk is really infinitesimal.'

'Nonetheless, it is there. I would prefer not to chance it. If we manage to recapture this woman, well and good.'

'So what am I to do? Sit here and twiddle my thumbs? Or shall I go back to Sweden?'

'No, I don't want you to do that. I suggest you take a holiday. But here in Germany. Go down to Munich and do some skiing. You do ski?'

'Of course I ski.'

'Well, then, spend Christmas in Munich, and stay on into January. I will come down and spend a few days with you.'

'You will spend Christmas with me?'

'Well, no. I must spend Christmas with my family. But I could come down for New Year. Yes, I will do that. Now I must hurry. I have a meeting.' He kissed her. 'I will make the travel arrangements, and bring them to you tonight.'

The door closed behind him. Joanna heaved a sigh of relief and poured herself another drink. As always, he simply believed everything she told him. She wondered how long that would last. Meanwhile, she opened her handbag and took out both the note and the pound. She reread the note, committing the telephone number to memory, then tore both pieces of paper into strips and carefully burned them, making sure that there was no shred left before crushing out the ashes. She actually did feel like a holiday, having skated on enough thin ice over the past few weeks. Fesster and London would have to wait.

'Good morning, Anatole,' Liane said. 'I hope you had a good Christmas.'

The baker gaped at the woman standing in front of him. She wore a hooded cloak that concealed both her hair and her body, but hers was not a face anyone could forget. 'Mademoiselle de Gruchy!'

'Pound Twelve, please.'

'But where have you been? There has been so much trouble . . .'

123

'So I understand. Take me somewhere private and tell me about it. Hello, madame.'

Clotilde had come into the shop to see who her husband was talking to. 'Mademoiselle de Gruchy! Oh, so good to have you back!'

'I am glad to be back.' Liane followed Anatole through the bakery itself, where several men and women were hard at work and the scent of fresh bread clogged the air, into the parlour beyond.

'There is hot coffee,' Anatole said, fussing. 'And you must be hungry.'

'I am more hungry for a hot bath.' Liane sat down. 'But report, first.'

Anatole poured coffee, gave her the cup. 'I hardly know where to begin.'

'Try the beginning. I left here in October, because it was necessary for me to go to Paris. That is only three months ago. And I left instructions that no one was to undertake any action until my return, or unless instructed by London. So what happened?'

Anatole sat down also. 'Nothing happened at all for a month following your departure. Your brother came to see me once or twice, to find out if London had sent any messages. But they had not. So he stopped coming. I did not find anything sinister about this. I knew that the Group had broken up since your coming here, but you gave me to understand that it could be reunited when required.'

'So it can be. Do you not have all their addresses?'

'They are not at those addresses any more. They all seem to have disappeared after the shooting of the German colonel.'

'They are saying that was done by my sister. Can this possibly be true?'

'I am afraid there can be no doubt of it. Madame Burstein was avenging the death of her husband.'

'What?'

'As I understand it, Monsieur Burstein visited Bordeaux, was either identified or betrayed, and was seized and hanged after being interrogated. It is not known whether he gave away any of our secrets, but the mere fact that he had been taken

124

caused the various members of the Group to disappear. As you know, the Vichy authorities in this part of the country are very co-operative with the Germans.'

'But what was Henri doing in Bordeaux in the first place?'

'I do not know, mademoiselle.'

'And Amalie sought to avenge him. Oh, poor, silly girl.' But she could not blame her. Amalie's marriage had lasted precisely ten minutes before Henri had had to join his regiment. *She* had driven him and Pierre and James Barron up to the Belgian frontier, together with Joanna and her half-brother, Aubrey, thus beginning the cataclysmic series of events that had carried her along ever since – and which, but for Aubrey's death – and more recently the sad execution of Hercule – she would not have missed for the world. How it was going to end, how she would be able to resume a normal, civilized existence, even with James to help her, she did not know.

But for Amalie, the war had been even more traumatic. After her attenuated marriage, she had gone to live in Dieppe with her new parents-in-law, on the assumption that whenever Henri was given leave that was where he would go. Instead he had been pronounced missing, believed dead, following the disastrous campaign in Flanders. Amalie had been distraught, her anguish accentuated when her Jewish parents-in-law had been deported to a German concentration camp. Always emotional and quick-tempered, she had struck one of the Gestapo officers carrying out the arrest.

That had brought her into the orbit of Johann Roess, then only a junior officer, but as vicious as he was ever to become. It had also brought her into the orbit of Franz Hoeppner, who was commanding the garrison in Dieppe at the instigation of his best friend, Frederick von Helsingen, already in love with Madeleine. That action had undoubtedly saved Hoeppner's life when Amalie had gone on the rampage.

But her experiences, however brief, at the hands of Roess had left mental scars. Amalie had only been nineteen and her life, up to that fateful May day in 1940, had been lived entirely in the perpetual sunlight provided by the de Gruchy millions and the loving protection afforded her by her older siblings.

With all of that stripped away, she had undoubtedly suffered a mental breakdown, compounded by the marriage of her sister Madeleine to one of the hated Boches. She had even contemplated suicide. Liane had rescued her from that and had taken her into the Massif Central to join the guerrilla band. She had cared for her and nurtured her, and had been rewarded when, after a six-month absence, Henri had got to them – a fugitive to be sure, but they had all been fugitives. To witness Amalie's restored happiness had been a joy. Yet Liane had never doubted that the basic instability had remained behind the smiling countenance.

'Does London know what happened?'

'Oh, yes, mademoiselle. Pound is very upset. Not only about the unauthorized killing, but at his inability to get in touch with any of the Group. He is so upset that a month ago he sent one of his British agents to find out what is going on.'

'A British agent has been here? What did you tell him?'

'I could not tell him anything, because I did not know anything. And it was a woman, not a man.'

'A Pound agent? What number?'

'Number Two. So she must have been important.'

'Rachel! Yes,' Liane agreed, 'she was important. So you could tell her nothing. How long did she stay?'

'I'm afraid she is still here. Or in Germany. If indeed she is still alive. She crossed the border and was captured by the Gestapo. I had not supposed she would do such a foolish thing.'

'How do you know this?'

'It was put out by the Germans, that they had captured a British agent. They did not name her, but as it was only two days after she disappeared, it had to be her.'

'What date was this?'

'December eighteenth.'

My God, she thought. *That was the day before Limoges!* She had been tempted to come here then, but had known it was too risky. Instead, recrossing the border, she had doubled back to the north and taken refuge for a month with another guerrilla band, certain the Germans would look for her in the south. As they had. But even if she had come here, she would not have been able to do anything about Rachel.

126

'So let me get this straight,' she said. 'Pound Two was put down . . . when?'

'December eleventh.'

'Right. So she spent virtually a week here, doing what?'

'Her cover story was that of a schoolteacher from Paris. I gave her a job here as bookkeeper.'

'While she sought some information on my people, presumably. But you could give her none. And then, one day, she just ups and crosses the border? That's not logical.'

'She left at night. And I believe she went with Monterre.'

'Monterre was here?'

'He suddenly appeared here, seeking information.'

'What information?'

'About you, actually. He wanted to know when you were coming back.'

'Which you could not give him, because you did not know. But you told him about Pound Two. Why did you do that?'

Anatole flushed. 'Well, we were talking, and I told him how anxious I was about what was happening, and about London calling to find out, and that they had actually sent an agent to investigate . . .'

'And you also told him where this agent was to be found.'

'Well, I gave him the address of where she was staying, yes. Monterre is one of us. Isn't he?'

'I will have another cup of coffee,' Liane said. She watched Anatole get up and go to the pot. There was no point in censuring Anatole. He was a good and loyal patriot. His problem was he trusted too easily. And Monterre *was* one of them. Or he had been. 'So you think that Monterre took Pound Two across the border. If she came here to make contact with me or with my brother, he must have told her he knew where we were. Was he also taken by the Germans?'

'There has been no mention of it. But then, to them, he would have appeared as just a guide.'

'A guide who knew where to go.'

'Do you wish to call London? They are most anxious to contact you.'

Liane considered. But, much as she would have liked to hear James's voice, she would have to bring him up to date on a fairly catastrophic situation. It would be better to leave it until she had more positive information to give him, both about Rachel and about the Group. 'I think we'll do that later.'

'And if they call?'

'Leave things the way they are, that you have been unable to contact us. Now let me have that bath and a meal. I must get back across the border.'

'Is that not very dangerous? Did you hear about that business of the Gestapo officer being assaulted by a woman? The whole area has been turned upside down for the past month. No one has had any Christmas. The police were here several times.'

'Why here?'

'Well, they are suspicious of me.'

'And did you tell them anything?'

'Of course I did not.'

'Well, continue not to tell them anything. Now, my bath, and a meal, and I will leave you in peace.'

'You are looking for your brother and sister. Is that not like seeking a needle in a haystack?'

'But at least I know where the haystack is,' Liane told him.

'This has been one hell of a fuck-up, James,' the brigadier grumbled. 'You should never have used that girl in the first place.'

'With respect, sir, you authorized it.'

'Very well, *we* should never have used her. She lacked experience.'

'I regarded her as very capable, sir.'

'Well, I can't say much for your judgement. It is now a month since she was taken. Has there been no further word?'

'There has been no word since our last contact with Pound Seventeen, before Christmas, when he informed us of her disappearance.'

'Then she is certainly gone for good, whether she managed to commit suicide, was shot by the Germans, or is in a concentration camp. The damnable thing is that supposing she did *not* manage to commit suicide, we have no idea how much they got out of her. That is what was so irresponsible about employing her. She knows the identity of every Pound agent.'

'I know, sir. But there has been no suggestion that any of them have been compromised. Their reports are coming in as usual.'

'Well, we shall have to keep our fingers crossed. Now, do you know what I have to do? I have to go and see General Cartwright and tell him his only daughter is missing, believed killed. He is going to go through the roof.'

'If she is dead, sir, she died in the line of duty.'

'I don't think that is going to make him very happy, as he will not regard being in France as part of her duties in the first place. However, life must go on. I have cancelled my requisition order for funds to support the de Gruchy Organization.'

'But sir, that means you will be virtually shutting down the Route.'

'You're not suggesting that we pour thousands of francs into the hands of a prostitute?'

'We don't know that the de Gruchys are out of business, sir. In fact, we know that they are very much *in* business. It is merely that they have been forced to go into hiding and thus have been unable to contact us. But they will, as soon as possible.'

'Your optimism does you credit. But our business demands realism. What is so damned annoying about this catastrophe is that there is something very big planned for this year, something in which the co-operation of a viable French Resistance movement is damned near essential. Now—' His intercom buzzed and he pressed the switch. 'What is it? I said I was not to be disturbed.'

The woman was breathless. 'It is Pound Two, sir. She says it is most urgent she speaks with Pound One.'

'Pound Two?' The brigadier looked at James.

'She means Jennifer, sir. Pound Two's replacement.'

'Oh. Very well. Put her through. And it had better be important.'

One of the telephones jangled, and, at a nod from the brigadier, James picked it up. 'Yes.'

129

'Pound Two here, sir. I've heard from Pound Two.'

'What? Say again?'

'Pound Two, sir. She's in Switzerland. The Embassy is arranging to send her home.'

James looked at the brigadier. He was incapable of speech.

'Good God!' the brigadier said.

James got his emotions under control. 'Thank you, Pound Two. That is excellent news.' He hung up. 'I would say we can review the situation, sir. She may well have up-to-date information on the de Gruchys.'

'Hmm. I suppose it's possible. And at least I won't have to face old Cartwright.'

James was pleasantly surprised. He had never expected to hear his boss sounding afraid of anyone.

Liane moved slowly through the bushes along the bank of the Gironde, some twenty miles downstream from the confluence of the Garonne with the Dordogne, and thus a further five miles away from Bordeaux. Here, close to the little town of Paulliac, the centre of the wine-growing industry, there was little traffic, either on the roads in the distance, or in the river at her back. The freighters that had once made this their main thoroughfare now had nowhere to go, except to creep round Biscay or along the north Spanish coast; the fishing boats were mainly based on the river-mouth port of Royan.

Every couple of hours a German patrol boat swept up or down, but this was usually at some speed, and they were always more intent on watching for the telltale ripples that indicated the many sandbanks that littered the river than in looking at the banks themselves, as they wove their way in and out of the tiny islets in the channels.

At this moment Liane was more interested in the house, large and four square, with myriad chimney stacks. Most of the windows were shuttered, and the whole structure looked decrepit. But then so did the considerable grounds by which it was surrounded. The grass on the lawns was uncut; the flower beds nothing but a mass of withered stalks and weeds. And there was no sound, where only two years ago her presence, even on the river bank, would have been detected by the dogs, who would have come bounding down to greet a friend or terrify an intruder. She missed them the most, even as she reflected how sad her mother and father would be to see the family home in such a state. But they were safe in England now, and when they finally saw their house again, they would be the victors, and able to commence its restoration with all the confidence in the world.

Now she saw what she had been waiting for. It was dusk and there was a gleam of light at one of the unboarded windows. Liane took her pistol from her haversack, checked to make sure the magazine was full – she was sure she would not need it, but one could never be too careful – and thrust it into her waistband. Then she left the trees and ran quickly across the lawn and up the wide, concrete front steps. The front door sagged on its hinges, the once-splendid mahogany scarred and in places shattered. That would have happened last September, when the Germans had been hunting for her, not realizing that she had already left, taking their commanding officer with her. She pushed it aside, and entered the hall, waves of nostalgia sweeping her mind. But, quiet as she had been, the broken wood had creaked, and a man appeared in the doorway to the dining room.

'Who is there?'

'Good evening, Jacques.' She rested her hand on the butt of the Luger.

The man came closer. 'Mademoiselle Liane? My God! But . . .'

'No ghost, Jacques. Just tell me that I am welcome.'

'But of course, mademoiselle. How . . .?'

'Later. Who is living here with you?'

'Just my wife. Paul comes in every day, but he does not live in.'

'And?'

'Well, mademoiselle . . .'

'Where are my brother and sister, Bouterre?'

'They are on the islet.'

She nodded. 'And you supply them with food and drink. How often do they come across?'

'Twice a week. They were here last night.'

131

'Ah. Do the Germans ever come here?'

'Not now. They came here after the assassination. They took the place apart. But Monsieur Pierre and Madame Burstein had not come yet, so they went away again.'

'Excellent.' Liane went up to the vineyard manager and embraced him. 'As you can probably gather, I have spent the last week in and out of ditches and sleeping rough. I would like a bath, and a square meal, and a bottle of Gruchy. And then a bed. Can you provide those?'

'Of course, mademoiselle . . . Liliane!' he called. 'You will never guess who is here.'

Pierre de Gruchy peered at his sister, then hugged her tightly. Though several years the younger, he was also several inches taller, and although very thin, had a great deal of strength; he lifted her from her feet to kiss her.

'Oof,' she wheezed. His face, as handsome as any de Gruchy's, was covered in several days' growth of beard.

'Thank God you are back. You have heard . . .'

'Most of it. How is Amalie?'

'As well as can be expected.'

'Then load this stuff and take me to her.'

'You are coming across?'

'That is why I am here. Can't you use another paddle?'

Pierre and Bouterre loaded the canoe, placing the food and bottles of wine and water in the centre of the slender hull. Liane got in, kneeling in the bow, her paddle ready. Pierre sat in the stern and Bouterre pushed them off. They drove their paddles into the relatively still water and raced along, their experienced eyes picking out the ripple of the sandbanks; this part of the river they had explored time and again as children. It took them only fifteen minutes to reach the islet, where Amalie waited, up to her knees in the water, to hold the boat steady.

'Liane!' she gasped. 'Oh, Liane!' She burst into tears.

Liane kissed her, then helped Pierre push the canoe into a gully in the rocks where it was invisible from the river. Between them, Amalie now helping, they unloaded the stores and carried them into the little cave, the entrance of which was also turned away from the river so that no one who had not actually landed on the islet could know it was there.

'This is our hot meal night,' Pierre said, unclipping the lid for the cooking pot.

Liane uncorked one of the wine bottles. 'Together again,' she said. 'I should never have left you in the first place.'

Pierre brushed his mug against hers. 'Probably.'

'Are you very angry?' Amalie asked. She, too, was taller than her sister, but had the least classic features of all the family, although she was quite pretty. But her face was drawn and pale, her eyes filled with tragedy.

'I should be. But perhaps you can explain it.'

'You know what happened?'

'I know what I have been told by various people. No one has told me what Henri was doing in Bordeaux in the first place.'

'He went with Monterre.'

Liane frowned. 'Monterre went home before I left for Paris. He said he was fed up with being a fugitive.'

'Well, I suppose things didn't work out at home, either,' Pierre said, refilling her mug. 'He suddenly showed up at the bakery. Neither Amalie nor I were there, unfortunately, so he saw Henri. According to Anatole, he told Henri that he had recruited some men who wished to join the Group, but they had to be sure we were genuine. So he wanted Henri to go and talk with them.'

'Anatole did not tell me this,' Liane said thoughtfully.

'If only I had been there,' Amalie said. 'If only . . .'

'So Henri went to talk with these people. Could he not wait for you to come home?'

'He was in such a frustrated and agitated state. Well, we all were.'

'Did he know he was going to have to cross the border?'

'I don't know. When we got home he was gone. Anatole could only tell us that he had left with Monterre. He didn't know where they had gone. So all we could do was wait.'

'Until you heard he had been arrested and hanged. What happened to Monterre?'

'There was no mention of him. He must have got away.'

133

'But did he not come back to tell you what had happened?'

'No,' Pierre said. 'We assumed that he had gone into hiding.'

Liane looked at Amalie. 'So then you went berserk.'

'What was I to do?' Amalie gulped some wine. 'They put the photo in the papers. Didn't you see it?'

'I haven't had much time to read newspapers recently.'

'They showed a picture of him, hanging. Henri! And those brutes standing around, laughing. I had to do something. You weren't here . . .'

'Do you require me to be at your side for the rest of your life?' Liane turned to Pierre. 'Why did you not stop her?'

'She left while I was out.'

'But you guessed where she had gone.'

'When I discovered she had taken the gun, yes.'

'So you followed. And found her.'

'Well, I knew she would not return to Vichy. The local authorities work very closely with the Germans. She would seek to hide somewhere in the Bordeaux area, and there was only one safe place . . .'

'You are a pair of inexcusable fools.' Liane squeezed both their hands. 'You realize that London has been going mad?'

'Because I shot a German officer?' Amalie asked.

'Because you did so without orders, and stirred up the entire Bordeaux area, and other areas besides. Do you realize that the Germans have shot a hundred men?'

'The hostages?' Pierre was aghast.

'How could they *do* that?' Amalie was no less horrified.

'Because you would not surrender. And because you, Pierre, promptly disappeared, London was not able to contact you. You must remember that we are not acting on our own in this business. We are fighting a war, in conjunction with our allies, who also happen to be our bosses. We do not know what plans they are laying, but we have to obey their orders, to fit in with those plans.'

'Well, they'll have to accept what has happened,' Pierre asserted. 'It is over and done with, and the furore will soon die down. Anyway, London can get as angry as it likes. It needs us.'

'It is not over and done with,' Liane told him. 'Because of

134

their inability to get hold of you, London dropped an agent to look for us. I am pretty sure that it was Rachel. She was sent to Anatole in the first instance, but then, like Henri, she crossed the border. And do you know why she did that? Because Monterre sought her out.'

'Monterre? But . . .'

'As you say, he must have got away when Henri was arrested. Or did he get away? Because this British agent, Rachel, was also arrested once she was across the border.'

'Oh, my God!' Amalie cried. 'She was hanged, too?'

'We don't know. Anatole said there has been no publicity, other than that a British spy has been arrested. That was a month ago. So she is probably dead. But before she died . . . She knew everything about us. If she told the Germans . . .'

'Rachel would never betray us,' Pierre said.

'Of course she will have, whether she wanted to or not. The only hope is that she managed to kill herself before they searched her. But that is done. It is what happens next that matters. I am going to return to Anatole and get in touch with James, tell him what has happened, and see what he wants done. I am also going to see if I can find Monterre. It seems to me that he has a lot of explaining to do.'

'And us?' Pierre asked.

'You stay right here.'

'You mean you no longer trust us.'

'I no longer trust you not to do something stupid, yes. After I have contacted James, I will return here to tell you what happens next.'

'How long will that be? Do you have any idea what it is like to be cooped up in this hole? We cannot even go out of the cave in daylight for fear of being spotted by a patrol boat.'

'It will take me a week to get back to Limoges, and a week to return here. Assuming I can contact James right away, I should be back in just over a fortnight. But allow three weeks just to be safe.'

'And if you are not back in three weeks?'

'You may assume that I am dead.'

'Or taken by the Germans.'

135

'If I am taken by the Germans, I will be dead. I have my capsule.'

'Oh, Liane!' Amalie burst into tears.

Liane hugged her. 'It will not happen. But if it does, Pierre, you will have to take command.'

'Command of what?' Pierre asked.

'Of the force I am about to start recruiting. Now take me back to the mainland before the weather changes.'

'Liane?' James asked, hardly able to speak above the beating of his heart. 'Oh, my dearest, darling girl! You're all right!' He could not even reprove her for using an open-voice key.

'That would seem fairly obvious. But I love you, too. We have problems.'

'So I gather. But as long as you are back in command—'

'I am in command of nothing, at this moment. Although I am hoping that will change. James, I am so sorry about Rachel.'

'What about Rachel?'

'Did you not know she was taken by the Germans?'

'Did you not know that she managed to escape?'

'What? Rachel escaped from the Gestapo? How did she do that?'

'We don't know yet. What we do know is that she managed to reach Switzerland—'

'From Bordeaux? That is incredible.'

'It does rather sound like it. She has refused to divulge to our people in Basle how it was done, but she did it. She is on her way home now, so we'll be able to debrief her when she arrives. Meanwhile . . .'

'Is there any news of Joanna? I mean, now that America is in the war, I assume you have pulled her out.'

'Ah, well, yes, that would seem to be the obvious thing to do.'

'James! Something has happened. Tell me what it is.'

'Nothing has happened. Yet.'

'You mean she's back in Germany? Oh, my God! They'll shoot her.'

'I do not think the Germans are going to shoot Joanna,' James said, speaking very carefully. 'However, her situation is top secret and cannot be discussed, even with you, my dearest girl. Now, listen. You say you can get your Group back together.'

'I think so. Most of them.'

'Right. Then I want you to select a couple of good men and send them to Code Marker C 47 DF on your map. The code name is Rutter. We require up-to-date, accurate and detailed sketches of the harbour and its defences. We also need as much information as possible about the number of German troops in both the town and its vicinity, and their situation. Can you do this?'

'I would say so. James, would I be right in supposing—'

'Please don't speculate, Liane. Have your people get that information and come back to me as soon as you can. And, Liane, I wish you to send people, not go yourself.'

'Yes, sir. Over and out.' Liane replaced the handset and looked at Anatole.

'Is it something big?' The baker had the map on the table. 'Dieppe? Do you think it is the invasion? They said it would come this year.'

'I would just forget about it, if I were you. Now, can you get in touch with Etienne?'

'Etienne is dead.'

'What did you say?'

'He was captured by the Germans and executed, oh, last November. Soon after you left for Paris.'

'Are you telling me that Etienne was another who just wandered across the border?'

'He must have had a reason.'

'I am sure he did,' Liane said grimly. 'Well, where is Jules? Don't tell me he is also dead.'

'I do not think so. I think he has gone to Arcachon. He was a fisherman before the war.'

'I know. Well, send someone to Arcachon and tell him I wish to see him, urgently. Who else do you know how to get hold of?' Anatole scratched his head. 'Well,' Liane said. 'Dieppe. I know someone who knows Dieppe very well.'

James would just have to forgive her.

* * *

137

James was on the dock to greet Rachel when she stepped off the boat from Lisbon. He was in civilian clothes, so could embrace her and kiss her and frown at her.

'You've changed your glasses.'

'These are Swiss glasses,' she explained. 'Mine got broken.'

He escorted her to the waiting car. 'We have a lot to talk about. But to have you back . . .' He settled himself on the rear seat beside her. 'There was a moment when I had given you up for lost.'

The car moved away to commence the drive up to London. 'Join the club. Only mine were several moments, fairly well separated. But for Joanna . . .'

'What? Joanna was there?'

'She suddenly popped up to do her Scarlet Pimpernel stuff. I may never have liked that woman, but right now she is my favourite person in the world. But listen, I must tell you about Monterre. You remember Monterre?'

'The Communist. You were telling me about Joanna.'

'Monterre first. You have to get a message to Anatole. Monterre is working for the Germans. It was he who handed me over. Oh, I know I was stupid. Incredibly naïve. He found out where I was staying, came to see me in the middle of the night, told me he could take me to the de Gruchys, drove me to the border, and handed me over to the Germans.'

'God Almighty! Didn't you realize you were going to the border?'

'Well, I did. But I trusted him. I mean, he had fought with us in the cave. It wasn't until he tried to rape me that the penny dropped.'

'He raped you?'

'I said tried.'

'But after you were taken by the Germans . . .'

'Nobody raped me,' Rachel said, speaking very deliberately. 'Would it have made any difference if they had?'

'Of course not, my darling. I was thinking of you. Now, about Joanna . . .'

'I happened to run into a most perfect gentleman. A colonel named Hoeppner.'

'Franz Hoeppner?'

'That's right. Do you know him?'

'I've heard of him. He commands the Bordeaux District. Or he did.'

'He still does. And like I said, he was a perfect gentleman. Oh, he had to lock me up. And he did say that if I wouldn't co-operate he would have to hand me over to the Gestapo.'

'And if you did co-operate?'

'He could promise me a painless death. A bullet in the back of the head.'

'As you say, a perfect gentleman.'

'He was only doing his job. You would have done the same.'

James sighed. 'You could be right. Now, about Joanna . . .'

'But then the Gestapo showed up, and things got very nasty. I have to say that they don't really prepare you for that sort of thing in training school.'

'You said you weren't raped.'

'Is that all you can think about? There are worse things than being raped, believe it or not. Have you ever had a lit cigarette pressed into your nipple?'

'They did that?'

'I'll show you when we get home. It was a nasty little rat named Roess. But just as things were really getting grim, Joanna showed up.'

'That's what I wanted you to tell me about. What was she doing there?'

'Well, you know she has this thing going with this very big wheel in the SD, which is actually superior to the Gestapo, so she informed this Roess character that I was to be taken to Berlin for interrogation. He didn't like the idea one little bit, but she pulled rank. So I was placed on a train with her, suitably handcuffed, and when we got to Metz she turned me loose. Oh, we put up a bit of a charade. I tied her up and gagged her and left her in our compartment.'

'She let you do that?'

'It was her idea. Then I got off the train, and made my way across north-eastern France into Switzerland. That took some doing, I can tell you. Joanna had given me her money and a travel pass, and I had my papers, but I still had to walk most of the way. And, as I told you, I'd lost my glasses, and deciphering things like road signs was a tricky business. As for the places I had to stay! The Germans may not have got around to raping me, but some of those Frenchies certainly had a go.'

James held her hands. 'Rachel, be a dear and concentrate. This is very, very important. Why did Joanna rescue you from the Gestapo?'

'Because she was there, and I was there . . . What did you expect her to do? Stand there and watch them torture me to death?'

'She knew you were there? She didn't just happen on you?'

'Of course she knew I was there.'

'How?'

'Hoeppner must have told her. They were very thick.'

'And she came all the way from Berlin to rescue you?'

'No, no, no. She came from Berlin to assist in the search for the de Gruchys. She didn't know I was involved until she got to Bordeaux.'

'So rescuing you was a spur of the moment idea.'

'Well, I suppose it was, yes. But thank God for it.'

'She didn't . . . well . . . you spent some time on the train together, didn't you?'

'All of one day and a good bit of a night.'

'And she didn't . . . ah . . . try anything?'

'You must be joking. In my condition? Anyway, neither of us was in the mood.'

'You do know her reputation.'

'I have heard of it. Mainly from you. She was interested only in getting me out. What's all this about, anyway? You think she was up to something? In my book, she's a heroine. In any event, where was the point? She let me go. Just like that.'

'I'm trying to work out why she did that.'

'Surely because she is Pound Three and I am Pound Two. We're in the same outfit, right?'

James studied her. 'You do realize that since America entered the war, Joanna has become a traitor?'

Rachel frowned. 'But you sent her back there. Didn't you?'

'No, we didn't. We ordered her not to return. But she ignored our instructions.'

'Then . . .'

'As I say, technically she is a traitor.'

'But we know she's not.'

'Do we?'

'She rescued me, for God's sake.'

'And we don't know why. But we have to find out, and quickly.'

'Is it that important?'

'Yes. She doesn't know it, but she is under sentence of death.'

Rachel stared at him with her mouth open. 'What did you say?'

'The brigadier has decided that while we do not know if she really is a traitor, we can no longer take the risk that she may be. So . . .'

'You mean the order has actually been issued?'

'I'm afraid so.'

'But it has to be rescinded.'

'I'm afraid that's impossible. The assassin has already left Basle, and there is no way of recalling him now.'

PART THREE

The Fellowship of Death

A living dog is better than a dead lion.
Ecclesiastes IX

Seven

The Assassin

Unlike Reinhard Heydrich, Heinrich Himmler was so mild-mannered as to be almost self-effacing, and Oskar Weber suspected that he actually thought of himself as the most tolerant and inoffensive of men. The rimless spectacles and the rather vacant, moon-like features helped. Only those who worked closely with him knew better. Oskar had never done that till now, but he had observed the great respect in which the police overlord was held by even so demonic a character as Heydrich, and there could be no doubt that, from the utterly flawless black uniform he wore, every belt polished to the highest of sheens, he held himself in considerable esteem. Yet his movements were languid, his hand seeming to droop from his wrist as he gestured Weber to a chair.

'I have just returned from Russia,' he remarked without preamble. 'It is dreadful there. Quite dreadful.'

'You have been to the front, Herr General?' Oskar hated himself, but with this man it was necessary to be ingratiating.

'No, no. That is not my province. We are policemen, you and I, Oskar. Our business is the keeping of the peace behind the lines, the ensuring of the flow of supplies *to* the front, which is actually far more important than squatting behind a wall with a rifle. But it also entails rooting out the subversives, the enemies of the Reich, the Communists and the like. And, of course, the Jews. You no doubt know that the Führer has taken the decision that the only hope for the future of Europe is to eliminate that accursed race completely.'

'Ah . . . I had heard a rumour . . .'

'It is supposed to be top secret,' Himmler said mildly. 'There must be no rumours. However, the policy – which was

145

actually recommended by Heydrich, you know – is being put into effect, to begin with, in Russia. There are a great number of Jews in Russia, you know, Oskar.'

'So I understand, sir.'

'My people have been given the task of rounding them up, in their hundreds, their thousands, and disposing of them.'

'May I ask, sir, how does one dispose of a thousand people at a time?'

'With difficulty, Oskar. With difficulty. They are first of all made to dig large ditches.'

'You mean they are forced to dig their own graves, sir?'

'Well, they do not know it is their grave. They are merely told to dig a ditch. This could be for any purpose. Then they are made to undress. Men, women and children.'

'They do not object to this?'

'One or two hotheads do. But they are shot. The others . . . they do not seem to understand what is going on. Or what is going to happen. Even when, in numbers, they are made to stand on the edge of the ditch to be shot, they seem mesmerized, as if they cannot believe such a thing is happening to them. Have you ever attended a mass execution, Oskar?'

'No, sir, I have not.' *Nor do I wish to*, Oskar thought.

'It is horrible. It makes you want to vomit. But at the same time it stirs all the senses. All those naked bodies, about to be torn to pieces. Some of the females are quite attractive, you know. I remember one young female . . . my God she was well built. But there it is.' Weber was slowly realizing that this man did actually regard the Jews as a different species entirely. 'Anyway,' Himmler went on, 'we have been given a job to do, by the Führer, and we must do that job, and all the other jobs we may be given, to the very best of our abilities, because we are German officers and gentlemen. Do you agree?'

'Of course, Herr General.' Weber braced himself; he had an idea what was coming next.

'Before he went to Prague, General Heydrich left me a complete breakdown of his, and your, activities and problems. I have been reading it on the train.'

'May I ask how General Heydrich is, sir?'

'General Heydrich is very well, and he is doing his duty in stamping out Czech insurgency. Now, as regards you, I am concerned about this Bordeaux business. Last November a German officer was shot in broad daylight. It is now February and no arrest has been made. Yet we appear to know the name of the assassin.' He opened the folder on his desk. 'A woman named de Gruchy. As I understand it, she and her family have been on our most-wanted list since we took over France. Yet *none* of them has ever been arrested, at least not permanently. It appears that this very woman was once arrested, and then released. It also appears that her parents were also arrested and sent to a concentration camp, as they should have been – and then released! That is an intolerable situation.'

'Those decisions were made by General Heydrich, Herr General, as part of a plan to capture the leader of the group, the woman Liane de Gruchy, who was wanted for every crime imaginable. Sadly, the plan miscarried. Still, we did eventually get her. She was shot by my people when we attacked the Group's lair, last September.'

'That is very reassuring. However, this sister of hers is setting up to be a new menace.' Another glance at the folder. 'It says here that Roess was placed in charge of the case. In December. Without results. I understood that he was a good man.'

'He is, Herr General. But he . . . ah . . . met with an unfortunate accident on his way to Bordeaux, and has had to spend some time in hospital.'

'What sort of accident?'

'I believe he hit his head.'

'Good heavens! You say he is in hospital? When will he be fit for duty?'

'I believe very soon, sir. Meanwhile, Colonel Hoeppner, who is the Wehrmacht commander in Bordeaux, is continuing the search.'

'What has he been doing?'

'Well, sir, he has been interviewing people, offering rewards . . .'

'My dear Oskar, people who murder German officers are not going to be enticed by offers of reward. They can only

147

be cowed into surrender. That is what General Heydrich is doing so successfully in Prague. Has Roess taken any hostages?'

'Yes, sir. The local commander took a hundred hostages before Roess ever got there.' He felt it worthwhile to add, 'That was on orders from me.'

'Very good. I think it is time to shoot one or two.'

'Ah . . . I'm afraid, sir, that they have all been shot.'

'All of them? A hundred? You ordered that?'

'No, sir. Roess ordered it on his own initiative.'

'But that is brilliant. The man must be commended.'

'Yes, sir,' Oskar agreed doubtfully. 'But shooting the hostages has not brought any results.'

'How odd. These must be very strange people.'

'The fact is, sir, that the de Gruchys have attained a sort of mythical status in the eyes of the French people.'

'Even with this woman dead? And now this other woman has taken over her sister's mantle, eh? Well, she must be brought to justice, even if it means shooting everyone in Bordeaux.'

'I think there is a way to bring her out, Herr General. I suggested it to General Heydrich, more than once, but he felt it would not be acceptable to the Führer.' Himmler raised his eyebrows. 'You are aware, I suppose, sir, that Amalie de Gruchy's sister is living in Berlin?'

'If you are speaking of Frau von Helsingen, then of course I am aware of it. I am also aware that she has entirely broken with her family. Or they with her.'

'With respect, sir, I do not believe that is true.'

'Explain.'

'Well, sir, you know she visited her parents in Paulliac last September. That was my idea. We were seeking information on the whereabouts of her brother and sister, and we felt she might be able to unearth something.'

'And it all went very wrong.'

'Well, sir, we got the information we needed.'

'From Frau von Helsingen? All that she accomplished was to be humiliated by her own family.'

'I have always wondered how genuine that was, sir.

148

Consider. Frau von Helsingen returns to Paulliac for the first time since her wedding to Colonel von Helsingen. She is not welcomed. We know this, both from her own evidence, and from what she told Colonel Hoeppner at the time. However, she elects to stay on for a few days, and actually invites Hoeppner to dinner at the de Gruchy chateau. They are, of course, old friends; Hoeppner was her husband's best man. So what happens? Hoeppner innocently goes to dinner and finds himself the prisoner of none other than Liane de Gruchy, who no one had any idea was even in the vicinity. She uses Hoeppner and his car to get herself and her parents across the border into Vichy . . .'

'Where you followed her, illegally, and killed her and most of her associates. Yes, yes. It is all here in this file, and I congratulate you. But am I not right in recalling that when they left the chateau, they also left poor Frau von Helsingen tied to her bed? That is hardly evidence of collaboration.'

'Well, sir, it is very easy to tie someone to a bed. The point I am making is that Liane de Gruchy must have already been in the chateau when the dinner invitation was issued to Hoeppner.'

'You are suggesting that Frau von Helsingen was acting under duress, from her sister?'

'I am suggesting that she was a willing participant in the plot to get her parents to safety, in defiance of the Reich.'

Himmler stroked his chin. 'You are aware that Colonel von Helsingen's father is one of the Führer's closest associates?'

'Yes, sir.'

'And you wish me to tell him that she is a member of the Resistance?'

'No, sir. I do not think that will be necessary. I believe sufficient pressure can be brought to bear upon her to co-operate fully with us, if you will give me permission to do so, without any publicity. She is not a very strong character.'

Himmler surveyed him for several moments. 'She is a handsome woman.'

Weber refused to show any emotion. 'Yes, sir, she is.'

'And when she complains to her husband?'

'I think she can be persuaded not to do that. The point is, sir, that this is an opportunity to prove her loyalty once and for all. It is not possible for Amalie de Gruchy to have so completely disappeared if she is, shall I say, on the loose. I believe she has found a place of concealment, which even our very complete searches have been unable to locate. Logic dictates that such a place will be within the area in which she was born and grew up. We know it is not in the chateau or the grounds. We have searched them from top to bottom a dozen times. But it has to be somewhere close. And if it is a childhood haunt of Amalie's, it will also have been a childhood haunt of her sisters. Madeleine must know of it. If she is willing to assist us by telling us or showing us where this place is, then we can be sure of her loyalty. If she will not co-operate, or attempts to betray us . . .'

'You are asking her to deliver her own sister to us, for execution.'

'I am asking her to deliver to justice a woman who has denounced her as a collaborator, who has committed at least one murder, and who is an active and dedicated enemy of the Reich. We are fighting a war, Herr General. In wars it is necessary to stand up and be counted, on one side or the other. Frau von Helsingen claims to have done that. Now is the moment she should be required to prove it.'

Himmler considered him for several more moments. Then he nodded. 'Very good, Colonel. You have permission to use Frau von Helsingen to assist you in the search for Amalie de Gruchy. But I strongly recommend that you prove all the points you have made.'

'Fräulein Jonsson,' said the clerk at the reception desk, 'there is a gentleman to see you.'

Joanna was carrying her skis on her shoulder, her boots in her right hand. Never had she felt more relaxed, a combination of local exhaustion and a complete lack of tension, which had slowly grown on her over the past month – since Oskar's departure. But even his company, divorced from business, had been a pleasure in these delightful circumstances. Now it was coming to an end, but there were still two days left. And then . . . But she had determined not to think about 'then' until she was actually back in Berlin. She had not even allowed herself to wonder if Rachel had made good on her escape. But she must have. If she had been recaptured, Oskar, and thus she, would have known about it. But all that contentment could disappear with a single sentence. She turned to survey the hotel lounge. There was only one guest to be seen, a prosperous-looking man, seated and reading a newspaper.

'That one?' she asked.

'No, no, Fräulein. Colonel Hoeppner is in the bar.'

'Colonel Hoeppner? Oh, good lord! Will you look after this stuff for me, please, Hans?'

'Of course, Fräulein.' Hans knew who was paying for her stay, and who had spent a week with her over the New Year. As for this new situation, well, it might turn out to be interesting.

'Thank you.' Joanna strode into the bar, a place of soft lights and aromatic scents. 'Franz! What are you doing in Munich?'

'Visiting you.' He embraced her, but as there were several other people in the room, contented himself with a kiss on the cheek.

'No one is supposed to know I am here.'

'My dear, *everyone* knows. Or at least, everyone at the Albert. When I telephoned to let you know I had leave and was told you were not in residence at the moment, I simply asked where you were and was told the Majestic in Munich. Schnaps? But of course, you prefer cognac.'

'Thank you.' Joanna accepted the glass and led the way to a table in the corner. 'You know I am here as a guest of Oskars?'

Franz sat beside her. 'But he is not here at the moment. I checked.'

'Nonetheless, we cannot be seen to be having an affair.'

'But you can at least dine with me.'

'I should think that will be all right.'

'And if I were to drift along the passage at, say, midnight . . .'

151

She patted his hand. 'You are incorrigible. Just let's take it as far as dinner for the time being.' She drained her glass. 'Now I simply have to get upstairs and have a hot bath. I have been on the piste all day. Shall I meet you here at seven?'

'That is three hours away.'

'Am I not worth waiting for?' She blew him a kiss. 'Seven o'clock.'

She went upstairs, turned on the bath water, and undressed. Franz really was becoming a problem, she thought. He seemed to have fallen in love with her, which was totally unexpected after their somewhat prickly relationship over the past year or so, when he had so obviously distrusted her. If he had now decided to trust her after all, that was very gratifying; he was an attractive man. But there was no way she could allow him to come between her and Oskar. Oskar was her reason for existing, at least until the war was over.

But there remained the Secret. Franz had the knowledge to destroy her relationship with Oskar . . . To destroy her, in fact. Would he ever use it? He was, above all else, a gentleman. But spurned lovers often found it difficult to remain gentlemen. She tested the water, switched off the taps, and there was a gentle rap on the door.

'Shit!' she muttered, pulled on her dressing gown, and walked across the bedroom. 'Who is it?'

'I have a pound for you, Fräulein,' said the man's voice.

Joanna stared at the door, less in alarm than annoyance. That James should be chasing her here, when she was on holiday . . . Then it occurred to her that it must be something very big for him to do so. She unlocked the door, stepped back, and was again surprised. The man entering the room looked less like a British agent than anyone she had ever known – even Schmitt, the homosexual pimp, who had acted as a messenger boy for the SIS had had a somewhat sinister air. This man merely looked middle-aged and prosperous, carried a briefcase, and made her think of a travelling salesman. He even raised his hat.

'Fräulein Jonsson?'

It was the man sitting in the lobby! 'You are from Pound?'

'Indeed.' Carefully he closed the door. 'I have come at a bad time.'

'Is there a good time when my bath water is getting cold? And you have come to me here? Don't you realize how dangerous it is?'

'How so?' He laid his briefcase on the settee. 'No one save you knows who I represent, and you are never going to betray me. When I finish my business here, I am simply going to walk away, and no one here will ever see me again.'

'And of course, you found me by asking at the Albert. Boy, am I going to have a word with them.'

'I have been trying to contact you since before Christmas, Fräulein Jonsson.'

Joanna pointed. 'Fesster!'

'Exactly. But you have proved an extremely difficult woman to get hold of.'

'That is because I do not expect to be got hold of, except in cases of extreme emergency. So tell me what it is, and beat it. Like I said, my water's getting cold.'

'Would you not like to pour yourself a drink?'

'As bad as that, is it? Can I get you anything?'

'I will have the same as you.'

'Shows taste.' She turned to the table, on which there was a selection of bottles and glasses, and heard a movement behind her. Instantly her instincts reacted, but Fesster had moved with amazing speed and Joanna soon found herself on the floor, her brain a dull mass of pain, but still capable of working. She had been coshed. As the pain was dull rather than sharp she reckoned it had been a small sandbag, but she was, for the moment, utterly at his mercy so she kept her eyes shut.

She smelled his aftershave as he knelt beside her, and a moment later he touched her. Predictably, although there were several pulses available, he opted to open her dressing gown and hold her breast to make sure of her heartbeat.

'What a beauty,' he remarked 'It is a tragedy.'

The fingers released her, the scent moved away. Now she heard a faint rasping sound, and again recognized it immediately; he was screwing a silencer into the muzzle of an automatic pistol. She had only seconds to live. Her brain was not as clear as she would have liked, but the rest of her was unharmed.

She moved with all the speed to which she had been trained. Even with her eyes shut she knew exactly where she was in relation to the settee, on which he had placed his bag. He would be standing immediately in front of it as he prepared the pistol. Now she swivelled on her backside, swinging with both legs together, opening her eyes as she did so. Her flailing ankles stuck him on the calf and knocked him over, to sprawl across the settee. He recovered quickly and even squeezed the trigger, but did not take the time to aim, and the bullet smacked into the ceiling. Then Joanna was astride him, kneeling across his thighs, chopping down with her right hand to strike his arm a paralysing blow, which caused him to drop the gun. Instantly she seized it and leapt away from him, turning to face him, the pistol levelled.

Fesster sat up. 'I was warned you were dangerous.'

'And you did not heed the warning. How did you get hold of our password?'

'I am employed by your organization.'

'To do what, exactly?'

'My business is executive action. I would have thought that was obvious.'

Joanna lowered the gun. 'You were sent by Pound to murder me? Was there a reason?'

'I am not given reasons.'

'You bastard.' Joanna backed away from him, again pointing the gun at him, and with her free hand poured herself a glass of cognac. 'Do you wish one?'

'That would be very acceptable.'

'Don't move until I tell you to.' Joanna poured another glass and placed it on the table beside the settee. Then she backed away again. 'All right.'

Cautiously, Fesster took the glass. 'What happens now?'

Joanna appeared to consider this. 'Well, you understand that I cannot just let you go. Because you'll just try again, right?'

'You mean to turn me over to the police?'

154

'Well, you see, I can't do that either, because they might just be able to persuade you to tell them who I am.'

'Well, then, we are at an impasse, are we not?'

'Not quite. Why don't you finish your drink?' Fesster looked at his glass as if surprised to find he was still holding it, then raised it to his lips. As he did so Joanna shot him in the chest, and once again before he hit the floor.

'My dear girl,' Oskar said, holding Joanna against him. 'My dear, dear girl. You are trembling.'

'Do you realize that I have never killed anyone before? But that man . . .' She shuddered, and it was not *all* play-acting.

'Silly girl,' Oskar said. 'You shot several people in the battle in the cave, remember? Including one of my men, who lost his head. Not to mention Liane de Gruchy.'

'That was different. It was a battle. But to have a man, in my own bedroom, telling me that he is going to kill me . . .'

Oskar half-forced her into a chair as the blood-stained settee was covered in a dust cloth. It was the next morning, and Joanna was fully dressed. Oskar, on the other hand, had travelled overnight from Berlin after receiving her telephone call, and was both dishevelled and unshaven. 'I wish you to tell me exactly what happened. That police inspector was incoherent. As for the hotel staff, they all seem to be hysterical. The only sensible person I have spoken to is Hoeppner. What is he doing here, anyway?'

'I have no idea. He was here when I returned from the ski slopes yesterday. He was as surprised to see me as I was to see him. He invited me to have dinner with him, and I accepted. And then this happened.'

'I am still waiting to find out what did happen.'

'I was drawing a bath when there was a knock on the door. I opened it and this man came in.'

'You let a strange man into your bedroom?'

'He said he had a message from you.'

'He used my name?' Weber stroked his chin. 'The inspector said he had been drinking.'

'Well, perhaps he had. But I gave him a drink.'

'Why? Did he ask for one?'

'I always give people drinks. It is my nature.'

'Then he said he was going to kill you. Did he give a reason?'

'I didn't give him time. When he drew the gun I took it away from him. And when he came at me again, I shot him.'

'You took the gun away, just like that? Where did you learn such skills?'

'I think he thought I was just a frightened woman. He was careless. What are we going to do?'

'The business will have to be investigated. It is important to find out where he came from, who sent him, and how he knew of our relationship. But . . .' He snapped his fingers. 'Of course, he did *not* know of our relationship. He was sent after *you*. The British have discovered you are working for me.'

'Oh, really, Oskar, how can they have done that? And if they had, would they not merely have waited for me to return to England, and then arrested me there?'

'Those are questions the man would have answered, if he were alive. It is a pity you are so accurate' He ruffled her hair. 'I am not blaming you. It must have been a terrifying experience. But as of now you will be under twenty-four-hour protection.'

'I'm sure that isn't necessary.'

'And I shall issue you with a gun. Now, get your things together. You are coming back to Berlin with me.'

'To be placed in a glass bubble?'

'We have a job to do. Something that will interest you. Now hurry.'

Joanna went into the bathroom and peered at herself in the mirror. She looked absolutely normal, facially. But her hands still trembled. This had nothing to do with having shot Fesster; he had been a nasty little man, and, however it had actually happened, it had been self-defence. Had she not killed him he would undoubtedly have come after her again. Nor had it anything to do with the trauma of the night, when her privacy had been invaded by the hotel staff and the local police. That had been Weber's decision, when she had first telephoned to tell him what had happened. Nor was it because of poor Franz's helpless expression as he had hovered in the background, desperate to get involved, but unable to risk it, as a so-called casual acquaintance. And he, too, had clearly been wondering about the whos and the whys of the situation.

Wondering! Someone in the SIS had issued a contract for her to be killed. She could not believe James would have done that. How could he possibly suspect her of being a traitor, especially after the way she had risked so much to rescue his Rachel? But suppose Rachel had not yet arrived home. Or suppose she was not going to get home at all. She might be quite certain that, had she been re-arrested, Oskar would have told her about it. But suppose she was just dead in a ditch somewhere? An attractive, single woman, walking across France, possibly hitching rides where she could . . . She would be a perfect subject for rape and murder. But Rachel, alive or dead, had nothing to do with her relations with the SIS. So it had to be because of her refusal to return to England instead of continuing to Germany back in December. The bastards had determined that she meant to abandon them for good. Therefore, if they had decided on her execution as a traitor, once they realized that Fesster had failed, they would send someone else. At the very best they would be waiting for her when the war was over.

The situation simply had to be sorted out as quickly as possible. But how was she going to do that if she was going to have a bodyguard foisted upon her, and if, as seemed certain, Oskar was not going to allow her to return to England? She packed up her toiletries and returned to the bedroom.

'So what is this big job?'

Oskar grinned. 'Something I have wanted to do for years. You will enjoy it.'

Madeleine von Helsingen lovingly changed her baby's nappy. She allowed no one else, not even Hilda, to touch the child. Especially not Hilda. Her so-called friends – they were friends of the Helsingen family, and felt obliged to call and admire the baby and exchange gossip, but she knew that none of them really liked her – kept showing critical amazement that she was not employing a nanny, at least to do the dirty work. But in the absence of Frederick, Helen was all she had, the only alleviation from her dreadful loneliness. Hilda was hovering. Hilda always hovered, but this morning she was breathless.

'There are two gentlemen here, Frau.'

'Not more people from Switzerland?'

'Ah . . . No, Frau. They are not from Switzerland.'

'Then who are they?'

'I think they are from the Gestapo, Frau.'

Madeleine straightened, her heart pounding, but the colour in her cheeks could have been caused by bending over. What could have happened? Only her sisters knew anything of her involvement in that business last September. But of course, Joanna knew as well. Suppose Joanna's double game had been found out, and she had been arrested? Joanna thought she was indestructible, but no one was indestructible if they fell into the hands of the Gestapo. If that had happened, she was about to fall into the hands of the Gestapo herself.

She felt quite sick, and this apparently showed in her face, for Hilda asked, almost solicitously, 'Are you all right, Frau?'

'Of course I am all right,' Madeleine snapped. 'Show the gentlemen in.' Hilda hurried off and Madeleine went into the bedroom to straighten her dress and add some powder to her cheeks. Then she drew a deep breath and went into the drawing room. The two men stood together, looking embarrassed. Madeleine determined to seize the initiative. 'You have news of my husband? He is hurt?'

The men exchanged glances. 'Why, no, Frau von Helsingen. We have no news of the colonel. We have come to ask you to accompany us.'

'Accompany you where? Am I under arrest?'

'No, no, Frau von Helsingen. We are asking for your help.'

'And what if I say that I do not wish to help you?'

'I think for you to do that would be a very grave mistake, Frau.'

Madeleine gazed at him. He was being entirely polite, but once they got her into their cells . . . 'Will I be returning here?' she asked.

'Certainly, Frau.'

Madeleine hesitated a last moment, then went into the hall and put on her mink; she could not believe they would beat up a woman who was wearing a mink coat. 'Baby is asleep,' she told the hovering Hilda. 'I will be back in a little while, but listen out in case she cries.'

The two men came into the elevator with her, carefully avoiding touching her or even brushing against her. 'It is very cold on the street,' the spokesman remarked, indicating his approval of her choice of garment.

To her relief the black Mercedes had tinted windows, so that no one could possibly identify her, while those people around as she crossed the pavement carefully looked the other way, as was always best where the Gestapo was concerned. And a few minutes later they were at headquarters, where no one seemed to be the least bit interested in her.

'It is just one flight of stairs,' her escort said.

At least she was going up instead of down, and a few moments later she was being shown into a spacious office, to be greeted by Oskar Weber, and, to her consternation, Joanna.

'Frau von Helsingen.' Weber came around his desk to take her hand. 'It is very good of you to come.'

'Did I have a choice?' Madeleine glanced at Joanna. But Joanna surely could never betray her without betraying herself. Or could she?

'You know Joanna, of course,' Weber said. 'Did you also know that she works for me?'

Madeleine decided that it was best to lie. 'I did not know that.'

'Well, now you do. But sit down, sit down.' He held a chair for her. 'We wish to discuss your sister.'

Madeleine's head jerked. 'My sister is dead.'

'I am speaking of your younger sister.'

'I was told she too is dead.'

'Sadly, she is still alive. I say sadly, because she has followed the example of your other sister and become a murderess. She has killed a senior German officer. You are sure you did not know of this?'

Madeleine managed a frown. 'Are you speaking of that man Kessler in Bordeaux?'

'That is correct. You understand that this sort of behaviour is not something the Reich can accept, and the people who are going to suffer for her mad behaviour are her own. Her crazy act has already cost a hundred lives.'

'A hundred . . . How can my sister's murder of a German officer cost a hundred lives?'

'A hundred hostages were taken, against her surrender. When she did not surrender, they were shot.'

Madeleine looked at Joanna with her mouth open.

'It is true,' Joanna confirmed.

'But that is mass murder!'

'Caused by your sister,' Weber pointed out.

'She cannot possibly have known such a thing would happen.'

'The fact that the hostages lives depended upon her surrender was well publicized. Now, it may be that she did not believe we would carry out our threat. In that case she has made a very serious misjudgement. But that does not exonerate her from the responsibility of causing those deaths.'

'I cannot believe it,' Madeleine muttered. 'But . . . you think she should have given herself up, to be tortured and then publicly hanged?'

'That is between her and her conscience. But the fact is that orders have already been issued to Colonel Hoeppner to take another hundred hostages, and shoot them too if Amalie does not surrender within the month.'

Joanna turned her head sharply.

'Franz Hoeppner would never do that,' Madeleine declared.

'Colonel Hoeppner is a soldier, Madeleine. Soldiers often receive orders they do not like. But they carry them out nonetheless.'

Again Madeleine looked at Joanna. 'You knew?'

'No. But I knew it was a serious matter. *Is* a serious matter.'

'And what am I supposed to do about it?'

'You can save the lives of a hundred innocent Frenchmen. Probably more.'

'By betraying my own sister? Even if I knew where she is . . .'

'That, too, is a matter of conscience. Your conscience. You cannot shirk the facts. Amalie is guilty of murder. Were this peacetime, she would be arrested by the *gendarmerie* and guillotined. Now we are at war, and things are different. But the end result will be the same. Amalie will be caught, eventually. But every day she evades capture is going to cost the lives of Frenchmen. Your Frenchmen, Madeleine. Can you stand by and see that happen?'

'There is nothing I can do.'

'There are two things you can do. One is to give us some idea of where she might be hiding. We know it is not in Paulliac. We have taken the chateau and the grounds apart, and found nothing. But a place for her to be concealed for so long . . . We are sure it has to be some place she knows very well, and obviously she is being supported by someone – or several someones. Can you not think of such a place?'

Madeleine hesitated. 'No.'

Weber studied her. 'You understand that if you deliberately withhold information that could lead to the arrest of an enemy of the Reich, you too could be classed as an enemy of the Reich. Even you, Frau von Helsingen.'

'I have already said, I do not know of any place my sister could be hiding.'

'Very good. Then would you be willing to go to Bordeaux and make a personal appeal to Amalie to surrender?'

'That would be to make myself utterly reviled by everyone.'

'My dear Madeleine, you are already personally reviled by everyone, at least in France, for marrying a German.' Madeleine swallowed. 'But I imagine that will change when they realize that you are trying to save their lives. And until it does, you will be under Franz Hoeppner's personal protection. And Joanna's, of course.'

'Joanna's?'

'She will be coming with you, as your personal bodyguard.'

Joanna gave her a reassuring smile. 'And my daughter?' Madeleine asked. 'Who is going to look after my daughter?'

'Your daughter will be cared for by the State, until your return.'

*   *   *

161

Joanna gazed across the railway compartment at Madeleine. 'Weber knows you were lying,' she remarked.

'Lying about what? I have not laid eyes on Amalie since the day of my wedding. And then she refused to attend the ceremony.'

'But you know where she is hiding. Where she has to be hiding. Because it must be a childhood haunt, and it must be somewhere close to the chateau, from where she can be sustained by those of your people who are still loyal. That is logical. And besides, you gave it away when you hesitated in response to his question.'

'He accepted my reply.'

'Oh, my dear Madeleine, you cannot go through life taking people at face value. Especially with a man like Oskar Weber. His whole life is a self-created charade. He holds secrets pertaining to almost every member of the government locked away in that brain of his or in his private files. I do not know if he ever intends to use them; he just enjoys the feeling of power it gives him.'

'Are you saying he knows *our* secrets? You have told him?'

'He does not *know* anything about you, although he would like to know everything. But he has his suspicions. He cannot believe you have so turned your back on your family, just as he does not believe your version of what happened at the chateau in September. But there is another factor. He wants you. He dreams of you. He used to dream of Liane. It is a mixture of class hatred, envy, and pure sexual desire. Do you know that he once actually had sex with Liane?'

'That is absurd! And obscene!'

'Obscene, perhaps. But not absurd. You obviously do not know that when she visits Paris, Liane stays at a brothel operated by an old friend of hers.'

'You are saying that my sister is friendly with a brothel-keeper, and that she stays at her house? Now I know you are lying.'

'How well do you know Liane?' Madeleine bit her lip. 'I know her better than anyone,' Joanna said. 'I know all of her secrets. So you may believe that on one occasion last year, Weber was in Paris and visited the brothel, and, being given

– because of his rank and position – his pick of the girls, he naturally chose the most beautiful of them: Liane. Was that not amusing? Liane finds it so.'

'And Weber knew who she was?'

'Not then. He found out afterwards, when it was too late; she was already dead, as far as he knows. And do you know what is the worst thing for him? Because he had been drinking when he went to the brothel, and because, for all her looks, he thought she was only a whore, he can remember very little of what they did together.'

'Why are you telling me this? You work for him. And you are his mistress.'

'I carry out both of those functions as part of my job.' Joanna had a strong temptation to tell her that she actually worked for James Barron. But that would have been an unforgivable breach of security, and she had sufficient bridges to mend if she could ever regain England. 'I am telling you this because he has now transferred his hatred, and his lust, to you.'

'If he were ever to lay a finger on me . . .'

'You have powerful friends – or at least, your husband does. Weber is well aware of this. But suppose your Freddie were to stop a bullet in Russia?'

Madeleine stared at her, all the colour draining from her cheeks.

'And he is already laying the groundwork for your arrest, whether anything happens to Freddie or not. He has persuaded Himmler that you do know where Amalie can be found. So now, you see, he has you across a barrel. Which is where he would like to have you in the flesh. He is a cautious man, and he is proceeding cautiously. He knows that the final judgement will have to be passed by Hitler himself. Thus he is giving you enough rope to hang yourself, and the only way you can avoid hanging yourself is to hang Amalie. Either way, it will be a great triumph for him.'

'While you gloat,' Madeleine said bitterly. 'And once I thought you were my friend.'

'I am your friend. And as you know, I work for the British

163

Government. They require me to play a double game. But I believe I know a way in which both Amalie, and the people who are to be shot if she does not surrender, may be saved. To do that you will have to trust me absolutely. Are you prepared to do that?'

Eight

The Lovers

'Herr Colonel!' Captain Marach stood to attention. 'It is good to have you back, sir. But . . .' He peered at his superior. 'Are you all right?'

Roess hung his cap on the hook behind the door. His head was still shaved, but instead of a bandage he now wore a strip of thick plaster. 'They tell me that I am.'

'But after all this time . . .'

Roess sat behind his desk. 'Five weeks and three days, Hermann. Most of which I have spent in hospital. It seems that I did not take the wound I received seriously enough. Hence the collapse. But, as I say, I have been pronounced fit.'

'That is excellent news, sir. Excellent. And the investigation?'

'There is no trace of Amalie Burstein anywhere in Gascony. It is my belief that she is dead, lying unburied and unnoticed in a ditch somewhere. I have reported this to Berlin, but they will not accept it. Well, they can find another investigator. I have work to do here. I wish you to arrest Constance Clement.'

'Sir?'

'Do not make silly remarks. I wish the whore arrested, now. I wish to see her standing in front of me in one hour's time.'

'Yes, sir.' Marach hurried from the room, and Roess lit a cigarette. There would be no interference in his enjoyment of the next few hours.

As always Constance presented a confident front, even if, as it was the middle of the afternoon, she had had to dress in a hurry. 'Why Colonel,' she said, 'I did not know you were back. What have you done with Jeanne? And . . .' Like

Marach earlier, she peered at his head. 'What has happened to you?'

'I have been hit on the head, Constance,' Roess said pleasantly. 'I have really been quite ill.'

'Oh, I am so sorry. But . . . is Jeanne all right?'

'Has she not told you?'

'She has not come back. I have been so worried. But then I thought, she is with Colonel Roess, she will be all right.'

'Close the door, Marach,' Roess said. 'And remember that every word you hear from this moment is confidential.'

'Yes, Herr Colonel.' Marach closed the door.

'Now tell me,' Roess said, 'how is you father, Constance?'

'Ah . . . I expect he is dead.'

'You have not heard?'

'Well, as we told you, he and I have not spoken in years. You mean he *is* dead? Is that what Jeanne is doing? Tidying up the estate?'

'Suppose I ask you, did your father ever exist?'

Alarm bells started to ring in Constance's ears, but she kept her face expressionless. 'I do not know what you mean.'

'Your father does not exist. Not that father, anyway. Just as you have no family in Limoges. And you have no sister at all.' Constance was lost for words. She could only stare at him. 'The bitch who pretended to be your sister gave me this.' He touched the plaster on his head. 'Now tell me who she was.'

Constance licked her lips. 'I do not know.'

'Very good. Marach, take this other bitch downstairs and prepare her for interrogation.' Marach's hand closed on Constance's shoulder.

'No, wait!' Desperately she tried to think while waves of terror threatened to overwhelm her. 'I am telling the truth. She appeared suddenly and asked for work. Well, she is a knock-out. You know that. So I gave her a place.'

'And pretended she was your sister. Downstairs, Marach.'

'Up, madame,' Marach said, tightening his grip on Constance's shoulder.

She gasped and stood up. 'What is going to happen to me?'

'Why, you are going to suffer. And amuse me.'

166

If only they would give her time to think. She had to come up with some acceptable answers. But there was no time. Marach was marching her through the door and snapping his fingers at the secretary. She immediately pressed some kind of buzzer on her desk, and by the time they reached the outer door they had been joined by four men. Marach now released her arm and she was seized by two of the men to carry her forward. When she tripped and lost her footing, one of her high-heeled shoes coming off, they simply continued. She had not regained her balance by the time they reached the stairs, and so they went down with her toes bumping so that her other shoe came off. Then she was in a cellar, lit by a single un-shaded electric light bulb, but filled with unpleasant-looking instruments, and unpleasant odours, too.

Think, God damn you, she told herself. *Think like Liane. Act like Liane. Do what Liane would do.* Liane had made the instant decision that Hercule's death was necessary to save the Route. Only the Route mattered. And *she* was now capable of running it. She had been doing so for the last several months. She simply could not allow herself to be tortured, when she might well reveal its existence – there were three British airmen hiding in her attic at that very moment.

Yet the Gestapo had to be given something, or they *would* torture her. Were the circumstances reversed, Liane would sacrifice her without hesitation. And what difference would it make? Liane was already on the run. So she would never again be able to use Constance's house as a base. But that would be safer for everyone, and Liane, with her brains and her beauty, would soon find another Paris home.

Roess had followed them down. 'Strip the bitch,' he commanded.

'No!' Constance gasped. 'Wait. The woman who pretended to be my sister was Liane de Gruchy.'

The men, surrounding Constance to begin taking off her clothes, checked to look at their commander. There was no Gestapo agent in France who did not know the name Liane de Gruchy.

'What did you say?' Roess asked, his voice low. 'You are a lying bitch. I am going to cut off your breasts, slice by slice.'

167

'It is the truth!' Constance shouted. 'I swear it on my mother's grave.'

Roess stood immediately in front of her. 'Liane de Gruchy is dead. She was killed in the battle in the Massif Central.'

'She was not killed. She was not even wounded.'

'Her body was seen by . . .' He checked himself, frowning.

'By her accomplice, who claimed to have shot her.'

'And you know the name of this accomplice, no doubt.'

'She would never tell me that. But she said it was someone very important.'

'Someone very important,' Roess mused. 'So, you have been sheltering Liane de Gruchy in your brothel?'

'What was I to do? She came to me, told me she wished somewhere to stay, and threatened to kill me if I would not assist her. She is a terrifying woman. You have seen that with your own eyes. You saw the way she shot that man, the expert way she handled the gun.'

Roess continued to stare at her for some moments, but she could tell that he was beginning to believe her. 'Why did you not inform me of the situation?'

'I dared not. She told me her people are everywhere, and if anything happened to her, they would execute me.'

'And do you not suppose I am going to execute you?'

'You cannot,' Constance cried. 'I am telling you everything.'

'She assaulted me. She is the one who gave me this wound in the head and sent me to hospital for five weeks.'

'I did not know that. You mean she has been arrested?'

'No. She escaped. But she is on the run.'

'Has she not been on the run for nearly two years now?' He scowled at her. 'Listen,' she said. 'I can deliver her to you. She will come back to me. She must.'

'Why?'

'Because . . . because we are lovers.'

Again he gazed at her for several seconds, but again she could tell that he knew enough about Liane's background to believe her. Then he said, 'She can never work for you again. Any one of my officers will recognize her.'

'I know that. But I am still certain she will return to me whenever she can.'

'And you will hand her over to me?'

'Yes. I swear it.' They gazed at each other, then Constance asked, 'May I go home now?'

'No,' he said. 'Strip her and spread-eagle her,' he ordered his men.

'But . . .'

'I am going to whip you anyway, for what your "lover" did to me. But . . .' He grinned at her. 'I will not execute you, at this time. You will have your chance to deliver Liane de Gruchy to me.'

Roess sat at his desk. He was bathed in sweat and his muscles were still jumping. This was only partly from flogging the woman, listening to her screams, watching her dissolve into tears. It was mainly because what she had told him was only just truly sinking in. Liane de Gruchy, the most beautiful woman he had ever seen, was alive! He had actually fondled her naked body, and she had knelt between his knees to fellate him. He had held her in his hands, and he had allowed her to get away. But she was alive! The implications of that were almost too great for him to grasp. The implications of *his* knowing that, when everyone else thought she was dead, were almost too great to believe. How she, and the Resistance, must have been laughing these past few months. The question was, what did he do with such knowledge? What could he do? Who could he most harm?

Would it be best to wait until she simply returned and walked into his arms? But for all Constance's confidence, that might take a long time, supposing it ever really happened. No, the time to use his information was now, in order to have maximum effect. But Oskar Weber! He would have preferred to go over Weber's head, to Heydrich. But Heydrich was in Prague. He did not know Himmler, and, like everyone else, he was vaguely afraid of the man. So to Weber. Weber believed that Liane was dead, but he had never seen her body. He had acted on the information of that succubus he seemed to feel necessary to have around, who had to be the accomplice Constance had mentioned – the two women had been close friends before the war. Weber's reaction to learning that he had been hoodwinked by his mistress would be very amusing. Better yet, it would mean the destruction of the American bitch. The fate that a man like Weber would devise for a woman who had so betrayed him was even more amusing to contemplate. It would have to be something medieval.

More important even than that pleasurable prospect, it would put Weber for ever in his debt. He picked up the telephone.

Pierre de Gruchy, standing on the riverbank in the dusk, looked from his sister to Joanna to Bouterre, his expression a mixture of anger and consternation.

'It is not his fault,' Madeleine said. 'I knew where you had to be hiding.'

'And how many of your German friends also know?'

'If any of my German "friends" knew, do you suppose you would still be alive?'

Pierre looked at Joanna. 'But she knows.'

'I'm on your side, remember?'

'And I would say Liane knows,' Madeleine said. 'As she used to play on the islet as a girl.'

'Mademoiselle Liane has been here,' Bouterre said. Pierre gave him a dirty look.

'Liane is here?' Joanna cried.

Bouterre looked at his employer. 'She has been here twice,' Pierre said. 'Once in January, and then again a week ago.'

'But she is not here now. Did she say where she was going?'

'She said something about Dieppe.'

'Dieppe?' Joanna looked at Madeleine.

'That is where Amalie lived, after her marriage, and before the arrest of the Bursteins.'

'Did she tell Amalie it was to do with her in-laws?' Joanna asked Pierre.

'She did not discuss it at all. She told me that it was time to start reorganizing the Group, and that she would be back in a few weeks. I think it is something quite big. The code name is Rutter, and it is top secret.'

'Which you have just confided to us.'

'Well . . .' He looked from Joanna to his sister.

170

'All right. We aren't going to tell anyone. And have you started recruiting? You cannot do it from here.'

'It is a matter of getting across the border, really. There has not yet been an opportunity.'

'You mean you have been afraid to leave your hideaway,' Madeleine said scornfully.

'You do not know how dangerous it is.'

'Do you know that the Germans have shot a hundred hostages?'

'Liane told me about it. But what was I supposed to do? Hand over my own sister?'

'Does Amalie know?'

'She knows. But there is nothing she can do about it either. She is in a very depressed state.'

'And do you know that the Germans are planning to take another hundred hostages, and shoot them too? And then another hundred, until she is handed over.'

'My God! Are they savages?'

'They are determined to make it very plain that their people, especially their officers, are not to be killed without their exacting a terrible retribution.'

'What are we to do?'

'I think,' Joanna said, 'that I can solve the problem.'

'You?'

'Not me, personally, but I believe I have a solution. The Germans say they are going to go on shooting people until Amalie is handed over. But if Amalie is proven to be beyond their reach, they will have no reason for the shootings. They may be very angry, and they may be capable of extreme savagery, but they are still susceptible to world opinion. They are claiming that Amalie must surrender, or every German officer in France is at risk. But if Amalie *cannot* be surrendered, I believe they will call off their present campaign.'

'You mean if we claim that Amalie is dead.'

'That will not work. They will demand to see the body. But if we can get Amalie to England, and have her picture published in the newspapers, and her identity confirmed by her parents, they will have to accept that she is beyond their reach, no matter how many people they shoot.'

171

'And how do we get her to England?'

'We take her into Vichy, and call London, and ask for her to be picked up.'

'Just like that? The moment she leaves Paulliac she will be arrested.'

'No she will not. She will travel with us. She will wear a veil . . .'

'That is suspicious in itself. You will be stopped.'

'If we are, it will not be for very long. I am travelling on official SD business, and have a warrant to prove it. No German soldier will dare interfere with me, or anyone who is with me. You will come with me as well, and you can start your recruiting from Limoges.'

Pierre hesitated, chewing his lip.

'You must do this, Pierre,' Madeleine said.

'Does it matter to you?'

'Yes, it does.'

'Do you wish to speak with London?' Joanna asked as they parked outside the bakery. She had hired a car in Bordeaux, and returned to Paulliac at night to pick up Pierre and Amalie. Now it was the following evening, but as she had prophesied, they had crossed the border without difficulty.

Madeleine shook her head. 'It would require too many explanations, and be too dangerous. These people must not know who I am.'

'They can hardly not deduce that you are my sister,' Pierre pointed out. He and Amalie were seated in the back.

'Then I will remain in the car.'

'Why do you not ask London to take you out as well?' Amalie asked. 'I know they would.'

'And what about my husband? And Helen?'

'Well . . .'

'Just don't say it,' Madeleine recommended.

'You will all stay in the car,' Joanna said. 'Until I have made my number.' She got out, went into the shop. There were two other women there, so she waited for them to be served and leave.

'Madame?' Anatole asked.

'Pound,' Joanna said. He stared at her in consternation. 'Come along,' Joanna said. 'You are Pound Seventeen. I am Pound Three.'

'Three?' Startled as he was, he understood that she was a very senior member of the unit. 'But . . . here?'

'I am everywhere. I need to call London.'

'Now is not the usual time.'

'If it were not urgent, I would not be here. Madame.' She smiled at Clotilde as she entered the shop.

'Mind the till,' Anatole said to his wife. 'This lady and I have business.' Clotilde did not look very pleased, but she made no comment. Anatole led Joanna through the bakery itself and into the parlour. 'This is a friend of mine,' he explained. 'He is one of us.' Joanna had to catch her breath.

'Mademoiselle Jonsson,' Monterre said, coming forward.

'You know each other?' Anatole was surprised.

'We are old comrades in arms,' Monterre said.

'Yes,' Joanna said.

'Well, then, that is very good. The wireless is here.'

It was actually concealed in a large cabinet, to the casual glance merely a receiving set. Joanna watched him setting it up while her brain raced. If what both Franz and Rachel had told her was accurate, Monterre was now working for the Germans, quite apart from being a would-be rapist. He would have to be dealt with immediately, but she could not do it herself and risk an imbroglio with the Vichy police – she was not supposed to be in Vichy at all. Pierre would have to handle it. But where did that leave Anatole? First things first.

'What I have to say is confidential,' she announced. 'I am sorry, Monterre, but you must leave the room.' Monterre hesitated, then nodded and went outside.

Anatole opened the key. 'I will speak,' Joanna said. Her Morse wasn't good enough for what she had to say.

Anatole was through. 'Pound Two.'

'And you also,' Joanna said. 'I will call you when I am finished. And close the door.' She waited for it to be shut, then took the mike. 'Pound Three.'

There was a moment's silence. Then Rachel said, 'My God! Joanna! You're alive.'

'Yes,' Joanna said. 'Put him on.'

'Joanna!' James shouted. 'Listen, I can explain.'

'Keep it. Your man didn't make it.'

'You mean . . . Good God!'

'Your guys trained me, remember?'

'I remember. What are you doing now? If you're in Limoges . . .'

'I need a plane.'

'You're coming out. That's the best news I've heard in years.'

'It's not for me. But we have to get Amalie out.' A brief silence. 'You with me? OK, so she broke the rules. But her remaining here is bad for all of us. You have to do it, James.'

'And you're coming with her?'

'Can't be done. For me to disappear now would compromise too many people.'

'And what about yourself? You do realize you're in deadly danger?'

'Only from you.'

'That's been cancelled.'

'Then there's no problem. I'll be back as soon as it can be done, legitimately. That is, from a German point of view.'

He sighed. 'I hope to God you know what you're doing. Is Liane around?'

'Of course she isn't.'

'What do you mean?' His voice took on a note of alarm.

'Didn't you send her to Rutter?'

There was a moment's silence. Then he asked, 'Are you telling me that Liane has gone to Rutter? I specifically forbade her to go herself.'

'Well, I guess she couldn't find anyone else.'

'Shit, shit, shit! She'll be picked up.'

'They haven't managed to do that yet. What's it all about?'

'Sorry. Top secret. I don't even know myself. Brune will be there tomorrow night. Signing off.'

'Hold it one moment. I can't hang about here, so I'd like you to have a word with Anatole.'

'What about?'

'I want you to tell him that it is his duty to put Amalie on that plane tomorrow. That should he fail to do so, he will be held responsible.'

Another brief silence. Then he said. 'You think this is necessary?'

'Ask Rachel what she thinks.'

'If Anatole is on the blink, we could be in big trouble.'

'I don't think he is actually on the blink. I just think that from time to time he needs reminding who he's working for. I'll get him.'

'Here's where we say goodbye, for the time being,' Joanna told Pierre and Amalie. 'Hopefully I'll see you, Amalie, when next I'm in England,' She kissed her, and hugged Pierre. 'Take care.'

'We shall never forget what you have done,' Amalie said, and embraced her sister. 'And you. Will you be all right?'

'Yes. Take care. And give my love to Mama and Papa.' Madeleine turned to Pierre. 'And you.'

'I will remember what you have done.'

'Thank you.'

Pierre turned to Joanna. 'Oh, please remember me as well,' she said.

'How could I forget?' He remembered the night they had spent together in his Paris flat, so long ago.

She kissed him. 'Remember about Monterre. He is a traitor.'

Pierre nodded. 'I will deal with Monterre.'

Joanna and Madeleine got into the car. 'What do we do now?' Madeleine asked.

'We continue to Bordeaux as if this interlude had never happened.'

'My dear Madeleine!' Franz Hoeppner embraced his best friend's wife. 'Joanna.' Another hug. 'Where have you been? I was informed that you would be arriving two days ago.'

'I didn't know you two knew each other,' Madeleine remarked.

'Franz and I have worked together quite closely in the past,' Joanna explained. 'We actually went directly down to Paulliac. Madeleine felt that she would be able to see if there was any evidence that Amalie had been hiding there.'

175

'My men have searched both the chateau and the grounds time and again.'

'It was still worth trying,' Madeleine said. 'I am sure I know the whole area much better than your men, with respect, Franz.'

'Oh, I have no doubt about it. And did you turn up anything?'

'No. I would say she has never been there.'

'And if she had? Would you have told me?'

Madeleine met his gaze. 'I came here to find my sister.'

'Knowing that if you do, and allow me to capture her, I am going to have to hang her in public?'

'Knowing that if she is not caught, you are going to shoot another hundred of her, and my, countrymen.'

Franz looked at Joanna. 'It wasn't an easy decision,' Joanna said. 'But surely it was the right one.'

Franz clearly did not agree.

They dined together after Madeleine had gone to bed early.

'I never did know Madeleine very well,' Franz confessed. 'But I am bound to say that I always estimated her as a woman who shrank away from big decisions, and certainly as a most loyal member of the family. I have always had a suspicion that she only married Freddie because she thought it might help her parents.'

'You're probably right.'

'And then to discover that her family were past helping . . . But actually to turn over her sister to be hanged . . . I cannot imagine what Freddie will say.'

'She was forced to it, by Weber.'

Franz frowned at her. 'Are you serious?'

'Absolutely. He bullied her into coming here.'

'Good God!' He filled her wine glass. 'And you?'

'Please don't ask questions.'

'Do you love him? *Can* you love such a man?'

'I can be the lover of such a man.'

He studied her for several seconds, as was his habit. 'Will you tell me what really happened in Munich?'

Joanna shrugged. 'Certainly. Someone tried to kill me, but I killed him first.'

'Just like that?'

176

'When one realizes that one is about to be killed, one is inclined to act first and work things out afterwards. Oskar is sorry that I did not manage to take him alive, so that he could be questioned. But he wasn't there, to know what it was like.'

'Have you any idea who it could have been?'

'I have quite a few ideas. But nothing I can prove.'

'Tell me some of them.'

'Well, to a great many people, I have become a traitor.'

'But . . . well, then they will try again.'

'I guess they may. Then I'll probably have to shoot someone else.' She gave one of her wicked smiles. 'You're not going to pretend you thought I was a goody two-shoes as well?'

Franz put down his glass and held her hand. 'I would like to marry you.' For the first time that he could remember, Joanna looked genuinely shocked. 'Is the idea that distasteful to you?'

'I . . .' She drank some wine. 'It would raise a lot of questions.'

'You are worried about Weber? He does not own you.'

Joanna had always considered herself as capable of making instant decisions as Liane, while always acknowledging that Liane was the stronger character. But she had to wonder how Liane would deal with this. Here was a genuinely likeable man, who could possibly turn out to be a loveable one. Marriage to him could be her salvation here in Germany . . . But it would burn her bridges everywhere else. If only the situation had arisen before December 7th. How simple that would have made life. Even James might have gone along with that. Now . . . And yet she suddenly wanted to share with him. At least half of the truth, anyway. Perhaps he might be able to find a way out of the cul-de-sac into which she had managed to get herself.

He had been studying her expression. 'Is it that serious?'

'What I will tell you must be in the strictest confidence.'

'Of course.'

'So I cannot tell you here.'

'Ah. Well, where then?'

'Let's finish dinner.'

*   *   *

177

They went upstairs, and when they reached her floor, he held her hand. 'Do you know how eagerly I have waited for this moment?'

'Let's hope it stays that way.' She unlocked the door and switched on the light.

'Does Madeleine know about us?'

'I have no idea. Madeleine thinks I'm a whore, anyway.'

'Yet she came down here with you?'

Joanna locked the door, kicked off her shoes. 'You still don't understand. I work for Oskar.' She stepped out of her dress and watched him take off his tunic. 'I am his tame troubleshooter as well as his main courier. Surely you understood that.'

Franz, sitting down to take off his boots, looked up with a frown. 'I know you carry out certain jobs for him. I know that you have his confidence.'

'I am also one of his overseas agents. I am a spy, Franz.'

'How can you be a spy?'

'Because of the way I can enter and leave England at will, I carry information from him to his people in England, and bring theirs back to him. That situation no longer obtains, but I am still on his payroll. He sent me down here to keep an eye on Madeleine, to make sure she does not attempt to betray us.'

'Then you are a traitor to your own people.'

'I am now.' She stood in front of him, naked. 'Would you like to leave?'

He gazed at her groin, then held her hips and brought her down to sit on his knee, and was struck by a thought. 'Does Madeleine know all this?'

'Yes.'

'And does Weber have any idea that you betrayed him in the matter of Liane de Gruchy?'

'Good Lord, no. If he did he would skin me alive.'

'You are probably right. Why did you do it?'

Joanna took a deep breath. Her confidence was growing. 'Liane and I were at finishing school together. We loved each other. In many ways, we still do. And then we shared that pretty grim experience at the time of the invasion. If it hadn't

178

been for her, I'd have gone nuts, or committed suicide or something. I couldn't just shoot her.'

'Especially as she had just shot Weber.'

'Ah . . . yes. Are you going to tell him all of this?'

'I prefer your skin where it is, and I like sharing a secret with you. And, as you say, you are no longer of use to Weber as a spy.' He nuzzled her breasts. 'I will have a word with him, about letting you go.'

'Good morning, Roess,' Weber said genially. 'My God, what happened to you?'

'I was attacked.'

'Oh, yes, I remember, by some doxy you had on a train. You should pick your women more carefully. Has she been arrested yet?'

'No.' Roess pulled up a chair in front of the desk and sat down.

'I hope you have not come all the way to Berlin to tell me that.'

'I have come to tell you that I have positive proof that Liane de Gruchy is alive, well, and more active than ever.'

Weber leaned back in his chair. 'I'm afraid that woman seems to have hit you harder than you realized. Was it five weeks you spent in hospital? I think you need to return there for further treatment.'

'I am not joking, Colonel Weber. I recently had reason to arrest a brothel-keeper named Constance Clement.'

'I know Madame Constance. I have been to her house. What can she have done to upset the Reich? She only has German officers as her clients.'

'I am aware of that. But there was an . . . incident there, just before Christmas, and, after investigation, I found it necessary to take her into custody.'

'Now that is a shame. She was a fine-looking woman.'

'She is still a fine-looking woman. We did not harm her. Well, not so you'd notice. But she was very frightened, and she volunteered the information. She was recently joined by someone she called her sister. This was a strikingly good-looking woman who proved a great attraction in the house.

179

Then she disappeared, immediately after the incident. Now Constance has confessed that she was not her sister at all, but Liane de Gruchy.'

'And you believe her,' Weber remarked contemptuously.

'Yes. Because it is the truth. Apparently de Gruchy has been to Paris several times, and always stays at the brothel.'

'If that *is* true, Roess, Constance is an active traitor to the Reich and should be hanged. But I'm afraid it is obvious that this woman dreamed up this ridiculous story to get herself out of your clutches.'

'I said I have proof. With your permission . . .' Weber shrugged. 'First of all, there is the description of her, which ties in perfectly with other descriptions of her, and with that old photograph we have. Oh, her hair was dyed and her clothes shabby, but it all fits.'

'You have seen this woman?'

'Ah . . . no. But my deputy, that boy Marach, has.'

'I am still waiting for some proof.'

'The incident I mentioned was when a man broke into the brothel. This man was armed, and he shot his way through the reception room and up the stairs, and into the room where this woman was servicing a client. Without hesitation, she drew her client's pistol from his holster and shot the intruder dead.'

'You are saying that de Gruchy shoots her own people.'

'At the time it was supposed that he was after her client, who was a senior officer. She was regarded as quite a heroine by the other officers. But when the dead man was investigated, it turned out that his name was Hercule Coustace, and that he used to run the bar in Montmartre where de Gruchy hid when she was in Paris on a previous occasion. You may recall, Colonel, that when we raided that bar, de Gruchy and Coustace killed five of our people and escaped. You interrogated Coustace's sister personally.'

Weber stroked his chin. 'I do remember. She was an exciting little thing. We sent her to a concentration camp. But nothing she told us connected Coustace's murderous mistress with de Gruchy. Nor do I see the link now. This prostitute may well have been a woman who Coustace had fallen out with. These

French people are very emotional. What do they call them on the Left Bank? Apaches, eh? So it is quite possible that he broke into the brothel to avenge himself, in which case she can be said to have shot him in self-defence. De Gruchy was shot by my personal aide. I am sorry, Roess, but you are trying to create a situation that doesn't exist.'

Roess all but snarled. 'You refuse to believe me. Because you are infatuated with that American bitch.'

Weber raised a finger. 'Be careful, Johann. I placed you where you are, and I can place you somewhere else. You are a zealous officer and I respect you, but I am sure you are not entirely well at the moment. Go back to Paris and take it easy.'

Roess stood up. 'And if I produce Liane de Gruchy?'

'What are you going to do, find out where she is buried and dig her up? I really am not very interested in exhumations. I think when a person dies or is killed, he or she should be left undisturbed.'

'I am not a fool, Oskar. Why do you think I released Constance? It is because she is certain that Liane will return to Paris, return to the brothel. The moment she does that, Constance will inform me.'

Weber sighed. 'If you believe that will ever happen, Johann, then perhaps you *are* a fool.'

'But if it does?'

'Why, then, I will salute you, call you a genius. I may even reward you.'

'Anything I wish?'

'Within reason.'

'If I deliver Liane de Gruchy, thereby proving to you that Joanna Jonsson lied to you about killing her – and about how many other things, we do not know – I wish the right to interrogate Jonsson myself. Twenty-four hours, and then I will hand her back to you for execution.'

'Supposing that she is still alive to be executed. And this will be after you have already interrogated Liane de Gruchy? Do you know, Johann, that if we lived in a normal, civilian-oriented world, as it will be again one day, you would be locked up, and probably executed yourself, as a sadistic sex maniac. However, I will agree to your request, on two conditions. One is that until you manage to unearth Liane de Gruchy, Fräulein Jonsson is not to be questioned or harassed in any way. The other is an order. You may hold both women for twenty-fours hours. Not a second longer. Then they must both be delivered to me, alive and, I suppose I can't expect them to be well, but certainly in one piece.'

Roess grinned. 'And how would you describe yourself, Oskar?'

'I,' Weber said, 'am a dreamer.'

'You are a fool to come here so often,' Anatole said.

'Are you not my oldest friend?' Monterre asked. 'My partner?'

'I do not like what I am doing. It is too dangerous. Do you not know that Monsieur Pierre is back, and reconstituting the Group?'

Monterre frowned. 'I did not know that. How long ago did he come?'

'Oh, a month now. You were here the night he returned.'

'You did not tell me. What about his sister?'

'He brought her here to be flown to England.'

'Which sister?'

'The wanted one. Amalie.'

'And you did not tell me that, either?'

'Well, by the time I understood what was happening, you had gone. Why did you leave so quickly?'

'I do not trust that American woman.'

'Well . . .' Anatole grinned. 'She does not trust you, either.'

'So what was her business?'

'I have told you. Both to bring Monsieur Pierre out of Bordeaux, and to get his sister to safety.'

Monterre stroked his stubbly chin. 'And you say he is recruiting? How many people has he got?'

'Twenty or more. Jules has rejoined. There is no news of Etienne.'

Etienne is dead, Monterre thought. But he did not say so. He was as unsure of Anatole's politics as anyone. He knew that the baker worked for the British because of the retainer he received, and because there was just a chance that they

182

could still win the war. He also knew that Anatole gave him information about the Resistance, at least in this part of the country, just as he had betrayed the woman Cartwright – on the strict understanding that he was not involved – because it was more likely that the Germans were going to win, and *he* wanted to win in either eventuality. 'So where is Pierre now?' he asked.

'That is what I am saying. He is in Limoges, and he comes here regularly to use the radio. If he finds you here . . .'

'I will volunteer to rejoin. It will be ideal.'

'You fool! He will shoot you on sight. Don't you understand? He knows all about you. That woman you betrayed to the Germans, Rachel Cartwright, escaped and got back to England.'

'What are you saying? She escaped the Gestapo? How could she possibly have done that?'

'I do not know. The business was hushed up, as you may imagine.'

'But you know of it.'

'Well, they told me of it, when they came in February.'

'They?'

'I have told you,' Anatole said, with some impatience. 'Pierre and Madeleine, Amalie and Joanna.'

'Who is this Madeleine?'

'Madeleine de Gruchy, that was. Amalie's sister. She is Madeleine von Helsingen now, the wife of a German officer. She lives in Berlin.'

'And she was here, in Vichy, with her sister. Holy Jesus Christ! They are a nest of vipers.'

'Or patriots, according to your point of view. But as I say, they certainly know all about you.'

'Jonsson saw me here, and did nothing. She did not even say anything.'

'But she sent you out of the room while she spoke to London. You knew she was going to find out about you. Isn't that why you left so suddenly? I think you had better accept that they have your number. As for when Liane gets back . . .'

'She has been here too?'

'You know she has. Then she went off to Dieppe . . .'

'Why Dieppe?'

'I have no idea. It is something very hush-hush.'

'Dieppe,' Monterre said, thoughtfully. 'Yes. I can see that it would be. Very good, Anatole. You have been most helpful, as always. I will take your advice and leave before anyone knows I am here.'

He left the room, and Anatole wiped sweat from his brow.

Franz Hoeppner stared in utter consternation at the report that had been placed on his desk. His initial reaction was disbelief that such a thing could have happened. His second was relief that St Nazaire was not his responsibility. But it was close enough. He raised his head to look at Major Holzbach, his second-in-command. 'There is no doubt about this?'

'None, Herr Colonel. It was a bold stroke. But we gave them more than they bargained for. One ship sunk, over a thousand men killed, many taken prisoner . . .'

Franz was studying the report again. 'This indicates that the destroyer was sunk deliberately, rammed against the docks after being stuffed full of explosives. And equally, that the dry dock was destroyed. That was obviously what they meant to do. I think you must give them credit for a successful operation. And our people do not seem to have known what was going to happen.'

'No, sir. There will have to be an inquiry.'

'Which, thank God, should not involve us. Thank you, Major. This will have to be kept quiet until a general release from Berlin.'

'As you say, sir. Heil Hitler!' Holzbach saluted, and was replaced by Eva.

'Monterre is here, Herr Colonel.'

Monterre, Franz thought. Should he have known of it? Only if the de Gruchy Group had been involved. But as far as he knew, the de Gruchy Group no longer existed. 'Well, Monterre,' he said. 'Where have you been, these last few weeks?'

Monterre hesitated in the doorway. 'I have been gathering information, Herr Colonel.'

'Well, let us hope that some of it may be useful.'

'I would use the word sensational, Herr Colonel.'

'I am sure you would. Are you sure that what you are going to tell me has not already happened?'

'Herr Colonel?' He was clearly bewildered.

'Then tell me what it is. You may sit down.'

Monterre sank into the chair before the desk. 'One hardly knows where to begin.'

'The beginning is normally useful.'

'Ah, but is there a beginning? Will there be an end?'

'Monterre, you do not have the intellectual capacity to be a philosopher, and I do not have the time to listen to drivel. Either get on with it or get out.'

'Very good, sir. Amalie de Gruchy is in Vichy. With her brother, Pierre.'

Franz frowned. 'You are certain of this? You have seen them?'

'I have not seen them myself. But my source is absolutely reliable. Pierre is reconstituting the de Gruchy Group.'

'And how are they supposed to have reached Vichy? Every border crossing is on the lookout for them. For Amalie, certainly.'

Monterre drew a deep breath. 'They were taken across the border, sir, in a car driven by Joanna Jonsson and Madeleine von Helsingen.'

Franz gazed at him with a look of such venom that Monterre shifted uneasily in his seat. 'Get out,' Franz said. 'Get out, and do not let me see your face again, you unutterable little rat.'

'I am telling you the truth, Herr Colonel. Have I not always told you the truth in the past? You did not believe me when I told you that Liane de Gruchy had survived the battle in the cave. That was claimed by this same Jonsson. She is a traitor, sir.'

'If you ever make a statement like that again, Monterre, I will have you shot. Now I have told you to get out. Do you want to be thrown into the street?'

Monterre scrambled to his feet and backed to the door. 'Would you not like to know where Liane is now, sir? She is on her way back from Dieppe, where she has been carrying out a secret mission for the British. Dieppe, Herr Colonel. Dieppe. A seaport just across the Channel from England. Why do you suppose she was there?'

'Eva!' Franz called. 'Summon some people and have this cur thrown out. He is not to be admitted to these premises again.'

Monterre ran from the room.

Eva closed the door, and Franz gazed at it for several moments. He was conscious of several different emotions at the same time. Anger and outrage, certainly, but directed against whom? Despair and a sick feeling in his stomach, equally certainly. For the first time in his life, he had fallen in love. He had already informed OKW that he needed some leave, and he intended to go to Berlin the following month. There he would see Weber and inform him that he intended to marry Joanna.

Monterre had not lied about the survival of Liane de Gruchy. Why should he be lying now? Besides, it all fitted so terribly well. It had been Madeleine who had invited him to dinner at the chateau on that fateful September night. She had been shocked, horrified, by the sudden appearance of her sister, by his being taken prisoner, and when found the next morning she had been tied to her bed, apparently as much a victim of her nefarious family as himself. Madeleine, his best friend's wife, but a de Gruchy to her backbone.

It had been Joanna who had claimed that Liane was dead, shot by herself. It had been Joanna, Oskar Weber's right-hand woman, who had taken charge of the British agent Cartwright, and so mysteriously allowed her to escape. Weber had accepted her explanation, but then Weber had also accepted Joanna's version of what had happened in the cave, and regarded her as utterly trustworthy. It had been Joanna who had come down to Bordeaux as Madeleine's minder, just as it had obviously been Madeleine who had known exactly where to go to find her brother and sister, and with Joanna's help spirit them across the border to safety. And it had been Joanna who had shared that horrifying ordeal with Liane at the beginning of

186

the war, when not only had the women been raped, but her brother had also been killed.

Joanna claimed to have been big enough to accept that such tragedies were a concomitant of warfare, which could not basically affect her Fascist beliefs – something else that had apparently been accepted without question by Weber. But was any woman – or any man, for that matter – that big? The experience had certainly turned Liane into an avenging angel, moving around France like a shadow, striking as and when she chose, even as high as the chief of the Paris Gestapo, and then contemptuously sparing his life.

And then there was that unexplained business of the attempt on Joanna's life, which she had handled with masterly cold-bloodedness. Had she really not known who had sent the assassin?

The two most important women in his life. He knew that he would give a great deal to see Liane again. That was not love, it was sheer lust. With Joanna it was different. She was the sort of woman he had always dreamed of meeting, such a contrast to the stiffly amoral girls with whom he had grown up, whose only ideals had been Hitler and Nazism. Joanna was more amoral than any of them, but her amorality was entirely hedonistic, and she had no more respect for political jargon and clichés than she did for the rules of society. She was the sort of woman who made a man glad to be alive.

And now he was being required to destroy her, along with Liane, and Madeleine – and, by association, Freddie von Helsingen as well. Why? If Madeleine was covertly helping her family, did she really deserve to be hanged for that – even if they were outlaws? If Joanna was secretly helping the Resistance, would her execution make a bit of difference, especially if he could stop her activities by the simple means of marrying her? And if Liane was actually carrying out a mission for British Intelligence, well . . . He frowned.

Dieppe. As Monterre had reminded him, it was just across the water from England, and it was a place in which he had a personal interest, as he had commanded there, briefly, just after the occupation. But the British had just carried out a most successful raid, on St Nazaire. Would they be contemplating another so soon? Or was all this a build up to the day every German soldier knew had to come?

Nine

Dieppe

The Lysander dropped out of the night sky, skimming the treetops before bumping across the meadow to come to a halt. Instantly several men and women ran forward, some to the aircraft, others to replenish the oil in the flaring landing lights – they knew the plane would be taking off again immediately.

The pilot came out of the after door. 'Pound Twelve?'

'I am here, Mr Brune,' Liane said. 'Are you alone?' She was disappointed.

'Yes, I am. I was told to pick up your material and return immediately.'

'I have it here.' She handed him the satchel. 'Is there no message?'

'Ah . . . yes.' Brune, a chubby young man made to look even chubbier in his flying suit, looked left and right. 'It is of a confidential nature.'

'Then come over here.' She led him away from the men, while Pierre looked after them curiously. 'Well?'

'The message is from Pound One. He says to tell you that you are a very naughty girl, but if what you have is as good as I am sure it will be, congratulations.'

'It is everything he wanted. Why were we not informed of St Nazaire?'

'You had no group formed. Now he wants to know how many people you have available, and how soon they can be ready to move.'

'Tell him that I have thirty-one people, and that we can move at twenty-four hours' notice.'

'That's splendid. You will receive your orders in a few days.'

189

'I was expecting news of my sister.'

'Oh, yes. Pound One said to tell you that she is being well looked after, has seen your parents, and is in the best of health.'

'Thank you. But why has there been no publicity of the news of her escape to England? He has had her now for several weeks.'

'I have no information of that, mademoiselle.'

'Well, I wish information on this, and urgently. My sister's escape was to be given the maximum publicity, but not a word has been released. Do you know that a hundred men have been shot because of the Nazis' inability to capture her?'

'That is barbaric.'

'It is also history, now. The point is that another hundred men have been taken hostage, and they will be shot if Amalie is not surrendered, or if she is not proved to be beyond the reach of the enemy by being out of the country. That news *must* be released, and substantiated, within a week. Do you understand me?'

'I will report what you have said, mademoiselle. But I would say that the decision regarding releasing the news of your sister's escape is probably out of Pound's hands.'

'Then he had better get it back. Tell him I love him dearly, but if he expects me to lead my people into battle on his behalf, and probably get killed, I have to have some co-operation from him. OK?'

'Yes, ma'am.'

Liane kissed him on the cheek. 'I'm not blaming you, stupid. Have a safe flight home.'

'If you'd care to come in, Major Barron,' the secretary invited.

James stood up, put on his cap – today he was wearing uniform – and entered the large office. 'Major Barron, gentlemen,' the brigadier announced, with the air of a magician producing a rabbit from a hat.

James gulped as he saluted; he had never faced quite such a collection of brass – no fewer than six general officers were seated at the table in front of him.

190

'At ease, Major,' one of these now said, a thin-faced man with a long nose, whose name, James knew, was Montgomery, the commanding officer of south-east England. 'Take a seat.'

'Thank you, sir.' James sat down, placing his cap and brief-case on his lap.

'The brigadier says you have something for us.'

'Yes, sir.' James opened the briefcase and laid several papers on the table.

The generals passed them around. 'Who made these sketches? These harbour plans seem to be very detailed.'

'I can vouch for their accuracy, sir. She is the very best agent we have.'

'She?' The question indicated distrust of the idea of using a woman.

'A pretty woman has access to areas beyond the reach of a man, sir.'

There was some clearing of throats, then another general tapped another piece of paper. 'Do you expect us to believe this? That there is only one arsenal in the town, and all the munitions are stored there?'

'If that is what she says, sir, then that is the situation. Or was the situation when she was there, several weeks ago.'

'Why has it taken so long for this information to reach us?'

'My people operate out of Vichy, sir. Dieppe is on the Channel coast. My agent had first of all to cross France to get to her destination, spend some time in Dieppe accumulating this information, and then make her way back across France to her base. This is a lengthy operation, certainly for someone who is already wanted by the Gestapo.'

'And if she were to be captured by the Gestapo, she would of course be forced to divulge her activities.'

'She has been sought by the Gestapo for nearly two years now, sir. And they have not caught her yet.'

There was some more throat-clearing, then someone asked, 'Brigadier?'

'I have the utmost confidence in Major Barron's people, sir.'

'Then we will accept your recommendation. Now, tell us what support we can receive on the ground.'

'There are several guerrilla groups who appear ready to respond,' the brigadier said. 'Monsieur Moulin, who has returned to France, is handling this.'

'I hope none of these know what we intend?'

'No, sir. They are merely awaiting a signal to take action against German lines of communication, on a given date.'

'Quite so. Is Major Barron's Pound group included in this?'

'It is my opinion,' the brigadier said, 'that Major Barron's group should actually take part in the assault. They have the experience, from St Valery last year.'

'St Valery was a disaster.'

'That was not the fault of the Resistance, sir.'

'Why was this group not employed at St Nazaire?'

The brigadier looked at James. 'They were attacked by German forces and virtually destroyed last September, sir. Since then they have been reforming, but were not yet ready last month.'

'Hmm. And you feel these people would be prepared to undertake the support of another . . . ah . . . raid?'

'My people will undertake whatever I require them to, sir.'

'I see. They will require a competent commander, who will need to understand our plans. As these must remain top secret, you will have to arrange for this fellow to be brought over here, so that we can interview him in person.'

'That will not be necessary, sir. I will command the group myself.'

The generals looked at the brigadier. 'I should point out that Major Barron has twice been wounded in this war. It is not our policy to send wounded soldiers back into battle.'

'With respect, sir, I am perfectly fit again, and while my people will follow me anywhere and carry out my orders without question, after the St Valery fiasco and the events that followed, which, as I have said, led to the virtual extermination of the Group as it was then, they will need me to lead them in a new venture of any size.' He paused as the generals stared at him. 'I am assuming that this is the case.'

'It would be better if you did not assume anything, Major. You will be briefed nearer the time. How long would it take your people to move from their Vichy base to within striking distance of Dieppe?'

'I would say four weeks, sir. As I have said, it requires a movement right across France, and this movement cannot be undertaken as a single body. They will have to split up into small sections, and rendezvous at an appointed place. Again, this is what they did for the St Valery raid.'

'Hmm. Four weeks. Today is the first of May. They will have to begin their journey a month today.'

'Very good, sir.' James looked at the brigadier. 'With your permission, sir.'

The brigadier sighed. 'Oh, very well. We can discuss your department later.'

He turned to the generals. 'The last week of this month, sir.'

Montgomery nodded. 'The brigadier will inform you of the exact date, and you will be fully briefed before you leave. However, you will convey no information to your people other than that they must be prepared to undertake an offensive manoeuvre, commencing at the beginning of June. Absolutely no information as to the destination must be revealed to *anyone*. The entire success of this operation depends upon absolute secrecy. Is that understood?'

'Yes, sir.'

'Very good. And thank you for your information, Major. Good day.'

The brigadier and James shared a taxi, but of course they could not discuss the conference. But as James obviously had a lot on his mind, the brigadier asked him into his office.

'Is this what I think it is, sir?' James asked.

'You were told not to think about it at all. However, if it will put your mind at rest, this is not the invasion. It is not even another raid, as at St Nazaire, which was made for the express purpose of destroying the dry dock and the U-boat pens. It is, if you like, a reconnaissance in force, to find out just what we will face when we do invade. The idea is to seize Dieppe, hold it for a couple of days, and then withdraw. This will enable us to determine the speed of the enemy's response, and we are also hoping to draw in a considerable part of his available air force, and, as the RAF will be supporting in strength, inflict heavy losses. The same goes for any naval units he may have in the vicinity. Of course we understand there will be casualties, but we would hope to inflict more on him than he on us. Does that answer your query?'

'Yes, sir. But there is a small problem. As I understand it, I am required to tell my people to prepare to move, then join them and lead them into occupied France, without telling them where they are going. However, they're not stupid. Liane certainly is not. She has been required to go to a particular place and make those sketches and notes. Now she is to be told to prepare her people to undertake an offensive manoeuvre. Obviously she is going to realize our destination.'

'Hmm. However, as I believe you trust her absolutely, tell her to keep her thoughts to herself. We have a serious domestic matter to consider. You are likely to be away for several weeks. Who is going to run Pound during that time?'

'Rachel.'

'I hope you're not serious.'

'She is a most capable young woman, sir.'

'She is also hot-headed and impulsive. Anyway, it is simply not feasible to have a sergeant who is also a woman running such an important department.'

'I'm not quite sure in which order you wish me to answer that point, sir. As to the rank of Pound One, I should like to remind you that when I was away in France for a considerable period last autumn, and you drafted in an officer of commensurable rank, he proved to be a disaster, and the unit was only kept going by Rachel. If her actual rank bothers you, well, you can always promote her. As to her being a woman, well, I suppose we can't do much about that, but I have discovered over the past couple of years that when it comes to doing difficult jobs, women are every bit as good as men.'

'You are thinking of your de Gruchy friend, I suppose.'

'She ranks very high, yes, sir.'

'And what about your other friend? Jonsson?'

194

'She also ranks very high. I will be forever grateful that your hit man didn't make it.'

'There is a hell of a row brewing about that. He has just disappeared.'

'That's understandable. He's dead. He attempted to carry out his orders to kill Jonsson, only she killed him first. She can be quite deadly. We trained her to be deadly.'

'But then . . .'

'Oh, she knows he was acting on our orders. But she doesn't appear to bear a grudge. I only hope you will never issue such an order again, sir.'

'And you are prepared to go on trusting her. But not to the extent, I hope, of revealing any of our current plans to her.'

'She is not involved in our current plans, sir.'

'Thank God for that. Very good, James. You may place Cartwright in charge during your absence, but she must understand that she is to undertake no action, no action at all, without reference to me.'

'I will do that, sir. And her promotion?'

'I will have to consider that.'

'There's just one thing more, sir. The business of Amalie de Gruchy. We've had her now for several weeks, and the fact has not been released. The guerrillas only sent her over in the hope of obviating the necessity for sacrificing any more hostages. But as yet no one knows we have her . . .'

'I'm afraid that, too, has to stay under wraps for the time being. The top brass consider that the amount of time and energy the Gestapo are putting in to finding this young woman is taking their minds off other matters, which could involve our new project. When that is completed, we will release the whereabouts of Amalie de Gruchy.'

'And the hostages?'

'James, we are fighting a war. And in war people get killed, some innocently. That is a regrettable fact of life.'

'Well,' Rachel said. 'How was hobnobbing with the high and mighty?'

'Very interesting,' James said. 'Sit down and listen very carefully.'

195

She obeyed, but was showing explosive signs before he had even finished. 'Are you out of your flipping mind? You are no longer fit for active service.'

'I'm as fit as a fiddle.'

'The last time you got involved in an op in France you were seriously wounded.'

'Lightning never strikes twice in the same place. From your point of view, the important thing is that you will be in sole charge during my absence.'

'Do you mean that?'

'Well, subject to the brigadier's overrule, of course.'

'Cheer me up.'

'I'm sure you'll grow to like him when you know him better.'

'I do know him, better than you.'

'How so?'

'He's a friend of my parents. He used to come to tea and play croquet when I was younger. And,' she added darkly, 'when Mummy and Daddy weren't looking, he'd squeeze my bottom. He's a dirty old man.'

'One learns things every day. But I'm sure he's only a dirty old man outside of office hours, and in office hours he is normally on the end of a telephone rather than a clutching hand. Now, enough of this chat. We have things to do.'

'Like getting hold of Liane, and telling her you're on your way to shag her,' she said bitterly.

'Now that,' James said, 'is exactly what I had in mind.'

'What brings you here?' Oskar Weber asked.

'I happen to be on leave,' Franz Hoeppner said.

'And you decided to pay me a visit? How very civil of you. Have you come to offer your condolences?'

Franz sat before the desk. 'You mean about St Nazaire? It seems odd that you knew nothing about it.'

'St Nazaire was the Abwehr's business, not mine. You mean you have not heard that Heydrich is dead? Murdered in cold blood. It was a carefully laid ambush, not like that hit-and-run affair in Bordeaux. He was seated alone in the back of his open car. There were outriders before and behind. But when the car slowed at an intersection, these three criminals stepped out of the crowd. Two had automatic weapons, which they used but without hitting anyone. But the third had a grenade, and this he lobbed into the back of the car, where it exploded.'

'And Heydrich was killed?'

'Well, not outright. But he was too badly injured to be saved.'

'What happened to the patriots?'

'You mean the criminals? Oh, they are dead. They holed up in a church and were surrounded by our people and shot.'

'Well, I suppose they knew what they were risking. What does Himmler make of it?'

'He is furious. But not so angry as the Führer. He is resolved to make the Czechs pay in blood. He is talking about destroying an entire town – men, women, and children. You will understand that we have a lot on our minds at the moment. So if you have called simply to say hello, I will say hello and goodbye.'

'I called, in the first instance, to discuss Dieppe.'

'What has Dieppe got to do with me?'

'I have a suspicion that it is to do with all of us. A month ago I received information from a source I am bound to regard as reliable, that British agents were engaged in filing reports on the defences and military establishment of Dieppe.'

'There are British agents in almost every seaport in France.'

'As there were in St Nazaire? This was one of their best people.'

'Very well. I assume you forwarded this information both to the commanding officer and to OKW.'

'I informed Rinteler, certainly. As regards OKW, well, I am sure you know that I am not the most popular of their officers at this time. I am surprised that I am still in Bordeaux, and not in Russia.'

'You are in Bordeaux because I wished you left there until this Amalie de Gruchy business has been sorted out. I presume you have still made no progress in that direction.'

'Unfortunately, no. I received no reply from Rinteler,' Franz went on, 'so I took leave, and before coming back to Germany

I visited the port. You know I commanded there immediately following the invasion?'

'Yes,' Weber agreed. 'And even then you were interfering with the Gestapo.'

'Who needed to be interfered with. I did not come here to discuss the Gestapo. I am here because, although I repeated my information to Rinteler, he pooh-poohed it. He insisted that there has been less enemy activity in the Channel than usual this year. He said that does not indicate the likelihood of an invasion. I would have said quite the opposite. However—'

'Just one moment. Did you use the word "invasion"?'

'I believe it could be that, yes. Dieppe is a seaport, reasonably close to England, and points like a dagger at the heart of France. And it fits in with the raid on St Nazaire, which was clearly a reconnaissance in force. Have your agents in England not turned anything up?'

'I think you have been letting your imagination run away with you, Colonel. If I receive any supportive information I will look into the matter. However, thank you for bringing it to my attention. Have a pleasant holiday.'

Franz remained seated. 'There is another matter.'

Weber raised his eyes. 'Yes?'

'I would like you to release Joanna from your employment.'

Weber frowned. 'What interest have you got in Joanna?'

'I wish to marry her.'

Weber stared at him for several seconds, then gave a shout of laughter. 'Is she aware of this ambition?'

'Yes, she is.'

Another stare, then a snap of the fingers. 'Munich! You were with her in Munich! The bitch!'

'There have been other occasions. We are in love. I know that is an emotion you will find impossible to understand, much less appreciate, Oskar. I know that Joanna has been your mistress . . .'

'Joanna *is* my mistress.'

'But you do not love her. She is a beautiful woman, and she works for you. In that capacity she once saved your life. I am sure you are very grateful. Now you can show your gratitude by releasing her to make a decent life for herself.'

198

Weber continued to stare at him for several seconds. Franz could see no change of expression, but that went with such a cold-blooded creature. Yet he was taken by surprise when Weber suddenly smiled. 'Of course, Franz. You are absolutely correct. I have had the best of her. You are welcome to take her over.'

'That is very civilized of you, although I would have put it differently. I shall go and see her now.'

'By all means do so. However, I am afraid I cannot release her right this moment. She has certain duties to perform, and I must find adequate replacements.'

'How long?'

'I should think a month will do.'

Franz stood up and clicked his heels. 'Again, thank you for your co-operation, Herr Colonel.'

Weber watched the door close, and leaned back in his chair. *The poor fool*, he thought. But that bitch, betraying him time and again with that fop . . . He leaned forward again, frowning. Roess had said she was betraying him, had betrayed him from the beginning, and he had not been referring to any clandestine love affair. Well, if the pair of them assumed he was incapable of dealing with them, they were gravely mistaken. Between them, they had given him all the ammunition he needed. He picked up his phone. 'Put me through to General Himmler.'

He had to wait for some time, but at last a woman said, 'General Himmler's office.'

'Is the general available? This is Colonel Weber, and the matter is urgent.'

A moment later Himmler's quiet voice was on the line. 'Have you something for me, Oskar?'

'I am calling about Hoeppner, Herr General.'

'Hoeppner? Are you referring to General Hoeppner?'

'No, no, sir. I am speaking of the general's nephew, Colonel Franz Hoeppner, who commands the Bordeaux area.'

'Oh, him. Don't tell me he's managed to crack the de Gruchy business.'

'No, sir, he has not, and frankly, I do not believe that he

199

ever will. His heart isn't in it, he is against taking hostages, and I regret to say that he seems to have missed or overlooked several important leads. It is my opinion that he should be replaced as soon as possible.'

'Hmm. I shall of course act on your recommendation, Oskar. I will speak with Halder.'

'I think the transfer should be made immediately, Herr General.'

'I have said that I will attend to the matter. Do you have a replacement in mind?'

'That is a matter for the Wehrmacht. Anyone has to be better than Hoeppner.'

'Very good. But you should brief the new man. I will keep you informed.'

Weber put the phone down and returned to his intercom. 'Call the Albert Hotel,' he told his secretary, 'and tell Fräulein Jonsson that I wish to see her.'

'Here, Herr Colonel?' The woman was well aware that when her boss wished to see his mistress, he invariably called on her.

'That is what I said, Fräulein.' He had no wish to encounter Hoeppner again.

Franz was waiting in the hotel lobby when Joanna returned from Gestapo headquarters.

'Franz!' she cried. 'What a pleasant surprise. I had no idea you were in Berlin, until Oskar told me just now.'

He embraced her. 'You have been with Weber?'

'He sent for me.'

'To tell you what?'

'Come upstairs.' She led him to the lift. The reception clerk looked astounded, and somewhat apprehensive, but he was not up to date on the situation. The lift doors clicked shut. 'He told me he had given permission for us to marry. Oh, Franz! I am so happy there has been no unpleasantness.'

'I have to say that his reaction surprised me too. But do you mean he sent for you just to say that you could marry me?'

'Well, no. He has a job for me to do. A last job, and then I'm free.'

He followed her along the corridor. 'What sort of job?'

Joanna unlocked the door of the suite and led him in, then she closed the door. 'What the hell? As this is my last one. I told you, I'm his private courier. Because I can travel so freely, I take his messages to his various agents in the field, and I bring their replies back. It's all very simple, really.'

'So where is he sending you now?'

'England.'

'What did you say?'

'I've been there often. Cognac?' She poured two glasses.

'You cannot go to England. You'll be shot as a spy.'

She handed him his glass, drank from her own. 'There is no one in England who has the least idea that I am anything but the daughter of a Swedish diplomat. Believe me, Franz, I have done this often before, without the least bit of trouble. Well, now that we are officially engaged, would you like to come to bed?'

'But why England, now?'

'Oh, he seems to feel there could be something big on, and he wants to find out what it is.'

Franz snapped his fingers. 'Dieppe!'

Joanna had kicked off her shoes. Now she turned to face him. 'Say again?'

'The official reason for my visit to Berlin is that I have obtained information that the British may be planning an attack on Dieppe.'

'What sort of attack?'

'I have no idea. But it could be a big one. It could even be the invasion.'

'What makes you say that?'

'Because they sent their leading agent to Dieppe, almost certainly to check out the port installations and the garrison dispositions. Do you know who that was? Your friend Liane.'

Joanna sat down on the settee, somewhat heavily. 'Who told you all this?'

'Monterre. I loathe the man, but he is a most fruitful source of information.'

'And you believed him?' *Why isn't Monterre dead?* she asked herself.

'Almost every thing he has told me in the past has been accurate.'

'And what have you done about it?'

'About Liane?' He sat beside her, put his arm round her shoulders. 'Nothing. I am not going to betray your secret, my dearest girl. But I had to do something about Dieppe. Only no one would listen to me, or at least they pretended not to listen to me. But Weber . . . he really is a devious character.'

'Yes,' Joanna said thoughtfully. 'And is he also taking steps to strengthen the defences of Dieppe?'

'I have no idea. But it really isn't his province. He can supply the Wehrmacht with information, but he cannot influence what they do with that information.'

'Well, no doubt he will get his act together in due course. And you have done all you can. Let's go to bed.'

Liane read the transcript of the coded message. 'Oh!' she said. 'Oh, Pierre!' She hugged her brother. 'He's coming himself.'

Pierre scanned the paper. 'This is not very informative.'

'Well, of course he can't be informative. It's top secret. But we have our instructions. We are to be ready to move at the end of the month, and he will be coming himself to lead us. Into battle with the Boches!'

'At Dieppe.'

'Sssh!' She glanced at Anatole, who had done the decoding. 'He has repeated twice that this is top secret. No one is to know of it outside the three of us. That includes Clotilde, Anatole.'

'Of course, mademoiselle,' Anatole agreed anxiously.

'He says nothing about Amalie,' Pierre commented morosely.

'Of course he does. He says she is well and with Mama and Papa, but that for reasons he cannot at this moment divulge her presence in England cannot be publicized. I am as sorry about that as you, but I am sure they have their reasons. Why are you so grumpy? This could be what we have been waiting for for two years.'

'I am remembering St Valery.'

'These things happen. And it was the British who suffered, it was James who was wounded, not us and not you. Now I want no more defeatist talk. Our business is to alert each of our people that they must be prepared to move by May thirty-first. Right?'

Pierre looked at Anatole, who waggled his eyebrows.

'Well,' James said. 'All correct?'

'I have packed your gear, sir,' Rachel said frostily. 'Including a suicide capsule for when you are captured.'

'You really must try looking on the bright side. I shall be wearing uniform and will thus be a prisoner of war.'

'And what about Hitler's directive after St Nazaire that all Commandos are to be shot when captured?'

'I am not a Commando. Now, you know that I'm going to be gone for several weeks. You're sure you can manage? I gather that Jennifer is coming back as your assistant. Mind you only use the bed one at a time.'

'Yes, sir. With the brigadier's permission, of course.'

'Eh?'

'You said I was to do nothing important without first referring to him, sir.'

'Remind me, the moment I'm home, to put you across my knee.'

'Do I have to wait that long?'

He took her in his arms, and was interrupted by a gentle cough from the doorway.

They turned together. 'Good God!' James cried.

'Joanna!' Rachel released him to run forward and embrace her friend. 'I never expected to see you again.'

Joanna kissed her and hugged her, then released her to look at James. 'No welcome for the prodigal daughter?'

'I'd like to know what's going on. It's been six months.'

'A long time. You guys got a drink?'

Rachel went into the flat and Joanna sat down. 'As you can imagine, there was a bit of a flap after Pearl Harbor, so I was sidelined for a while. Now I'm back in business.'

'How did you get in?'

'I'm using my Swedish passport.'

'And you're again posing as a courier for Weber?'

Rachel returned with a glass.

'I *am* Weber's courier.' Joanna sniffed the glass. 'This is whisky.'

'I'm sorry. It's all we have in the alcohol line. It's Johnnie Walker Black.'

Joanna made a face, but took a sip.

'Of course we are very grateful for the help you gave Rachel,' James said. 'Does this mean you'll be returning regularly from here on?'

'I don't know about that. I thought I'd been pulled out of this business for good, and would have to spend the rest of the war behind a desk . . . You guys are going to win, aren't you?'

'I don't see how we can lose, with your people behind us. But there's the point. There have been questions.'

'From whom?'

'Well, from your mother for a start. Seems she's been in touch with your dad, but all he could tell her was that you'd gone back to Germany. Obviously she couldn't get the US embassy in Berlin on to it, because they'd packed up and left. So she's got the State Department working. She seems to think that you have been kidnapped, but why she cannot say.'

Joanna nodded, finished her drink, and held out the glass. 'I know. Poor old girl. I'll make it up to her when this is done.'

'Do you realize that you are well on the way to becoming an alcoholic?'

'Do you realize the stress under which I live? Stress created by you.'

'Let's get our facts straight. You volunteered. And I told you to pull out last December.'

'I felt I had a contribution to make.'

'What you mean is, you enjoy the life you are living, the glamour as much as the danger.'

Joanna took the glass from Rachel's hand. 'You could be right.'

'What I am trying to tell you is, at the moment the State

Department seem to be going along with your mother's ideas, but they have their own people in Berlin, who pretty soon are going to discover that, far from being under duress, you are living high, wide and handsome, and even that you are Oskar Weber's mistress.'

'Not any more. I'm getting married.'

'You?' Rachel and James asked together.

'Well, why not? You remember Franz Hoeppner, Rachel?'

Rachel sat down. 'You intend to marry Franz Hoeppner?'

'He's asked me, and I have agreed. Oskar has given his blessing.'

'But . . .' James scratched his head. 'Hoeppner is a German officer. A Nazi.'

'I'm not sure about that. He's a real nice guy. You remember that, Rachel.'

'Yes,' Rachel said absently. 'He said he would shoot me in the back of the head rather than hang me.'

'Well, he had to say that. You were a spy. And you agreed that James would have done the same thing.' Both women looked at James.

'There are times,' he agreed, 'when I feel like doing just that to certain women. You are, therefore, intending to become a Nazi.'

'I am intending to become a German housewife.'

'Which will be regarded as an act of treason to the United States.'

'You'll have to sort that out. I'm your baby, remember. You haven't asked me why I'm here.'

'I assume you are carrying a message to your friend Burton. Have you ever met him?'

'Nope. And I don't want to. It's the message that's important.'

'I thought you never knew what was in the messages,' Rachel remarked.

'I don't. They're in a code for which I don't have a key. But I have a pretty good idea what this is about. Dieppe.'

There was a moment of absolute silence in the office, then James asked quietly, 'What about Dieppe?'

'Oskar has the idea that you guys could be planning an

205

attack on the port.' She looked from face to face. 'Don't tell me you are!'

'You think this fellow Burton is being instructed to find out what he can about a projected attack?'

'I would say so, for me to be sent. Will he be able to find anything?'

'I have no idea. I have no idea if there is anything to find.'

'Have it your way. Well, I'll see you guys.' She finished her drink and got up.

'I'm afraid,' James said, 'that you will have to stay for a while. Only a week or so.'

Joanna sat down again. 'So there *is* something planned. And you think I'd leak it? Shit!'

'We just can't take that chance. Not that you'd leak it, but that, supposing you were to fall out with your boss, he might just screw it out of you. Like I said, it will only be for a week or so.'

'So it's to go ahead right away. What are you scared of? The Germans could hardly react quickly enough now.'

'I'm sorry. If it were ever to be discovered that I had allowed you to return to Germany with any knowledge about Dieppe, I would probably be shot. I would certainly be cashiered.'

'And afterwards?'

'You go back to Germany, if you wish. You were delayed, and thus any information Burton may be able to produce will be delayed also. That will just be bad luck for Jerry. These things happen.'

Joanna sighed. 'OK. I take your point. I'll tell the Dorchester I'll be around for another week.'

'Ah . . . I'm afraid not.'

'Would you say that again?'

'We may be quite sure that you can be trusted. Others may not. We have to do this by the book.'

Joanna stared at him. 'You mean you are actually arresting me? Putting me in prison? You have got to be joking.'

'I am putting you into protective custody. You will be taken to a safe house, and held there until it is time for you to leave.'

'And Burton's reply? He sends them to the Dorchester.'

'I will arrange for it to be picked up and delivered to MI5. Once they have read it, it will be kept for you to take back to Germany when you go.'

'What a shitting mess.'

'You don't have to go back to Germany at all, you know. You can opt out, right this minute. We'll still have to keep you here until after the raid, but then we can sort it out with the State Department, and you can go home.'

Joanna shook her head. 'I have to go back, James.'

'Because of Franz?'

'There is that. Oh, not because of any love between us. But he's a decent guy, and he shares some of my secrets, which could get him into deep trouble if Weber got the idea I had defected and started asking questions. And then there's Madeleine. You were in love with her once, right?'

'I thought I was.'

'Well, she too is closely connected to what I've been doing, and her survival is linked to my loyalty and behaviour. You wouldn't like to think of her standing on a scaffold, would you?'

'It would be pretty grim. But I wouldn't like to think of you in that position, either.'

Joanna blew him a kiss. 'I can take care of myself. So what happens now?'

'You'll go with Rachel.'

'Great.'

'And Joanna . . . no funny stuff. Until we say so, you play this by our rules. We have scaffolds in England too, you know.'

She gazed at him for several seconds, then nodded. 'I reckon you do.'

James telephoned the brigadier. 'Pound One, sir.'

'Ah, James, I was about to call you. Is there a problem?'

'I hope it won't be a problem, sir. It concerns Jonsson.'

The brigadier snorted. 'Well?'

James repeated the relevant conversation. 'As I say, it really is just a hiccup. As soon as the raid is over, she can be released. A month in the clink won't do her any harm.'

'Ah. Yes. Unfortunately, James, it may be a lot longer than that.'

'Sir?'

'Operation Rutter has been postponed, James. For at least a month.'

Ten

The Raid

'**S**hit! James cried. 'Shit, shit, shit!'

'I know exactly how you feel,' the brigadier said. 'But these things happen. The raid will now take place in the middle of August. You'll have to stand your people down. Just for a month.'

'They're ready to go now. *I'm* ready to go now.'

'James, you are a professional. And you say your people will follow you anywhere. Well, now they'll have to wait a while. But only a month. You'll make your move at the end of June.'

'You do realize, sir, that a delay like this increases the risk of a leak?'

'Nothing has been leaked so far, has it? The same security applies. Leave the worrying to us.'

'Yes, sir.' He replaced the receiver and looked at Rachel. 'As you say,' she agreed. 'Shit, shit, shit. What first?'

James looked at his watch. 'Pound Seventeen won't be listening for another four hours.'

'But Liane will be all ready to go.'

'She knows she's not to assemble until she's certain I'm on my way.'

'She'll be spitting mad.'

'Don't you think I'm spitting mad? But there's something else we have to do. Get me MI5.'

'Loring,' said the slight young man leaning against the bar.

'Barron,' James said, looking around the room with some distaste; it was just a shade too clean and tastefully decorated.

'SIS?'

'What makes you think that?'

'The fact that you had our phone number.'

'Good point. Do you people always meet in places like this?'

'Safest, old man. Everyone in places like this has a secret, and everyone else knows better than to ask questions. What are you drinking? I'm on a Pink Lady.'

'I'm sure she's enjoying it. I'll have a pint of bitter.'

Loring chose not to take offence, but merely remarked, 'I'm not sure they serve that here.' But they did, and the two officers retired to a table in the corner of the bar, which at this early hour had only a handful of customers. 'Now then,' Loring said, 'do you have something for us, or do you wish something from us?'

'You have recently received a visit from one of my people. Joanna Jonsson.'

'One of yours, is she? I say, old man, you do like them large.'

It was James's turn to decide not to take offence. 'She gave you, as usual, a letter for a man named Burton.' Loring sipped his drink. 'I would like to know what was in that letter.'

'Sorry, old man. Classified, you know.'

'Look, the letter was delivered by my girl.'

'Then she is the one you should ask for its contents.'

'You know she hasn't got a clue what she's carrying.'

'Then perhaps you should change your rules.'

James finished his beer. Getting angry with this twit would be totally counter-productive; he was only doing his job. 'Well, will you tell me this: was the letter anything to do with troop movements, or a possible attack on the French Channel coast?'

'Sorry, old man. Can't be done. Another drink?'

'I would choke,' James said, and left.

'Shit, shit, shit,' Rachel muttered. 'How can we fight a war when every department regards itself as a world of its own and won't share its secrets?'

'He was only doing his job.'

'You are too fair-minded. I'd have wrung the bugger's neck.'

'Out of the mouths of babes and sucklings . . .'

She snorted. 'Can't you pull rank? Get the brigadier on him?'

'No, I can't. The last thing anyone would want is a row between SIS and MI5.'

'So we still don't know if Jerry really has the wind up or if it's a routine exchange of views. What about Joanna? You're going to have to go along and tell her she's in hock for two months instead of one.'

'I have decided to delegate that duty to you.'

'Oh, great. I'll have to see if I can borrow a suit of armour from the Tower. What about your other favourite woman? It's just about time.'

James sighed. 'Then you'd better get through.'

'Shit,' Liane said. 'Shit, shit, shit.'

'I couldn't agree with you more,' James said.

'We are all ready to go. Ammunition and food supplies have been issued . . .'

'But no routes compiled, I hope.'

'You said that must wait until you got here.'

'Good girl. So how many of you actually know the destination?'

'Me, Pierre and Anatole.'

'How much do you trust Anatole?'

'We have to trust him absolutely. He runs the radio.'

'Is he there now?'

'No. I send him out of the room when I am speaking with you.'

'Then you don't trust him absolutely.'

'What are you saying?'

'That I am aware that this delay is going to strain everyone's nerve. I know I can trust you and Pierre. I have never met Anatole, and I know that Rachel is unhappy about the part he played in her kidnapping. So just keep an eye on him. As for the rest, try to keep everyone happy. It's only another month.'

'I wish you were here.'

'I wish I was there, too. But I will be soon.'

'I love you, James.'

'I love you too. Over and out.'

He replaced the mike, looked at Rachel, who appeared to be sucking on a lemon.

'That,' James said, 'has been the longest month for my life.'

'I haven't enjoyed it either,' Rachel replied. 'You haven't had your mind on your work. Or on anything else.'

'How is Joanna?'

'Spitting blood. I've just told her she has at least another month in there.'

'We must make it up to her when she comes out. So, all set?'

'As always. Shall I enumerate?'

'As always, I have complete confidence in you. So—' The telephone jangled. They stared at each other. 'You'd better answer it,' James suggested.

'Maybe it's off. Oh, how I hope it's off. After such a delay there has to have been a leak.' She picked up the phone. 'Pound Two.'

'Pound. Put James on.'

Rachel handed James the phone, whispering, 'Maybe!'

'Pound One.'

'James, all ready for the off?'

'Yes, sir. Don't tell me there's another delay?'

'No, no. I have some news. Good news. Well, I suppose it's good news, for most of us. Tell me, have you been badgering MI5?'

'Ah . . . I contacted them about a month ago. I wanted to find out if Jonsson's contact had been instructed to find out what he could about the raid. So I asked MI5 for a release. They weren't the least bit co-operative.'

'Well, you seem to have put the wind up them vertically. Apparently there *was* a query regarding a possible descent on the Channel coast of France, mentioning Dieppe specifically. So they felt they should do something about it. The upshot is that after tailing Burton for some time, they have arrested him.'

'Oh my God! Without a reference to us?'

'I know. They do like to keep things to themselves. He's

on a technicality, drunken driving, and they'll release him once the show is over.'

'So they know about it.'

'Well, yes. They had to be briefed when they started asking questions. But what interests us is another part of the instructions to Burton. It's very cryptic: "release Jonsson, use number seven for reply". What do you suppose they meant by that?'

'Did that message ever get to Burton?'

'No. They just arrested him.'

'Well, sir, I would say that he has been instructed to betray Jonsson to us. That is, that the Nazis have decided she is of no more use to them.'

'But if they're shopping Jonsson, how will Burton get his message back to them?'

'Through this other agent they seem to have. Number Seven.'

'And who is he? Or she?'

'I'm sorry, sir. That's MI5's business.'

'Hmm. I suppose this could put Jonsson in a spot of bother. I mean, she hasn't been shopped, has she? Not yet, anyway. You'll have to warn her of the situation. I assume that she's intending to take Burton's reply back to Germany. But now there won't be one, will there?'

James looked at Rachel, who was listening on the extension. 'I think we can sort that one out, sir. Leave it with me.'

'Good man. Well, the best of luck, and I hope to see you back in . . . well, as soon as possible.'

The phone went dead. 'Has he ever fired a shot in anger in his life?' Rachel asked.

'I believe he was a subaltern in the Great War.'

'And Joanna?'

'Keep her until I get back. We'll discuss the situation then.' He took her in his arms. 'Aren't *you* going to wish me luck?'

She kissed him. 'Just come back, you great schmuck.'

'Shit!' Franz Hoeppner cried. 'Shit, shit, shit!'

'Sir?' Eva hurried in from the outer office. Franz handed her the sheet of paper with the official heading. 'Oh, my God!' she said. 'Oh, Herr Colonel.'

213

'It had to happen some time,' Franz said. 'I have been here too long as it is. And I actually applied for a front-line posting last July. It's just that it couldn't have happened at a worse time. Get me the Albert Hotel in Berlin, will you?'

'Yes, sir. Ah . . . that man Monterre is here.'

'Oh, fuck him. I beg your pardon, Eva. Let him wait. Put that call through first.'

Fifteen minutes later he was connected. 'Colonel Hoeppner,' he said. 'Is Fräulein Jonsson there?'

'I'm afraid the Fräulein is not in residence at this moment, sir.'

'But you still have her suite?'

'Oh, indeed, sir.'

'So you are expecting her back. When?'

'I cannot say, sir. She never gives a time of return. She just shows up.'

Franz hung up. 'Get me Colonel Weber,' he told Eva.

But when she returned to say that Colonel Weber was in a meeting and would not be free for another hour, he said wearily, 'All right. Send Monterre in. This had better be important.'

Monterre shuffled as he always did when in the presence of a German officer, and especially this German officer, after their last encounter. 'Several weeks ago I reported that the British might be planning an attack on Dieppe, Herr Colonel.'

'Based upon some supposition of yours.'

'With respect, Herr Colonel, my report was based upon the knowledge that Liane de Gruchy had visited Dieppe on the orders of British Intelligence.'

'A woman who is supposed to be dead.'

'A woman who, up until three weeks ago, was living near Limoges, where she was recruiting a new band of guerrillas to carry out an attack on forces of the Reich. And do you know who joined them three weeks ago? A British officer named James Barron, who is their control in London. He is also Liane de Gruchy's lover.'

Liane de Gruchy's lover! But of course a woman like Liane de Gruchy, however ambivalent her sexuality, would have a lover. A genuine lover, as opposed to the numerous men she had seduced over the past two years. Franz kept his voice even with an effort. 'And you claim they are on their way to attack Dieppe?'

'I would claim that it is too much of a coincidence that a woman as important to the Resistance as Liane de Gruchy should be sent on a mission to Dieppe and, having returned to Limoges, prepare her people for aggressive action, and then be joined by her British controller. These three things must be connected.'

Franz stroked his chin while subjecting him to one of his long stares. 'You say they left Limoges three weeks ago. Why are you only reporting it now?'

'Because they suspect me. I cannot go there when they are there, except very secretly. I last went there two weeks ago, when I learned about the Englishman and that they had left the previous week. Then I came here, but it takes time. Do you not think I deserve a reward?'

'There will be no reward,' Franz said. 'You will be paid, as always, for this information. If you learn anything more, bring it in. I will give you the name of my successor.'

'You are leaving Bordeaux, Herr Colonel?'

'Yes,' Franz said.

'Well, Franz,' Weber said into the telephone, 'what is the trouble now?'

'I thought you might be interested to know that I have been given a regiment and transferred to the Russian front. Did you know of this?'

'No, I did not. But I congratulate you. Certainly on the regiment. It is long overdue. As for Russia, well, at least it is summer. And we appear to be doing well. You will be in at the finish.'

'I would hope so. However, as I am to leave in the next week, I think it would be a good idea if Joanna and I were married before I go. Unfortunately, she does not seem to have returned. Why is this? You said she would be back in a fortnight, but it is now well over a month and I have not heard from her.'

'I know. It is inconvenient.'

'Are you not concerned?'

215

'She has been late before. I am afraid, Franz, that Joanna is a woman who does things her own way and in her own time. I am surprised you have not already learned this.'

'So you are not worried.'

'No, no. There has probably been some problem with shipping passages. I can understand how disappointed you are, but you know, a slight delay might not be a bad thing. It is always distressing when a couple gets married just before the husband leaves for the front . . . and then doesn't come back.'

'You are all heart, Oskar. Tell me, have you done anything about Dieppe?'

'Why should I do anything about Dieppe? You mean because of that cock and bull story dreamed up by one of your informers? My dear fellow, I have far more important things to do.'

'As you wish. I just thought that you should know that following my cock and bull story of a high-level member of the Resistance being sent to Dieppe, I have a report that they are preparing themselves for a considerable offensive movement within the occupied territory, a movement that is going to involve covering a considerable amount of ground. I have also learned that they have been joined by a British officer who is going to command their activities. Now, I am sure you will agree with me that there is no possibility the Resistance can consider a large-scale operation on their own. They must be expecting outside help. That can only come from the British, and it can only come from across the Channel. I leave you to draw your own conclusions. As I am in any event bound for Russia, I have put *my* conclusions in a memorandum, which I am forwarding to OKW. I have, of course, as I am duty bound to, reported the gist of my conversations with you on this matter. Good day to you, Oskar.'

Weber regarded the phone for several seconds. Sour grapes? But he kept coming back to the same story. And if he *was* submitting a report to OKW . . .

Weber picked up the phone again. 'Get me Colonel Roess, in Paris.'

* * *

216

James and Liane lay on their stomachs on a grassy knoll, looking down on the shallow valley and the railway line. Having reached their destination, James was in uniform, while Liane wore her usual trousers, blouse and beret.

'That runs straight into Dieppe,' she said.

'That's our initial target.'

She turned her head. 'I thought we were attacking Dieppe.'

'The Commandos and the Canadian brigade are doing that. Our business is to seal the port and prevent reinforcements getting in.'

'What about the roads?'

'The other groups have been allotted to handle the roads.'

'They have not arrived.'

'They'll be around. Only the leaders will come to the rendezvous, and that is not until tomorrow.'

'You are so confident.'

'One has to be confident, Li.'

'Oh, I am glad you are confident. It makes up for my lack.'

'You, lacking confidence? *You*?'

'I know that I am living on borrowed time.' She rolled over to lie on her back. 'And now I am less confident than ever. Because I have so enjoyed this past month.'

'Sleeping in ditches? Eating once a day? Bathing once a week?'

'Sleeping in your arms? Sharing every minute with you? Knowing that—'

'Confidence, remember. We've blown up a railway line before.'

'And just about went with it. I have been happier this past month than I have ever been in my life before.'

He kissed her. 'Hearing you say that makes the whole thing worthwhile. So, afterwards . . .'

'Afterwards,' she said, and took him in her arms.

Jules cleared his throat, embarrassed. He was a big man, with heavy features and broad shoulders and lank black hair, who had been one of the original members of the band, eighteen months before. Liane could remember with amusement how she had been afraid of him when they had first met, and

217

equally how he had become one of her most trusted aides. She pulled up her trousers and then sat up. 'Is there a problem?'

'Rostand is here.'

'Already? And what is this name, Rostand?'

'It's a pseudonym,' James explained, also dressing himself. 'They all use pseudonyms, except you. It is to protect their families.'

'But as I have no family to protect . . . Well, we had better see him.'

They made their way through the wood to where the Group were bivouacked. It was August 17th. To James's surprise, and relief, all thirty-one had arrived, and there had been no incidents – but then, he reminded himself, these men were all accomplished guerrillas, and their female leader even more so.

Rostand was with Pierre. He was a small, dark man, who, to James's concern, was clearly very tense.

'It is the invasion, yes?' he remarked. 'We have waited two years for this moment.'

'It is an assault on the port of Dieppe,' James said carefully. 'Our only concern is to prevent German reinforcements from reaching the town for as long as the battle continues. It is very important to remember this. However, as they do not know what is about to hit them, we do not expect any reaction for at least twenty-four, and possibly forty-eight hours.' He spread the map on the ground. 'This is the road for which you will be responsible. You will prepare a roadblock here.' He prodded the stiff paper. 'But it must be concealed and not erected until midnight tomorrow, August eighteenth. The same with this bridge.' Again he prodded the map. 'It must be blown, but not until after midnight. It is essential that you stick to that exact timetable.'

Rostand nodded. 'We will do it.' He peered at the map. 'It is a big road. They may have tanks.'

'Our information is that the nearest panzer formation is a hundred kilometres away. By the time it can arrive, if it ever does, you should have erected an impassable barrier. You have been chosen for this task because you have the most men and you have been equipped with bazookas. You must

218

hold that road for at least forty-eight hours after tomorrow night.'

'And afterwards?'

'If, at the end of forty-eight hours, the enemy continues to attack you in overwhelming strength, you may withdraw your people and send them home.'

'Just like that, eh? Leaving our dead behind. There will be some dead, Major Barron. Perhaps many.'

'I think you would be unwise to attempt to take your dead; the delays could be costly. Rostand, we know you to be a courageous and determined leader of your people. We know you will not let us down.' He held out his hand. 'Good fortune.'

Rostand shook hands, then embraced Liane, shook hands with Pierre, and left the bivouac.

Jules was hovering. 'Granville is here.'

'Another pseudonym,' Pierre remarked.

'All these strangers, knowing the map reference where we are to be found,' Liane commented. 'Do you realize that if there is a traitor in this lot we could all be slaughtered in a matter of moments?'

'If there is a traitor in the Resistance we are all dead in any event,' James told her. 'Let's see Monsieur Granville.'

'Herr Colonel.' Major Hans Rinteler stood to attention. 'Heil Hitler! Welcome to Dieppe.' He was a thin man with a hatchet face, who was sweating at the unheralded appearance of the Gestapo chief.

'Heil Hitler!' Roess acknowledged.

'Is this an official visit?' Rinteler asked anxiously.

'Yes, it is.' Roess drew off his gloves. 'I have been asked by Colonel Weber to visit you. You know Colonel Weber?'

'Ah . . . No, sir.'

'He is a senior officer in the SD. You know of the SD?'

Rinteler gulped. 'Yes, sir. But . . . you mean the SD has an interest in Dieppe? I do assure you . . .'

'I am sure you will. Shall we sit?'

He did so, and Rinteler hastily returned behind his desk. 'I had heard you were not well, Herr Colonel.'

'I am perfectly well, thank you. A couple of months ago

219

you received a visit from Colonel Hoeppner, who was then Commandant of the Bordeaux area.'

'That is correct, sir. Colonel Hoeppner was on his way to Berlin on leave, but he came up here first. He used to command here, you know.'

'I do know. I used to serve here myself. Colonel Hoeppner made certain comments. Do you recall what they were?'

'He seemed to feel that we might be attacked by the British.'

'And how did you respond to that?'

'Well, frankly, Herr Colonel, I found it difficult to respond at all. I mean, look out there.' The office was situated on the top floor of the headquarters building, and the window overlooked the harbour and the sea beyond. 'Have you ever seen such a picture of calm? Even six months ago there was usually some activity, even if it was only an MTB rushing by at great speed, but for the past few months, nothing.'

'And you do not find that suspicious? How far away from where we are sitting now is the English coast?'

'Perhaps sixty miles.'

'At sea, a distance that can be covered in a few hours.'

'I am sure you are right, Herr Colonel. But no military commander would attempt an assault without proper reconnaissance. As I say, there hasn't been any reconnaissance since before Easter. Not even aerial, and the RAF used to overfly us regularly.'

'There was no visible reconnaissance before the attack on St Nazaire. Has it never occurred to you that your position might have been fully reconnoitred from within by an English agent? A member of the French Resistance?'

'I hardly think that is possible, sir. All our installations are under heavy guard and cannot be infiltrated.' He frowned. 'There was one incident, a couple of months ago . . .'

'Go on.'

'Well, the sergeant in command of the guard at the arsenal was found to have a woman in his bed . . . Well, I reduced him to the ranks, of course. His was a responsible position.'

'I would say you were right. When you say the arsenal, how many arsenals do you have?'

'Well, just the one.'

220

'Are you saying that all your reserves of arms and ammunition are in one place?'

'Well . . . yes.'

'I shall refrain from comment. Very good. This woman was arrested, of course. Where is she now?'

'Actually, we let her go.'

'You did what?'

'Well . . . she was just a whore. Actually, she was rather an attractive piece. You know, excellent figure, yellow hair, a really handsome face, soft voice . . . I found it difficult to condemn poor Schultz as severely as perhaps I should have done . . . Is there something the matter, sir?'

Roess was staring at him with an expression that was almost frighteningly venomous. Then he opened his briefcase and took out a somewhat battered photograph. 'Do you recognize that woman?'

Rinteler studied the face. 'It is certainly familiar.'

'That,' Roess said, 'is Liane de Gruchy. I assume you have heard of Liane de Gruchy?'

'Why, yes, Herr Colonel. But . . . Liane de Gruchy is dead.'

'Liane de Gruchy is very much alive, Major.'

'You mean . . . Oh, my God!'

'Quite. She was here, on behalf of the British, noting everything about your defences. You had her in custody. And you let her go!'

'How was I to know? I thought she was dead! What am I to do?'

'What you must do, if you wish to save your miserable neck, is take immediate steps to put your command in a state of defence to withstand an imminent attack. How many men do you have?'

'I have a thousand men, officially. But there is a long sick list.'

'Get them out of hospital. Then get on the line to Paris and have them bring in reinforcements. You need at least a brigade of infantry and a panzer regiment. They must be here in twenty-four hours. Then get hold of Luftwaffe Coastal Command and tell them that you will require maximum air cover in the immediate future, and at no more than an hour's notice. Then get through to Le Havre, and tell them that you want the Channel swept tomorrow night, and every night after that until the order is rescinded. And then send out patrols. You can be certain there is a guerrilla concentration within striking distance of the town. Pay particular attention to the railway line. Oh, and get your munitions out of that one building.'

Rinteler was gulping like a fish out of water. 'You are speaking of generals, admirals, Herr Colonel. Are they going to take orders from me?'

Roess gazed at him for several seconds. Then he said, 'Probably not. Have a call placed to Berlin. To Colonel Weber. I will speak.'

The Group polished their weapons as the sun sank towards the western horizon, ate their evening meal and took their drinks of wine. They knew what lay ahead of them, and were not afraid, but none of them had yet had to sustain a full day of action. Even the battle at the cavern the previous autumn, in which the de Gruchys as well as Jules and James had taken part, had lasted less than an hour. But they were all both determined and confident.

'When do we move?' Pierre asked.

'Nine o'clock,' James said. 'We need to be in position by midnight.'

'And what is happening over the other side, do you think?'

'The troops will be embarked by now. They will also commence the operation at midnight, to be here at four tomorrow morning.'

'Listen!' Liane said.

The men stopped talking and listened to the low rumbling sound in the distance; it was a still night.

'Panzers!' Pierre said. He had served in the French Motorised Cavalry in the weeks leading up to Dunkirk.

'Moving at night?' Jules asked.

James and Liane looked at each other. 'It cannot be,' Liane said.

'It is,' Pierre said. 'We have been betrayed again.'

Now everyone looked at James. 'All right,' he said. 'Let's hope Rostand reacts. We certainly must. If they are putting re-

222

inforcements into Dieppe, we must stop them, or at least distract them. Liane, you and Jules come with me and we will blow up the railway line. Pierre, you take the remainder of our people and get down to Rostand; tell him my orders are countermanded. A few panzers aren't going to make that much difference, but the road must be closed before anything else can be brought in. Above all, the bridge must be blown immediately.'

'Understood.' Pierre hurried off to round up his people. James and Jules shouldered the haversacks containing the explosives. Liane took the one containing the detonators. Then they hurried into the darkness.

They reached their position just before eleven. Now they could hear gunfire from the south; as Pierre could hardly have reached Rostand as yet, that meant the guerrilla leader had indeed reacted, but he wouldn't have had the time to block the road. And now, distantly, they heard the whistle of a train, much later than a train would normally be making this relatively brief journey from Paris.

There was no time to reconnoitre the situation. James ran down the final slope and reached the bottom of the shallow embankment. Liane and Jules panted beside him. James clambered up the other side, took out the sticks of gelignite, and began placing them against the sleepers. Liane waited with the detonators.

'Hey, there!' someone shouted in accented French.

Jules immediately put down his haversack and levelled his tommy gun, sending a burst in the direction of the advancing patrol, one of whom gave a shriek of pain. But instantly fire was returned from the darkness. Liane went down, but James knew she wasn't hurt, merely lying on the ground beside him. Desperately he finished packing the explosive, trying to ignore what was happening about him, reaching for Jules's bag to add to his own.

The firing had stopped, and he heard the click of Jules fitting a fresh magazine to his gun. The train whistled again, now appreciably closer.

'Detonator.' Liane placed it in his hand, and he fitted it. 'Now go.'

'You come too,' she reminded him, and slid back down the slope carrying the plunger. Her movement attracted attention, and there was a fresh outbreak of firing, the bullets whining into the night, striking the rails and ricocheting to and fro. If one of those were to hit the gelignite . . .

Jules immediately returned fire. 'You go, Major,' he said. 'I will cover you.'

James hesitated only a moment; the train was now very close. 'Ten seconds,' he said, and followed Liane, paying out the wire as he did so. He reached the bottom of the embankment. Liane was already halfway up the slope on the far side. He ran behind her, pausing to look over his shoulder. Jules was still firing, lying flat behind the rail. And now the train could be seen, a glaring light rushing through the darkness.

James stood up. 'Jules!' he bellowed. 'Come on. I command you.'

Jules ignored him, continuing to fire into the darkness.

'James!' Liane screamed.

He scrambled up the slope, threw himself behind her, plugged the wires in. 'Down,' he commanded, remembering the last time they had done this, when they had almost blown themselves up. But this time they were further away. He pressed the plunger and lay beside her, head buried in the earth.

The noise was enormous, and as far away as they were from the explosion, they were still showered with debris. It was several minutes before they could move. Then Liane said, 'That was a big charge.'

'Are you all right?'

'I have a bump or two. Listen.'

Although there was noise in the distance, right here was absolutely quiet save for a loud hissing sound. The wrecked train was a mass of flames, carriages scattered to either side of the track, while a huge hole had been torn in the embankment.

'My God!' Liane said. 'Jules!'

'He covered our escape. But I don't think he's going to be the only hero tonight.'

Now sound returned, shouts and screams, overshadowed by a low moan.

'Do we attack them?' Liane asked.

'It's going to take them several hours to sort out that mess, much less get themselves organized again. The show could be over by then. Let's get to where the action is.'

It was half past three before they made contact with the rest of the Group. The shooting was desultory, but there were some small fires burning on the road itself.

'We've knocked out a couple of them with the bazookas,' Ronsard told them. 'But they came upon us so unexpectedly. What has happened?'

'I don't know for sure. Where are the enemy now?'

'They seem to have withdrawn for the time being. I think they are waiting for dawn.'

'What about the bridge?'

'There was no time. This should not have happened, Major.'

'Tell me about it. Did any get through?'

'Three or four.'

'Well, I know the British are bringing tanks with them, so that shouldn't be a problem.'

'Where are the British?'

James looked at the luminous dial of his watch, and held up his finger. 'Should be . . . now.'

The entire night sky lit up behind them as there came a huge paean of noise, out of which the explosions of guns and the staccato rattle of machine guns could be discerned.

'It is over!' Ronsard shouted.

'I'm afraid it has only just begun,' James told him. 'Can you hold here?'

'That depends on how hard they come on. We have suffered losses.'

'So have they. Do the best you can.'

'Where are you going?'

'I am going to get into the town and see what I can do. If we can knock out the arsenal, we can still win this.'

Ronsard looked at Liane. 'Where he goes, I go,' she told him. 'Besides, I know the way.'

'And so do I,' Pierre said. 'If the town falls, their attacks will cease.'

Ronsard snorted.

The three of them made their way down the road, which, behind the guerrillas, was clear of both people and vehicles. In front of them the sky was still bright with flame, while behind them the first faint streaks of dawn could be seen. The noise from the city and the beaches continued.

'What do you think happened?' Liane asked.

'We were betrayed again,' Pierre said, his voice thick with rage.

'James?'

'It certainly looks like it.'

'It can't have been one of ours. No one knew our destination until after we left Limoges.'

'Anatole knew it,' Pierre said savagely.

'I think,' James said, 'that we need to leave that until after it is over.'

They were well within sight of the town now, the glare of the fires being overtaken by the steadily lightening sky. 'Where do we go?' Liane asked.

'You tell me. We want that magazine.'

'Over there.' She pointed, and they broke into a trot, only to be halted when, still half a mile from the first of the houses, they heard a shouted command.

'Halt there! Throw down your arms.'

'Shit!' Liane snapped.

'He spoke English,' James pointed out. 'Raise your hands, but keep your weapons.' He set the example, calling out, 'I am Major James Barron. SIS.'

The Commandos approached, cautiously. But they could identify James's uniform. Now an officer came forward, also wearing the crown of a major on his shoulder straps. 'You're Pound! Whalley, Third Commandos. Bit of a snafu, isn't it? They were waiting for us.'

'So it would appear. What's happening down there?'

'Most of the Canucks are pinned on the beaches, taking whopping casualties. We got pretty shot up as well, but we got through.'

'Orders?'

'To come in behind the port. I was actually told to look out for you, or your people.' He beckoned the corporal carrying the radio. 'Get on to Jubilee HQ and tell them we have contacted Pound.'

The corporal set his gear on the ground and started sending.

'I beg your pardon,' James said. 'Jubilee? Don't you mean Rutter?'

'The name has been changed. After the delay, you know. The big boys felt there might be a leak.'

'Well, changing the name doesn't seem to have helped.'

'Jubilee says well done, and that we are to co-operate with Pound in any way he wishes, sir,' the corporal said.

'So tell us what you wish us to do,' Whalley invited.

'There's one big job we can do. Major Whalley, Liane de Gruchy.'

'I say.' Whalley saluted, and then squeezed her hand. 'Are you with us, madame?'

'I am with him. And it is mademoiselle.'

'*Enchanté.*'

Liane raised her eyebrows.

'And her brother, Pierre de Gruchy.'

'My pleasure, monsieur. You said you had a target, Major.'

'The arsenal. If we can get rid of that, Jerry won't have much to fight with in the town.'

'What about reinforcements?'

'We're doing what we can. Let's get in there.'

There were some hundred Commandos, and they moved through the suburbs with confident speed. Most of the houses were shuttered, and their inhabitants were clearly keeping their heads down, hoping that the battle would continue to miss them. The high rate of fire continued to rise from the town and on the beaches, where the Canadians were desperately trying to break through. From out at sea there came the heavier reverberations of naval guns. Now that it was broad daylight, the sky had suddenly filled with planes, both RAF and Luftwaffe, snarling and spitting, criss-crossing the clear morning sky with their vapour trails. More ominously, from behind them they could hear bursts of gunfire.

227

'Will your people hold?' Whalley asked.

'For as long as they can,' James promised.

Dieppe itself was as shuttered as its suburbs, but there were people about. Several houses had been hit and there had been casualties; they could hear the bells of a fire engine and also an ambulance. Those civilians who encountered the Commandos stared at them in consternation, and one or two shouted curses.

'Whose side are they on?' someone asked.

'Their own,' Liane told him. 'You are destroying them just as much as the Germans have ever done.' The soldier took off his helmet to scratch his head.

'But you don't feel that way,' Whalley suggested.

'No, because I – and my family – are amongst those the Nazis attempted to destroy. There is your target.'

Hitherto they had seen no German soldiers as the entire defence was concentrated, as had been intended, on the seaward side. But, rounding the corner and facing the arsenal building, they heard a burst of fire, and two of the Commandos went down.

'Take cover!' Whalley bellowed, and his men scattered to left and right. Whalley himself knelt beside James and the de Gruchys. 'How many men would be in there?' he asked.

'There were twenty when I was there,' Liane said.

'You were in there, mademoiselle?'

'Yes, but that was a couple of months ago.'

'We have to go in,' James said. 'You have grenades?'

'Of course. But if that building is packed with explosives . . .'

'There'll be a hell of a bang.'

Whalley hesitated, then nodded. 'Sergeant,' he called.

'Sir!'

'Prepare to assault on my whistle.'

'Sir!'

Whalley looked at Liane. 'Well, mademoiselle, wish us luck.'

'Why should I do that?' Liane asked. 'We are coming with you.'

Whalley looked at James, who winked. Then the major blew

his whistle. The Commandos left their shelter and raced forward, tommy guns chattering. The garrison returned fire, and several men fell. But the majority made the steps. James was to the fore, with Liane on one side of him and Pierre on the other. At the foot of the steps they hurled their grenades, as did Whalley and those of the Commandos who were close enough. The doors exploded and several men standing just within came staggering out, only to be cut down by the automatic fire. Then they were into the hallway.

Men appeared on the gallery above them, and again the tommy guns blazed. But the Germans knew by now that they were outnumbered, and several surrendered, including the lieutenant in command.

'You understand that this building is filled with explosive,' he said in French. 'We commenced emptying it yesterday, but only a small part has been removed. One careless move . . . and hurling grenades . . .'

'My dear lieutenant,' James said. 'That's why we're here. Outside.'

The prisoners, most of them wounded, were led outside. 'See to our people, Sergeant,' Whalley commanded. 'Get the wounded back a hundred yards. Where is the main magazine?'

'In the cellar,' Liane said.

'Right. We'll handle this. Off you go, mademoiselle. And you, Major.'

Liane looked reluctant, and James grasped her arm. 'It is their business. Come on.'

They left the building and ran across the street. 'What about those houses?' Liane asked. 'They are not a hundred yards away.'

'They've probably been evacuated,' Pierre said.

'We don't know that.'

'I'll check them out,' James said.

'*We'll* check them out.' They ran forward, Pierre reluctantly following.

'Hey!' the sergeant bellowed. 'Major! Mademoiselle!'

To their left Whalley was just emerging from the arsenal. He had no wire, so James realized he must have set a timed fuse. But it would only be for a short time.

There were four houses making up the part of the street that faced the arsenal. 'You take that one,' James told Liane. 'Check it out, and then get out the back. Full speed. Pierre, take that one. I'll do the other two.'

This time they didn't argue. James dashed up the front path of the third house. The door was predictably locked; he did not waste time in knocking, but blew the lock out with his revolver, and ran into a neat front hall. 'Is there anyone here?' he shouted.

There was no one on the ground floor. He was about to go upstairs when a man's voice asked, 'You are English?'

The man stood in the doorway to the cellar steps. 'How many of you are there?' James snapped.

'My family. There are six of us.'

'And that cellar is underground?'

'Yes. You wish to come down and be with us?'

'You get down there and stay there. There is going to be a hell of bang in the next five minutes. This house may well come down. You stay put until after it's over.'

He ran out of the back door and into a yard, cast a hasty glance to his right, and saw Pierre emerging from the rear of the next house. He gave him a wave, and vaulted the fence into the fourth house, beyond which there was an open space. The back door of this house was unlocked. He threw it open, dashed into the kitchen. 'Is anyone here?' he shouted

There was no reply. He looked into the cellar, but could discern no movement, so he ran through the two front rooms, came back to the foot of the stairs, and heard a woman's voice.

'Help! Help me, monsieur!'

James raced up the stairs and burst into a bedroom. There was an elderly woman, under the covers, wearing a mob cap and looking extremely agitated. She recognized his uniform.

'Ah, monsieur,' she said. 'You are English! I knew you were not a Boche.'

'Can you get out of bed?'

'I have not left this bed for two years, monsieur. I am old. Old!'

'Well, you'll have to let me take you out. This place is about to blow up.'

'They would not take me,' she grumbled. 'They all left when the shooting started. But they would not take *grand-mère*. It is that Daniel, you know. He said I would be too much trouble. Who would have a son-in-law, monsieur?'

'Who, indeed? Come along now.'

He threw back the covers, discovered to his relief that she was wearing a nightdress, dressing gown and stockings, scooped her into his arms . . . and then the arsenal exploded.

James found himself in the garden, lying in a rhododendron bush, which had broken his fall. His ears were dead, but he looked up at blue sky where there should have been the upper story of the house. Burning bits of this were still falling about him. He felt no pain, but some discomfort from the weight on top of him. He looked down, and discovered to his amazement that the old lady was still in his arms. Even more to his amazement, she was still alive, and saying something, but he could not hear what it was. He tried to get up with her, and fell back again. She got herself off him, still talking. For someone who had spent two years in bed, she moved with remarkable freedom. Now she stood above him, swaying slightly, but still speaking, or rather, he felt, shouting.

Then he saw Liane coming towards him. She had lost her beret and her hair was floating. But she did not appear to be hurt. She also was speaking. He touched his ears, and she nodded, then helped him to his feet. The old lady was still talking, and Liane nodded, and pointed to the back of the garden, where Pierre waited. Behind them the houses were gaunt wrecks, their walls shattered and in places collapsed, their upper floors fallen through, bits of broken furniture scattered about. But James decided that the people in the cellar would have survived, and would be able to get out.

They crawled through the rubble and encountered Whalley and his men. 'You all right?' the Commando asked, peering at them. James had lost his cap and his uniform was in tatters, while he was bleeding in several places.

'Just about. But we have this lady . . .'

231

'You go and fight the Boches,' the old lady said. 'I will be all right. That Daniel! I will hit him with a stick.' She hobbled off.

'What was that all about?' Whalley asked.

'It would take too long to explain. What are your plans?'

'We seem to have done all the damage we can.' Whalley gestured at the vast hole in the ground that had been the arsenal. 'Now I reckon we must try to hit these people in the rear. You with us?'

'I think we must get back to our own people. How long can you hold the port?' James asked.

'We haven't got it yet. But when we do . . .'

'Begging your pardon, sir,' the corporal said. 'There's a radio message.'

'Well?'

The telegrapher was clearly shaken. 'They're aborting, sir. Casualties have been too severe, and the RAF have reported considerable troop movements towards the town, far sooner than was expected. The Navy is also taking heavy losses, and cannot maintain its position much longer. All troops must return to the beaches for immediate re-embarkation.'

Whalley looked at James. 'What a fuck up!'

'You'd better get out while you can,' James said.

'*If* we can. Mademoiselle, I am most terribly sorry.'

'We will meet again. When you come back. For good.'

'I will look forward to that. Major . . .'

'There is a separate message for Major Barron, sir.'

'Give it,' James said with a sinking heart.

'Major Barron is required to evacuate with us, sir.'

'Fuck that. My place is with my people.'

'The order was repeated, sir.'

'You must go,' Liane said.

'And abandon you? You'll come with me.'

'You know I cannot do that, James. I brought my people here. I must take them back. But you . . . they cannot risk your being captured.'

James looked at Whalley. 'I think the lady is right. You must obey orders. And, with respect, we must move now, or we won't make it.'

James hesitated a last moment. Then he took Liane in his arms. 'You call the moment you get back to Limoges.'

'The moment.'

He kissed her, shook hands with Pierre, and followed the Commandos through the rubble.

Eleven

Aftermath

'Lucky for some,' Pierre commented.

'We have work to do.' Liane led the way back through the rubble, ignoring the people all around them. The sun was now high, the day bright, but clouds of smoke were billowing above the port, the guns were still booming and chattering, and the sky above was still filled with planes.

'What are we going to do?' Pierre asked.

'What James said to do: disengage and take our people home.'

'You mean you will still take his advice? Still trust him? Or any Englishman? This is the second time they have sacrificed our people – sacrificed us – to no purpose.'

'I think,' Liane said quietly, 'that they have sacrificed far more of their own. And the purpose is to defeat the Nazis. What is happening?' she asked a man who ran by them.

'The Boches!' he gasped. 'They are shooting everyone.'

She realized that the sound of shooting was suddenly very close. 'Down here.' She turned along a side street, Pierre at her shoulder, and checked at a shout.

'Halt there! Throw down your weapons.'

They both turned to see six men emerging from another side street. Black uniforms.

'We are done,' Pierre said.

'We are townspeople, who found these guns.' Liane laid down her tommy gun, and, after a moment's hesitation, Pierre did the same.

The men came closer, and Liane caught her breath. Roess recognized her in the same moment. 'Well, well,' he remarked. 'Does not everything come to he who waits? Jeanne! Or should I call you Liane? This is the best day of my life.'

Liane felt sick. After so much, to face what had to come
. . . But Pierre had also recognized the situation. He had laid
down his tommy gun, but there was still a grenade hanging
from his belt. He wrenched it off, drew the pin.

'Grenade!' one of the Germans shouted. They all opened
fire at once. Liane hurled herself to the ground, fingers scrab-
bling for her gun. Pierre, struck several times, had fallen to
his knees. But he had thrown the grenade. It burst immediately in front of the six men, scattering them into blood-stained
ruin.

Liane rose to her knees, gun levelled, and as she saw movement she sprayed the men with bullets. She wanted to kill
Roess, to make sure he was dead. But Pierre was more important. She slung the gun and crawled across to him. There was
blood everywhere, but he was still alive.

'Good shooting,' he muttered. 'Now your legend will grow.'

'We must get you to help.'

'I am done.'

'No one is ever done,' she said fiercely, putting her arm
round him to help him to his feet. But his knees would not
support him, and he was too heavy for her. Together they sank
back to the ground.

'You must leave me,' he said, his voice hardly more than
a whisper.

'I shall never leave you.'

'You must. You have a duty to the others. You must take
them home.'

Liane chewed her lip, for almost the first time in her life
incapable of making an instant decision. Then she heard shouts,
and more shots. The noise was coming closer.

'You cannot fight the whole German army,' Pierre said.
'Listen! You *are* a legend. You must live, and make the legend
grow. If you die, if you allow the Germans to expose your
body, publish photographs of it, the entire Resistance will
collapse. Do you not realize that every man dreams of meeting
you, every woman dreams of *being* you? Now go and do your
duty.' He smiled. 'I have my pistol. They will not take me
alive.'

Liane kissed him and stood up, tears streaming down her cheeks. She looked at where the dead Germans lay. Roess was amongst them. But was he dead? The temptation to go to them and make sure was enormous, but now she saw movement at the end of the street. To wait a moment longer would be to die. She wanted to die, to go out in a blaze of glory behind her chattering tommy gun. But Pierre's words were still filling her brain. Liane turned and ran down the street.

'James! Oh, James!' Rachel embraced him while Jennifer gazed at them with enormous eyes. 'You made it!'

'*I* made it, yes.' James sank into the chair behind his desk.

Rachel stood beside him, took in the various pieces of plaster on his face, and knew there had to be many more beneath his uniform. 'Was it terrible?'

He gazed at her for several moments. 'I was at Dunkirk. But at Dunkirk there was hope. There was no hope at Dieppe.'

'Would you like a drink?'

'If I were to start drinking, I don't think I would stop.'

'But what happened?' Jennifer asked.

'They were waiting for us. They were pouring men and tanks into the area before our people even got ashore.'

'You mean we *were* betrayed,' Rachel said.

'God knows.'

'Did Liane survive?'

'She was alive when I left her. She had Pierre with her. They were going to get their people out.' He raised his head. 'Do you know what I feel like?'

'You obeyed orders,' Rachel pointed out. 'And Liane will survive. She always does. Ah . . . About Joanna . . .'

The door opened, and the two women stood to attention. James responded more slowly, rising to his feet. 'Glad you got back,' the brigadier said. 'Bit of a bloody nose, eh?'

James vacated the desk, as he knew that was where the brigadier liked to sit. 'Have we a figure on casualties, sir?'

The brigadier sat down. 'It's not very pretty reading. As far as we can ascertain, we have one thousand, one hundred and seventy-nine known dead. The Germans are claiming two thousand, one hundred and ninety prisoners of war, but of the six thousand one hundred men involved, only one thousand, seven hundred and sixty got home, which leaves nine hundred and seventy-one unaccounted for. We have to presume that most of those are also dead. We also lost twenty-eight tanks, a hundred aircraft, and several ships, including a destroyer.'

'Oh, my God!' Jennifer gasped.

'Do we have any idea of the German losses, sir?' James asked.

'They are admitting around three hundred killed, and thirty-odd planes.'

'Oh, my God!' Jennifer cried.

'If you are going to have hysterics, Sergeant, kindly have them outside,' the brigadier said. Jennifer gulped.

'I assume those figures do not include French Resistance casualties, sir,' Rachel asked.

'We have no figures for those, although we do know they were considerable. Have you anything on that, James?'

'I know the losses must have been heavy. But I was pulled out before I could form any estimate.'

'And you are bitter about that. I understand your feelings. But you really are a valuable member of our organization, James. When will you hear from your people again?'

'When – if – they get back to Vichy.'

'Well, we must keep our fingers crossed. Now, as you may imagine, questions are being asked. How did Jerry know we were coming?'

'I have no idea, sir.'

'No doubts about your people in France?'

'We will hold a thorough investigation into that when they get home, sir.'

'Yes. We will require a full report. What about Jonsson? I know it looks as if her Nazi masters have decided to drop her, but could not that have been a ploy?'

'It does not matter whether it was or not, sir. Jonsson has been under guard in this country for the past two months.'

'So where is she now?'

'Still under restraint. But I would like to release her.'

'And do what with her?'

'Well, sir, we know that she did not betray the Dieppe business, simply because she could not have. But if she has lost her status with the Nazis, I don't see how we can use her again. So I think we should tell her how much we appreciate her help, and send her back to the States. We will have to give her, shall I say, a clean bill of health, establishing that she has been working for us and not the Nazis.'

'And suppose the Americans make that public?'

'We will have to ask them not to, and hope for the best.'

'Hmm. Well, I'll leave that with you. Bear in mind that she could earn herself a lot of money by spilling the beans to the newspaper she worked for.'

'Joanna doesn't need money, sir. And I don't think she will spill any beans that could harm Liane de Gruchy.'

'Well, I hope you're right.' The brigadier stood up and looked around the three faces. 'Stop looking so damned disconsolate. So we got a kick in the teeth. But we learned a hell of a lot. All of our mistakes will be corrected. And the next time, when we go in, it's going to be for good.'

'So I'm to be deported,' Joanna said over lunch at the Café de Paris. She looked as good as ever, although her confinement could hardly have been described as arduous. 'There's reward for two years' hard work.'

'You are being retired,' James said. 'And here's a cheque for your back pay.'

'Thrown aside like a worn-out shoe.'

'Look, I'm trying to save your life.'

'You expect me to believe that Oskar really meant to turn me in?'

'It's in writing.'

'The bastard. Sheer jealousy, you know. He'd rather stop me marrying Hoeppner than have me bring back news about Dieppe.'

'Supposing there was any to bring. But he does seem to have had an alternative.'

'Who is this Seven, anyway?'

'We're working on it.'

'And Burton?'

'I'm afraid he's for the high jump. Or you could say, the long drop. With you gone, he's of no more use to us, either.'

'Poor sod. And I never even got to meet him. Well, thanks for lunch. It's been fun. Just tell me that Liane is all right.'

'She was when I last saw her.'

'You don't sound convinced.'

'She'll be all right.' He had to keep believing that. He leaned across the table to squeeze her hand. 'It's been fun for me. Working with you, I mean.'

'Now that I never thought I would hear you say.'

'Look, your boat leaves tomorrow evening at six. You'll have to catch the noon train. I could take you to the station.'

'And we'd have hugs and kisses and tears all round?'

'You have to be seen off by somebody.'

'Tell you what. Send Rachel.'

Rachel entered the office and threw her hat in the corner.

'How did it go?' James asked.

'She's gone.'

'Well, don't sound so gloomy. You'll make me think you had something going for her.'

'You don't understand. She's gone. After she lunched with you, she went straight out to Harwich and caught a boat for Gothenburg.'

James's jaw dropped, but he snapped it up again. 'That's not possible. I dropped her at the Dorchester myself, and there was a detective waiting.'

'What you forget is that she knows the Dorchester, and they know her. She must be just about their favourite customer; she's been staying there for years. So she gave the detective the slip. With some assistance, I imagine. I would say she's in Sweden by now.'

'Shit, shit, shit.'

'There is, of course, the possibility that she may just prefer to retire to Sweden than the States. We didn't give her a choice.'

'Do you really believe that?'

'Frankly, no. Do you want to do something about it?'

'Such as?'

239

'Well, Pound Twenty-Three could possibly set something up.'

'Rachel, that woman saved your life.'

'I know. Just making sure you feel the same way.'

'Anyway, it wouldn't work. There have been two contracts out on Joanna. The first survived, just, because he happened to be Pierre de Gruchy, and she decided to remember old times. The second didn't. Let her get on with it. If she's stupid enough to go back into Germany, well, it's her funeral.'

'You know,' Rachel said, 'I think that, deep down inside that tortured psyche of yours, *you* have something going for her.'

'Ah, Oskar!' Heinrich Himmler beamed. 'Come in and sit down.'

Weber sat in front of the desk. He had actually expected a summons before this. But it had been worth waiting for.

'So,' Himmler said. 'We have gained a great victory.'

'Oh, indeed, Herr General. Mind you, it was a near-run thing.'

'So I gather.' Himmler tapped the file on his desk 'Our reinforcements got there in what could be called the nick of time. Roess performed brilliantly. How is he, by the way?'

'Remarkably well. There was a man standing in front of him, who took the full force of the grenade blast. Roess has a broken arm and some facial injuries, but is otherwise unhurt. I believe he will be fit for duty again in a fortnight.'

'Excellent. I should like to commend him personally.'

'Of course, Herr General. I should point out that everything he did was on my orders.'

Himmler turned over the first page of his folder. 'Rather belated orders.'

'Well, finding out these things take time.'

'So it would appear. But were you not warned, two months ago, by Colonel Hoeppner, that he had information that such a raid might be imminent?'

'Well, sir, you know what Hoeppner is like . . .'

'But he repeated the warning only a fortnight ago, and this time submitted his information to OKW.'

240

'Yes, sir. It was then that I decided to act.'

'Because he had gone over your head? And when you decided to act, you did not go to Dieppe yourself, or even send Roess at that time. You sent the woman Jonsson to England. With what result?'

'I sent Jonsson to England following Hoeppner's first report, Herr General.'

'With what result?'

'There has been no result. I have heard nothing from her, or from any of our agents in England, for very nearly three months. I am worried that something has gone wrong.'

'I hope nothing has happened to her. She is such a beautiful woman. Is she your mistress?'

'Ah . . .'

'You are a lucky man. Perhaps . . . Well, we shall consider the matter. But you are right to worry. We are fortunate it was a raid. Had it been the invasion, the Allies could have been at the Rhine by now. The only person who comes out of the whole sorry affair with any credit is Roess. Abwehr didn't have a clue what was going to happen until it happened. You sat on vital information for two months! And you have managed to lose your best agent.'

'Well, Herr General, as regards Jonsson, I have serious doubts . . .'

Himmler waved his hand languidly. 'Your doubts do not concern me, Oskar. I have doubts of my own, as to whether you are truly suited to this job.'

'Sir?'

'This is a highly responsible position. It carries great power. To exercise such responsibility, such power, requires great judgement, the ability to make great decisions, instantly. It is my conclusion that you lack those necessary assets.'

Weber opened his mouth and then closed it again.

'And when, in addition, I learn that you have been badgering Frau von Helsingen, wife of one of our greatest war heroes . . . Did you know that Colonel von Helsingen is to receive the Knight's Cross with Oak Leaves for his courage and leadership on the Russian front?'

'I did not know that, sir. I will congratulate him when next

241

we meet. But as regards his wife, may I remind you, Herr General, that you gave me permission to employ her in an attempt to winkle out Amalie de Gruchy?'

'You should remind yourself, Colonel, that I expressed grave doubts as to the usefulness of that plan. And what do I find? That all the time you were rushing about like a chicken with its head cut off, the de Gruchy woman was in England, and has now been there for six months. You have managed to make a laughing stock of the SD. That is not acceptable.'

Weber's expression was a mixture of consternation and terror.

'Well,' Himmler said, 'you have expressed a wish to congratulate Colonel von Helsingen. I am going to give you an opportunity to do that. You are seconded to the Russian front. Oh, I do not expect you to fight, Oskar, but you may be more successful at finding and destroying Russian guerrillas than you have been at dealing with the French Resistance. And winter is coming on. I am told that a Russian winter is an experience not to be foregone.'

Weber licked his lips. 'When Jonsson comes back, if you wish her services . . .'

'What an obscene idea. You are dismissed, Colonel.'

Weber swallowed and stood up. 'Am I allowed to ask the name of my successor, Herr General?'

'I have not made a decision yet. But I am sure I will think of someone. Good day to you, Oskar.'

'Fräulein Jonsson,' said the Immigration Officer jovially. 'It has been a long time.'

'It has been an even longer time for me,' Joanna assured him.

'Still travelling on a Swedish passport, I see. This gentleman would like to have a word.' He gestured at the man standing in the inner doorway.

'Oh, for God's sake,' Joanna said. 'Do we have to go through all of that again?'

'If you would be so kind.'

'Oh, well.' Joanna walked round the desk and into the inner room. 'You know the phone number. Get on with it.' She

242

really couldn't wait to see Oskar's expression when she turned up, after he had tried to shop her. As she had told James, she knew it was sheer jealousy, to stop her marrying Franz. Well, she was going to stuff that up his ass.

The Gestapo agent stood in front of her. 'That phone number is no longer accessible, for you, Fräulein.'

'I am not in the mood for jokes. I wish to speak with Colonel Weber. Now.'

The agent smiled. 'That would require a long-distance call. To Russia.' Joanna stared at him while beginning to wish she had not breakfasted. 'However,' he said, 'his replacement has left us orders that should you return to Germany, he wishes to see you. He also said that you were to be placed under arrest, the moment you set foot on our soil. So . . .' He snapped his fingers and his companion produced a pair of handcuffs.

Joanna drew a deep breath to prevent herself from panting – or screaming. 'Why is Colonel Weber in Russia?'

'You will have to ask his superiors that, Fräulein. Who knows, one of them may come to your hanging. Now.' He stepped away from her, and drew a Luger automatic pistol. 'We know all about your skills, Fräulein. If you attempt to resist us, I am empowered to shoot you, not fatally, but somewhere painful.'

Think, goddamn it, Joanna told herself. But this had to be a nightmare, one from which she could awake at will. She took another deep breath. 'I am a Swedish citizen. You have no right to arrest me. My father is a member of the Swedish Government. This mistake will cost you your job.'

'Alas, Fräulein, here in the Reich we are required to obey orders, not debate them. You should take up your situation with Colonel Roess.'

Joanna's jaw dropped. 'What did you say?'

'Colonel Johann Roess has replaced Colonel Weber as Executive Commander of the SD, Fräulein. Your wrists.'

Oh, Jesus, Joanna thought. *Oh, Jesus!* Before she could recover, her arms were pulled behind her back and the handcuffs clipped into place

'Now,' the agent said. 'Let us see what you have under

243

there.' Another smile. 'You robbed us of this pleasure the last time we met.'

Joanna could think only that she was in the hands of Roess. But now she was also in the hands of this slimy rat who was fondling and squeezing her breast before moving down to her groin. She considered kicking him, but again before she could make a decision she was turned round and forced against the desk, the other man grasping her hair so that she was bent over, the wood eating into her thighs, her face banging the blotter. She felt her skirt and petticoat being raised, hands searching under her knickers to caress her buttocks and slide between. She felt physically sick, less from the degradation, or even from the thought of what might yet happen to her, than because her persona of arrogant invulnerability was being stripped away. But she told herself that even that had to be a temporary glitch. She was Joanna Jonsson. She *was* a Swedish citizen. She *was* the daughter of an important man. Not even Roess would dare do anything more than humiliate her.

And yet the drive to Berlin was the longest of her life. She remained handcuffed, and was thus unable to adjust her clothing, which remained disordered, and she was accompanied by two agents who spent the journey staring at her, clearly having difficulty resisting the temptation to touch her. But at last the car rolled into that so well-remembered courtyard, and she was marched through that so well-remembered doorway, and up the stairs to the huge office. Roess sat behind the desk beneath a portrait of Hitler. His left arm was in a sling, but otherwise he looked better than when last she had seen him, in the Gestapo cell in Bordeaux. He did not get up to greet her.

'Fräulein Jonsson,' he said. 'Have you any idea how long I have waited for this moment?'

Joanna had prepared her defences. 'Well, now you've had your fun. Will you kindly remove these things?'

'Why should I do that?'

'Because if you do not—'

'You will appeal to your father and the Swedish Government? What do you suppose they will do? Send a

Swedish army to invade us and rescue you? My dear Joanna, in modern terms, you belong to a *little* country. Charles the Twelfth has been dead over two hundred years. Sweden is a cipher.' Now he got up and came round the desk to stand in front of her. 'Do you know, I made a deal with Weber that if I found Liane de Gruchy and handed her over to him, I would be given you in exchange. Isn't it quaint how things turn out? I have not yet found Liane, although I came very close to it a month ago, but I have still obtained you.' He ran a finger over Joanna's cheek, down her neck to her throat, and then across the bodice of her dress, pausing to locate and stroke the nipple. Joanna kept still with an effort. 'Now, I would like you to tell me where your old chum is at this moment.'

'I have absolutely no idea. But I am sure you will hear of her again.'

'Do you know, I believe you. But we are going to play a little game, you and I. I am going to assume that you do know where Liane can be found, but are refusing to tell me. So I am going to question you about it, again and again and again, using all the methods at my disposal to obtain this inform- ation.' Joanna could only stare at him, trying to keep her breathing under control. 'Some of our methods are very inter- esting,' he explained. 'One of them was a favourite of Weber himself. Do you know of it? Electricity?'

Joanna licked her lips.

'I have seen him use it on a young woman,' Roess told her. 'This girl was not by any means in your class, Joanna, either in breeding or in looks. But she was an attractive little thing, and her reactions were most stimulating. It is simply a matter of attaching a pair of wires to separate parts of the body, shall we say, one to each nipple. The wires are then jointly attached to a box capable of generating electricity. When this box is activated, an electrical current passes up the wires and into the body. I am told the pain is quite paralysing, although from the way that girl reacted I would say it is more *galvanizing*. Now that is what I am going to do to you, over and over. Something to look forward to, eh?'

Joanna realized that he meant what he was saying, and that there was nothing she could do about it. She had to make a decision, and hope for the best. In any event, she did not see how anything she could say could harm Liane. 'I can tell you where Liane was a month ago,' she said. 'She was in Dieppe.'

'I know she was in Dieppe,' Roess said. 'I was there. I saw her, standing in front of me, with her brother. That was when I broke my arm. They threw a grenade at me.'

'And you're alive? She must have been having an off day.'

'We found the brother's body,' Roess went on. 'But not hers.'

'You killed Pierre?' Joanna cried. 'Oh, shit!'

'But the woman got away. Again!' he suddenly shouted. 'Where is she now?'

'I have no idea. Don't worry about it. Next time she'll probably throw straighter.'

'Bitch!' he screamed. 'I am going to take the skin from your ass.' He stamped to the door and threw it open. 'Take this bitch—' He gulped. 'Herr General.'

'Good morning, Roess.' Himmler entered the office, drawing off his gloves as he did so. 'I am told . . . Good heavens. Fräulein Jonsson?'

'Yes,' Joanna said, suddenly breathless all over again. It was over a year since she had last met him.

'But why are you handcuffed?'

'She is under arrest, Herr General,' Roess said. 'For treason.'

'Oh, come now, Roess. You have made a mistake. Release her.'

'But, Herr General . . .'

'I have given you an order, Roess.'

Roess swallowed, took the keys from his pocket, and released the handcuffs. Joanna rubbed her hands together.

'I am so pleased to have you back, Fräulein Jonsson,' Himmler said. 'Joanna! You do not mind if I call you Joanna?'

'I should like that, Herr General.' Joanna's head was spinning.

'Excellent. Excellent. Your clothes appear to be disordered. These people have not . . . ah . . . interfered with you, I hope.'

Joanna smiled at Roess. 'Not seriously, Herr General. If I could be taken to the Albert, where I have a suite . . .'

'I will take you there myself. I wish to discuss your future employment. There is a vacancy in my office, and I have long been an admirer of your . . . ah . . . work.'

'Thank you, Herr General.'

'Herr General,' Roess ventured, his face purple.

'Yes, Roess, I will speak with you later.'

Himmler escorted Joanna from the room.

'Hello, Anatole.'

Anatole peered at his visitor, and leapt to his feet. 'Mademoiselle Liane! My God! I did not . . . well . . .'

'Expect to see me again?'

'Oh, mademoiselle!'

'Has no one else come in?'

'Two or three. Tales of disaster . . .'

'Yes, it was a disaster. But some of us have survived. I must call London.'

'Ah, yes. You must do that. I will just tune the set. If you will wait here . . .'

'I will come with you, Anatole. Good evening, Clotilde.'

'Mademoiselle Liane!' Clotilde looked almost as terrified as her husband. 'To have you back – is Monsieur Pierre with you?'

'He is not with me at this time.'

'But he is well?'

'I am sure that where he is now he is as well as at any time in his life.'

Anatole was gasping for breath. 'Mademoiselle . . .'

Liane pushed past him into the bakery and thence the inner room. 'Monterre,' she said. 'How nice to see you, after so long.'

Monterre had been sitting at the table, drinking coffee. At the sight of Liane he scrambled to his feet, overturning the cup and reached inside his jacket, only to find himself staring down the barrel of Liane's Luger.

'Draw it,' she said, 'and lay it on the table. And, Monterre, I am sure you know me well enough not to try to outshoot me. It would be a shame to make a mess on Clotilde's carpet.' Monterre waggled his eyebrows as he looked past her, but Liane had already moved away from the door. 'Come in, Anatole,' she said. 'Close the door.'

Anatole obeyed, standing against it. 'Now, Monterre,' Liane said. 'The gun. Slowly. On the table.' Monterre drew the pistol and laid it on the table. 'Now stand back.' Monterre obeyed, again looking at Anatole. But Anatole, faced with a choice between Monterre and Liane, had already made his decision. 'Thank you,' Liane said. She picked up the gun and dropped it into her pocket. 'Now, I think you and I should have a private chat. Is that your vegetable van outside?'

'Yes. Mademoiselle . . .'

'Keep it until we are alone. Anatole, I will be back in a little while. After you, Monterre.'

Monterre gave Anatole a last despairing glance, then walked through the bakery and the shop on to the pavement. Liane followed, her own gun in her other pocket. She got into the van beside him. 'Now, drive. Go west.'

'West? But that is towards the border.'

'I thought that was where you would like to go.' Monterre engaged gear and drove out of the village. 'This is the route you normally use, is it not?' Liane asked. 'Is this where you drove Henri Burstein? Oh, I almost forgot, and Rachel Cartwright?'

'I can explain, mademoiselle. The Germans made me do it.'

'How unfortunate for you. And Anatole?'

'Anatole has not betrayed you, mademoiselle. He is too afraid of you. And perhaps . . .'

'He is in love with me? How sweet.'

'As I would be in love with you, mademoiselle, if there was any chance . . .'

'If you felt there was any chance of my returning your love? But that is a charming sentiment.' Liane looked out of the window. 'I think this is a sufficiently lonely spot. Stop the car.'

Monterre obeyed. 'Mademoiselle . . .'

'Would this be about the place you attempted to rape Mademoiselle Cartwright?'

'Mademoiselle . . .'

'I think it probably is.' Liane drew the other pistol, changing hands to hold it in her right. 'Open your mouth.'

'Mademoiselle . . .'

'Open it.' Liane's voice, normally so quiet, suddenly sounded like the crack of a whip. Monterre opened his mouth. 'Thank you.' Liane thrust the pistol barrel between his teeth and pulled the trigger before he understood what she intended. She jerked backwards as his head exploded, then, as his body sagged against the door, she placed the pistol in his right hand, wrapping his fingers round the butt with his forefinger round the trigger. Then she got out of the car and began to walk back the way the way they had come.

'Liane!' James said into the mike. 'My God, it is good to hear from you. Are you all right?'

'I am perfectly well,' Liane said. 'But Pierre is dead.'

'Oh, my God! How?'

'We ran into a German patrol.'

'Damn! I am so very sorry. Look, you must come out. I'll arrange a pickup.'

'There is too much to be done here.'

'Liane . . .'

'Jean is here with me. Jean Moulin. You know he has been in France for some months?'

'Yes. But . . .'

'His task, set him by de Gaulle, is to bring all the guerrilla groups together, under one head. Him. This is to make sure that we are a united fighting force for when you come back. You will be coming back, won't you?'

'Well, of course we will. But I cannot say how soon.'

'And Joanna is all right?'

'Ah . . . As far as we know, she's in Sweden.'

'Well, I'll be waiting for you. With Jean. And an army. I love you, James. Over and out.'